THE HOUSE WHERE DEATH LIVES

Edited by
Alex Brown

PAGE
PAGE STREET YA

PAGE STREET YA

For the ghosts—those who tell their stories,
and those who can't.

We are listening.

ATTIC
Good Morning, Georgia *by Courtney Gould* 1

DOWN THE STAIRS
Vanishing Point *by Traci Chee* 29

Cradle and All *by Kay Costales* 46

After Midnight *by Liz Hull* 65

SECOND FLOOR
The Grey Library *by Nova Ren Suma* 91

The Phantom's Waltz *by Rosiee Thor* 114

Mirror, Mirror *by Nora Elghazzawi* 141

Smartmonster *by Sandra Proudman* 163

FIRST FLOOR
Let's Play a Game *by Shelly Page* 189

What Lies in Silence *by Justine Pucella Winans* 208

me i'm not *by g. haron davis* 224

Like Mother *by Gina Chen* 244

GROUNDS
In Deep *by C.L. McCollum* 263

Bloom *by Tori Bovalino* 282

The Shoe *by Alex Brown* 297

A Helping Hand *by Linsey Miller* 321

About the Authors 342

Attic

GOOD MORNING, GEORGIA

Courtney Gould

THERE IS A GHOST IN LEAH'S MIRROR.

Despite what they say, Leah's ghost isn't scary or violent. It doesn't break her furniture or wake her in the middle of the night, sweaty and afraid. At first, Leah didn't even realize she was being haunted. It was a cold morning just like this one, the sky stale and gray, cotton sheets crisp at her legs. She woke, rolled over, and she saw it: a huff of fog across the bottom corner of her sticker-crowded mirror and, in the center of the fog, a heart.

This morning, Leah waits for the ghost to show itself again, sitting at her vanity while breath clouds from her chapped lips. Her wooden chair is stiff enough to keep her from sitting comfortably, even with her fuzziest blanket tucked under her thighs. The wind groans outside, whistling through the buckled siding of her family's farmhouse. The attic is cold this morning—even colder than it was in the night—and blue-tinged light leaks through the narrow window, cutting hard lines into the gapped wooden floor.

Normally, Leah would be dressed and out the door by this time. She'd be biking down her street with her little brothers in tow, racing to see if they could beat the school bus. But Leah hasn't left this room in at least a week. The soreness of staying still aches in her shoulders and knees. Her mother didn't say how long she'd be grounded, but Leah isn't going to mope about it. She has more pressing matters to attend to. Today, she's going to learn her ghost's name.

Leah grips the edges of her blanket, leans forward, and breathes against the mirror. Once the fog is thick enough, she writes her first message: *good morning*

Sometimes this works and sometimes it doesn't. Leah waits until the letters drip and the fog ebbs away, until a dogwood branch made bare in winter scratches at her window, reminding her that there is a world outside this room. This winter is deep. Leah can't remember the last time she saw green in the fields. The frost bleaches away everything, leaving the sprawling mass of her family's farm white as bone.

"Please," Leah whispers. "Please don't be gone."

After a moment, the fog thickens again and Leah's message fades away. A line clears through the cloud and Leah sighs in relief. The ghost's message is short:

hi

Leah beams.

i got scared you left, Leah writes.

i never leave, her ghost writes back. After a moment, it adds, *did the door open yet?*

Leah looks behind her. The staircase down to the main floor is half obscured in shadow, the door at the bottom locked with a deadbolt on either side. The first few days of this grounding, Leah's little brothers scratched at the door every few hours. They told her about the latest episodes of *Recess* and *Gargoyles*. The first few days, her alone time was spent reading and writing in her journal, punctuated frequently by her mother bringing dinner up the stairs. She stared out the window at the swaying trees bordering the fields. She imagined seeing her friends again at school, imagined sitting on the floor by the fireplace to warm up with a bowl of Campbell's. But lately, it's been only quiet. No knocking, no scratching, no visitors, no dreams.

In her whole life, Leah has never felt so alone.

not yet, Leah finally writes. *i don't know how long it's been.*

i'm sorry, the ghost writes. *are you hungry?*

Leah doesn't want to talk about her parents and she doesn't want to talk about the staircase. She doesn't want to talk about how hungry she is. She breathes again on the mirror.

can i ask you a question?

ok

With a shaky hand, Leah writes, *what's your name?*

Again, the letters bleed and the fog blots away. Leah is left staring at the harrowing shape of her own face—cheeks gaunt, hay-colored hair matted and tangled. Without a hairbrush in her room, her usual glossy sheet of hair has devolved into a mess. Her thin lips are pale and chapped, her blue eyes glassy and far away. Leah wonders if her ghost can see her. She wonders if her ghost is disgusted.

When she focuses again, her ghost has written a message: *i don't know if i should tell you.*

Leah blinks. *why?*

i don't know you.

i'm leah, Leah writes. The glass is cold under the pad of her finger. *i'm sixteen. i have two brothers. i like nancy drew. what else do you want to know?*

Another moment passes, and then the fog thickens.

Slowly, the ghost writes, *nice to meet you, leah. i'm georgia.*

In the early morning hours, Leah waits for Georgia. She dusts her windowsill and watches the spindly, flowerless fingers of the dogwood tree outside her attic room as they stroke the window at her bed. She gathers her dirty clothes into a pile and places them beside the stairs—sometime in the night, her hamper disappeared. Her mother must've come upstairs to take the laundry while Leah was sleeping. A pang of sadness rings in Leah's chest. As angry as she is with her mother, a piece of Leah wishes she'd seen her come upstairs, just to have someone to talk to.

Leah walks tenderly, cautiously over the attic floorboards, careful not to wake her parents in the bedroom below. The house is so quiet today that Leah can hear the wheezing of her own breath. Her bare feet are cold and Leah wonders why her father hasn't lit the fire or turned on the heater downstairs.

On the mirror, her writing bleeds, condensation pooling in the crackled paint of her vanity.

good morning

good morning

georgia, wake up

She wanders to the top of the attic stairs and looks down the length of them. The door at the bottom of the stairs is still locked, and it's been days since she heard noise on the other side. She should walk down the stairs and knock at the door. She should ask her mother how much longer she'll have to stay locked in her room. But when her foot hovers above the first step, her stomach turns. The room shrinks. Her chest squeezes and she staggers back.

When she turns, the mirror has changed. Her layers of messages are gone, replaced by a single line:

good morning!

Leah scrambles back to her vanity, brushes her hair over her shoulders, and she begins writing. *did you sleep in?*

i didn't sleep at all, Georgia writes back. Before Leah can question it, Georgia keeps writing. *i wasn't sure if i should keep talking to you.*

Leah looks at the words for a long moment. She should feel

the same way, she's sure. In fact, *she* should be the one who's afraid. This is *her* room, after all. She should feel nervous about talking to an entity in her mirror that she can't even see. She should wonder if she's losing her mind. She should suspect that Georgia isn't real, and if she is real, Leah should be scared of her.

Deep down, Leah *does* feel all of it. The fear, the anxiety, the suspicion, the unease. But there's one feeling lodged like a stake in her chest, stronger than the rest of it combined. It's been days since she's seen another face, heard another voice, felt the warmth of skin against hers. The alternative is sitting completely alone, staring at the walls until her mind rots away.

She's spent so long aching for someone to talk to, *something* will have to do.

why? Leah writes.

Georgia doesn't write for a long while. Briefly, Leah wonders if she's scared her off. She expels a breath over the mirror, quick to change the subject if it means they can keep talking.

are you in the room with me?

i don't know, Georgia writes. *i think so.*

A chill scuttles over Leah's skin. Despite herself, she smiles. She runs fingers through her wispy tangle of blond hair, careful to lay it delicately over her shoulder. She wonders again if Georgia can see her. She wonders if Georgia lived in this room before her, if she's dead, if she even *knows* she's dead. If she could leave this room, Leah would go downstairs and ask her mother about other girls who lived in this attic. She'd find a picture of Georgia just to sample the feeling of looking into Georgia's eyes.

can you see me? Leah asks.

no

Leah swallows. She tries not to feel disappointed—in fact, she's not sure what there is to be disappointed about. If Georgia could see her, she would probably stop having these conversations. The days of isolation have been hard on Leah, and every morning, she wastes away a little more. Her cheekbones are sharp as a knife's edge today, eyes circled with gray, skin as pale as the frost in the fields. If Georgia saw her, she would be afraid. No one wants to be friends with a girl on the brink of death.

can you show me what you look like?

For a moment, Leah isn't sure what it means. And then, carefully, a fog covers the rest of the mirror from top to bottom. Second by second, Georgia smears lines into the fog. First, long legs and overlarge shoes. A T-shirt. A smiling face and a halo of hair around her perfectly circular head. It's just a stick figure, but something about it puts Leah at ease. It's not detailed enough to paint a picture, but at least it means Georgia sees herself as human. Or, at least, she wants Leah to see her that way. In the sliver of space above her stick figure's head, Georgia writes her name.

Leah does the same, carefully drawing her knee-length nightdress, the hair that hangs to the small of her back. When she reaches her face, she hesitates. In a single swipe, she draws a smile, and even though it's a lie, she hopes Georgia believes her.

The space on the narrow mirror runs out, forcing Leah to draw her arm overlapping with Georgia's.

The fog thickens at the bottom of the mirror and Georgia writes, *did you make us hold hands on purpose?*

Leah's eyes widen. *i'm sorry*

don't be

Leah smiles. Even after Georgia stops responding to her and even after the house quiets and the frost thickens and the sky turns gray like dust, Leah smiles. Her ghost is here with her. Her ghost is in the room with her, and when Leah climbs into bed, she imagines eyes raking over her. A hand meeting the curve of her jaw, a voice whispering *good night* against her ear.

And even though the room is empty, Leah knows she isn't alone.

LEAH'S LAUNDRY HAMPER ISN'T THE ONLY THING THAT VANISHES from her room. One morning, she wakes to find her bookshelf empty, a thin sheet of dust loose on the white wood. The next morning, her stack of folded blankets goes missing from the bottom of her closet. Eventually, it's the scrambled pieces of a school project she was in the middle of working on. It makes no sense— it must be her mother or one of her siblings coming upstairs in the dead of night to steal things from her room. But she can't fathom *why*.

After a few days of it, Leah tries to catch someone in the act. She finishes talking to Georgia and she settles at the foot of her bed as the sky darkens, legs crossed, determined to stay awake and catch her thief. And, inevitably, she wakes up each morning with no memory of how she fell asleep the night before. She wakes up and more of her world is missing. Every morning, her eyes find the mirror and there's a sliver of curiosity. Things started getting weird when she learned about Georgia. The house got quiet, her things started disappearing, her body got . . . different.

It's not just her sallow face. Despite going days without food, Leah isn't hungry. At first, Leah craved one of her mother's honey-butter sandwiches, but the idea of it now makes her mouth go dry. She knows it's cold in the room because her breath clouds and ice forms a crystalline border around her window, but she doesn't shiver. When she sleeps, she doesn't dream.

Something is wrong.

Leah sits at her vanity the way she does most mornings, knees tucked to her chest. She circles her knobby kneecaps with her thumbs and waits for Georgia. Today, it takes longer for Georgia to write to her. The sun rises over the fields, peaks in the center of the white sky, and is on its way back to the horizon before Georgia's breath finally clouds the mirror.

leah, are you there?

Leah blinks at the mirror. It seems oddly urgent. Oddly formal. Still, Leah writes: *i'm here.*

good, Georgia writes. *i've been thinking about you being trapped in that room.*

Leah sits back in her chair. Until now, she hasn't spent much time wondering what Georgia does when she isn't writing. She wonders how many hours Georgia has spent idle in this room, lonely, thinking of Leah. And maybe Leah hasn't felt cold in days, but the thought of Georgia's mind wandering over and over back to Leah makes her feel warm. She sucks in a breath, fights back a smile.

what if we could talk to each other? Georgia writes.

we are talking to each other, Leah writes back, but she knows what Georgia means.

There's a piece of Leah that imagines Georgia's voice like silk, light and smooth and comforting. She imagines how it might feel for Georgia—or *anyone*, for that matter—to say her name out loud. But the other piece of her knows she should be scared of the possibility. If Georgia isn't a girl her age also trapped in this room—if she's something else—speaking to her could be dangerous. Georgia must have a strange power over this house. Over this room. Leah could already be caught in her grip.

what if we could talk to each other for real? Georgia writes. *with our voices.*

would it be safe?

do you trust me? Georgia writes.

Despite herself, Leah does. She trusts Georgia without seeing her, without hearing her voice, without feeling her touch. Because whatever Georgia is, she's all Leah has. Maybe her family downstairs forgot about her, but Georgia remembers her every morning without fail. She's the only life in this unmoving room, the only thing wrinkling the still waters. Leah moves to the mirror and, trembling, she writes, *ok.*

For a moment, there's nothing.

Then, from the corner of the room, there's scurrying in the walls. It's small and frantic at first, something like a rat clamoring for escape. Then the air changes, thickens like molasses. The hairs on Leah's arms stand up, and she tastes iron on her tongue. The room buzzes. The room *breathes*.

"What is this . . . ?" Leah mutters.

The scurrying quickens and grows louder. Suddenly, the room fills with footsteps. Leah slides from the chair and crouches to the floor, cupping her hands over her ears. She should've known this would be something bad. She's too trusting, just like her mother said. She's too slow to have common sense. She let something into the house. Now none of them are safe. Her parents' room is right under the attic. She's sure her mother will hear the noise.

The footsteps stop.

"Hello?"

Leah freezes. The voice isn't how Leah imagined it. Georgia speaks with a rasp, almost quiet enough to be a whisper. It's deeper than Leah thought it would be, but not scary. It's like it comes from the walls. It comes from everywhere at once.

"Georgia?" Leah asks, though it comes out as a whimper.

The shuffling picks up again, and then quiets. Leah watches the walls, the ceilings, but nothing moves.

"Can you hear us?"

Us? Leah narrows her eyes.

"I can hear you," Leah says, this time a little louder. "Can you hear me?"

After a moment, the shuffling returns, punctuated with a *smack* at the vanity. In the thin shadow of early evening, Leah is sure she sees the mirror wobble. She staggers back until her shoulders meet the wall. Her breath is short. She knew Georgia was in the attic with her, but this is the first time it's felt like she's *here*.

"Leah, if you can hear us, can you write on the mirror?"

The fear clouding Leah's mind burns away for a moment, and all Leah can hear is Georgia saying her name. It feels like a hand brushing over her spine. Every inch of Leah's skin comes alive at the sound of it. Georgia can't hear her answering, can't see her, can't touch her. But whatever veil separates them thinned a little when Georgia said her name.

Leah breathes on the mirror and writes: *i'm here*.

In the echoes bouncing off the attic walls, Leah is sure she hears a sigh of relief. Another voice murmurs. Not Georgia. A boy's voice. Leah tenses, eyes darting to the staircase. Georgia isn't alone, and the second voice feels different. Threatening. If she were smart, she would dash down the stairs and call for her mother. She would admit she's invited something into the house.

But the thought of walking down the stairs makes her sick, and the thought of confessing her guilt to her mother and accidentally extending this punishment makes her even sicker.

what's happening? Leah writes, hand quivering.

"I think I figured out how to talk to you, Leah," Georgia says, and just like before, her voice echoes from every direction. "Can you understand what I'm saying?"

On the mirror, Leah writes: *yes*.

"Good." The scurrying noise returns and Leah's gaze snaps to the space in front of her bed. It's like something shifts from foot to foot there, invisible. Georgia continues, "Leah, can I ask you a few questions? You can write your answers on the mirror."

Leah clenches the collar of her nightdress in her fist.

yes

"Thank you, Leah. Can you tell me where you are?"

i'm in my room

". . . are you sure?" Georgia asks.

In an instant, it's like the room tilts. Leah grips the back of her chair and turns to face the rest of her room, but everything looks the same. Empty, white, coated in a thin sheet of dust. But it's like someone has turned it backward. Everything is wrong, but not in a way she can name. It's like she's never been here before.

Unsteady, Leah writes: *what's happening to me?*

"It'll be okay," Georgia breathes. "What's your last name, Leah?"

Leah presses her fingertip to the mirror and freezes. She grasps for the first letter of it, but the longer she waits for the memory, the further away it feels. She can't remember her last name. The emptiness makes the floor sink under her feet.

"Leah?" Georgia calls, and her voice is infinitely farther away. "Can you answer me?"

"I don't know it . . ." Leah mumbles out loud. Her fingertip is numb against the cold glass. She needs to give Georgia an answer, but her mind goes blank. "I can't remember."

"What about your siblings' names?" Georgia asks, quieter this time. "You remember their names, right?"

Just like before, when she reaches for their names, she comes up empty handed. She tries to remember the shapes of their faces, but it's a blur. It was only a few days ago her little brother smuggled her a packet of crackers, right? She didn't start forgetting until she met Georgia. She wasn't losing pieces of her room, pieces of her mind, pieces of her. Whatever power Georgia has, it's more dangerous than Leah realized.

"Leah, can you come back?" Georgia asks. "I can ask a different question."

Leah swallows. *i'm here*

"What do you want, Leah?" Georgia asks.

nothing, Leah writes.

"You want something," Georgia asks. "What do you want? Do you want to leave this room? Do you want to stay?"

The air crackles with electricity. Leah clings to her vanity and tries to answer what should be a simple question. Something is wrong here, and it's getting worse every day. But she knows without asking that leaving this room means the end of her time with Georgia. When she looks at the staircase, the nausea grows so deep she doubles over. When she manages to touch the mirror again, she writes: *i want you.*

Georgia gasps.

There's a clattering low and thunderous as a storm, and then the room begins to shake. The mirror splinters under Leah's fingertip. She stumbles out of her chair and across the room, but her heel catches on the top of the staircase. She loses her footing and tumbles to the bottom of the stairs as the room continues to shake. Immediately, it's like the world has shifted all over again. She looks up at the ceiling and her head spins.

Leah turns to the door and begins pounding with the side of her fist. Sobbing, she cries, "Mom, please let me out!"

From the top of the stairs, she hears Georgia yell, "Goodbye."

No one on the other side of the door answers. Leah slumps to the floor and cups her hands over her ears. She stays curled at the bottom of the stairs for what feels like hours. Eventually, the shaking and rumbling slows to a stop. She lays still and she breathes slow and she waits for her heart to stop racing. Her hair, coated in static, sticks to her damp cheeks. The voices stop, along with the shuffling and scratching. And despite the fear that stiffens in her limbs, Leah doesn't want to be alone. She doesn't want Georgia to be gone.

She pulls herself to her knees and crawls back up the stairs, breath shallow in her chest. Outside, specks of snow freckle the angled window. Winter light bathes the floorboards in white and it's like the snow is in her room, too. Dust swirls and coats the floor. The room is dead quiet.

The mirror is completely coated in breath, but nothing is written. After a moment, the first lines form and Leah expels a pent-up breath.

are you there?

Leah sits at the vanity. Cautiously, she writes, *yes.*

are you ok?

Leah closes her eyes. This is Georgia, the first person to talk to her in forever, the first person to care about her in . . . even longer.

She's not some terrifying monster. She's not a trick of the light or a trick of Leah's mind. Leah says the mantras over and over, but it doesn't quell the first spark of doubt fanning up in her. When she opens her eyes, she writes.

you scared me

She waits what feels like hours again, and then Georgia writes, *i'm sorry*.

Leah nods. She breathes over the mirror and their words cloud away. Before she can write anything else, though, Georgia is writing again. Line by line, her message comes together and Leah's stomach sinks. When the message is finished, the letters drip.

you scare me too

At a certain point, Leah stops counting days. Instead, she measures her time by the frost encroaching on her bedroom window. The snow has gotten thicker outside, blurring away the length of the fields and drawing a curtain over the trees on the horizon. Pillows of snow sit heavy on the dead branches of the dogwood outside her window. She can't remember the last time she saw the white flowers blooming. It's been winter so much longer than she expected.

Today, Leah decides not to worry about what's happening to her. What Georgia is doing to her. What it means to stay in this room. She sits at the mirror and she writes: *good morning georgia.*

In moments like this, when fog blows over the mirror like first frost and the rest of her bedroom falls away, Leah wonders. She wonders what Georgia's world looks like on the other side of the glass. She wonders if Georgia is cold in her ghost room, if the snow is coating the dogwoods for her. Board by board, her room comes apart and she can only see the glass, her own blurred face staring back at her. She wonders what Georgia looks like for real. If Leah squints, and if the breath on the glass is thick enough, she can imagine Georgia in her own warped reflection.

is it snowing? Leah writes in the fog.

God, she's nervous.

Eventually, Georgia's words form: *not for me.*

She wishes she could show Georgia the snow. It might be cold, but it's peaceful. It's quiet. She can't remember the last time her brothers scratched at her door. She can't remember her mother's face. The hushed sounds of branches at her window are quiet and, other than her own breathing on the mirror, Leah's world is silent. There's only Georgia. When she wakes up, when she goes to sleep, and every second in between, it's Georgia.

i want to try something, Leah writes on the glass. Her chest is almost too tight to breathe. She presses her free hand to the mirror, holding it there until her skin sweats away the fog. She breathes over her last words and writes, *can you touch my hand?*

She waits, but nothing happens.

did you do it? Leah writes.

A moment passes, then Georgia writes, *yes.*

Leah's stomach sinks. She doesn't know what she expected, but at night, she imagines feeling Georgia's fingertips ghosting over her palms. She imagines hearing Georgia's voice again, warm and soft at once. She imagines touching Georgia's hair, and she wonders if it's coarse or fine, what color it is. She wonders if she could run her fingers through it. She wanted to press their palms together and find that they fit perfectly together, but she feels nothing. No hand on the other side of the mirror. No Georgia.

A line forms in the fog.

i want to try something too

Under Georgia's words, Leah writes, *ok.*

And then, like a flower blooming, a spot in the fog darkens. It takes Leah a moment too long to understand what she's looking at. Her heart thumps so hard she can hear it. Georgia's lips pressed to the glass, waiting. And Leah has imagined it a thousand times already, but only in the vague way she imagines leaving this room. The way she imagines telling her mother she won't live like this anymore. More a dream than a wish, something so impossible it hurts.

She wants to kiss Georgia, but the thought of feeling nothing is worse than any other nightmare she's had.

Leah closes her eyes, leans forward, and she presses her lips to the mirror. She pictures the first dregs of spring crawling over the fields, the clusters of dogwood blooms opening to the sunlight outside her window. And, as she imagines it, she feels lips meet hers. *Georgia.* Real, living, breathing Georgia. It wasn't a figment of her imagination.

She gasps and lurches back.

When she touches the mirror, it's cold glass again. Leah leans in fast and kisses the mirror again, but it's only a mirror. She presses her face into her palms and groans. For the first time since this all began, she could *feel* Georgia, and she immediately ruined it.

are you still there? Leah writes.

A long moment passes, snow flickering outside the window, and Georgia doesn't answer. Leah's chest tightens. She swallows and writes again.

please come back

The fog on the glass thickens, but Georgia writes nothing.

please don't leave, Leah writes.

i won't, Georgia finally writes. *i need to think.*

Leah fiddles with the hem of her nightdress and waits. She can't remember much about her life before this winter began—since she met Georgia—but she knows that this was certainly her first kiss. Her heart thuds an empty beat against her ribs.

i think i can help you leave this room, Georgia finally writes. *do you want to leave?*

Leah swallows. *i don't want to leave you.*

we can leave together

Leah turns to look at the staircase and the door. Like always, her stomach sinks at the sight of it, but she closes her eyes and buries her fear. If Georgia goes with her, she doesn't have to be alone. If Georgia goes with her, she can escape without losing the one person she loves. Whatever comes next, they can face it together. Outside her window, just visible through the flurry of snow, Leah just catches the flush of white dogwood blooms. Maybe winter is ending, she realizes. A flutter of hope warms her.

Despite herself, she smiles.

ok, Leah writes. *i'll go.*

THINGS ARE DIFFERENT WHEN LEAH WAKES UP.

The room is dark, even when Leah opens her eyes. The frost coating the fields outside has crept closer, coating the metal posts of her twin bed and dampening her sheets. She sits up and scrambles to the window, but it's no use. She can't see the dogwoods outside or the fields or the white sky. The frost is so thick it masks the entire outside world, leaving only her attic room. Leaving only the cold. Leah's breath is a shudder, clouding immediately.

"Hello?" she whispers.

The room is silent.

Leah swings her legs over the edge of her bed, and when her feet touch the floorboards, she can't feel the cold. She can't feel anything. She presses her fingertips to the skin of her forearm and feels nothing. She smacks her palm against her cheek and feels nothing. Her heart slugs a slow beat.

At the mirror, Georgia is already awake.

good morning, leah

please don't be scared

Leah narrows her eyes. She isn't scared, exactly. She isn't anything. She waits for the pieces of her room to click into place and make sense, but the relief never comes. Sitting at her bed, scanning the shadow-webbed shape of her room, it's as though someone kidnapped her in the night. Everything feels foreign, wrong, confusing. But none of it makes her afraid.

Well, not *none* of it.

The dark of the staircase looms ahead of her. When Leah stands, she can just see the door at the bottom of the stairs. For the first time since this punishment began, the deadbolts are unlocked and the door hangs slightly ajar. The dark beyond it is thick and unending, an open throat waiting to swallow her.

Leah staggers to the mirror and thuds into her chair.

what's happening?

Georgia begins writing immediately. *i figured out how to get you out. do you still trust me?*

Leah swallows. *yes.*

do you remember what day it was when your mom locked you in here? Georgia asks. When Leah doesn't immediately answer, she keeps writing. *do you remember what year it was?*

Leah presses her fingertips into the cracked, frost-damp wood of her vanity. She should know this. Maybe she forgot her brothers' names and her mother's face and her own last name, but she should at least know what year it is. Her hands tremble and she fights back tears. Originally, she was counting the days she was trapped here. She can't remember how long it's been since she lost count. The room is empty now, shelves cleared out, windowsill clean, vanity drawers emptied. The clothes in her closet disappeared a long time ago, leaving only her nightdress to wear every day. Everything that made this room hers is gone, and it's only an empty white shell left, holding her in place.

i don't remember anything anymore, Leah writes.

i know

Leah writes: *i'm scared.*

Again, Georgia writes: *i know.*

Leah presses her hand to the mirror, and even though she can't see it, she knows Georgia meets her there. Leah tilts her forehead against the glass, too, listens to her breath as it curls against the vanity. She wonders what face Georgia is making on the other side of this veil. If she's sad for Leah, or if this was her plan all along. Whatever is happening to her, things in this room are getting worse. She's almost out of time.

She wishes she could've seen Georgia's face just once.

do you want to leave? Georgia writes. *i can help you.*

how?

you have to go downstairs, Georgia writes.

Leah stiffens. She turns to look at the stairs again and her gut twists. Quivering, she writes: *i can't.*

you'll be stuck here if you don't, Georgia writes.

Leah bites her lower lip. *stuck here with you?*

i can't stay here forever, Georgia writes. The dot of her first *i* dribbles to the bottom of the mirror and Leah focuses on that instead of the rest of Georgia's words. She can't do it—she can't leave Georgia. She can't go down the stairs. Her room is changing every day, but at least it's still her room. She doesn't know what's down those stairs. She can't even begin to remember what the rest of the house looks like. She doesn't know what, if anything, will be waiting for her.

just me isn't enough, Georgia writes.

Leah shakes her head: *it's enough for me.*

i'll go with you, Georgia writes. *i promise.*

In the quiet space between Leah's breaths, she tries to make a choice. She should want to leave this room—she's forgotten her friends' names, the types of crops they used to grow here, the name of the state they live in. But she hasn't forgotten Georgia. And maybe she can't remember what kinds of things used to make her happy, but she knows Georgia makes her happy now. She's kind and she's terrifying and she's the only thing Leah cares about. The world outside this room is unknowable, but the world inside is the one they share.

Georgia doesn't want to stay.

Leah closes her eyes and she slides into a calm. Into a decision.

ok, she writes. *let's go.*

Leah stands, brushes the dust from her nightdress, and she eyes the stairs. On the mirror beside her, Georgia writes: *i'm with you. i'll be with you the whole way. i won't let you go.*

And so Leah makes her way to the stairs. The atmosphere in the room simmers until it's crackling like an old TV. Her stomach twists and turns, but Georgia is right. The door at the bottom of the stairs is the only way out of this room. She has to be brave enough to walk through. She has to let the dark on the other side swallow her. She turns back to the mirror, breathes a final breath against the glass, and she draws a heart.

By the time Leah reaches the base of the stairs, the fear makes it nearly impossible to move. But in the dark, in the cold, she's sure she feels a hand slip into hers. She closes her eyes, presses her palm to the door, and she pushes it open.

The air on the other side of the door is warm as apple cider and Leah eases into it. Eases into the dark, past the fear and the loneliness, and as quiet as the snow falling on the dogwood trees, Leah fades away.

FOR TWELVE MONTHS, THERE WAS A GHOST IN GEORGIA THIEL'S mirror.

Despite what the movies say, Georgia's ghost was kind. She was gentle and she was scared and she was desperately lonely. She liked Nancy Drew and butter-honey sandwiches and watching the first snow fall outside her attic window, tufts of white slowly coating dead dogwood branches. When Georgia kissed her ghost, the glass was cold. Georgia's ghost was lost and she was fading away, but she had a name.

Leah Connor was seventeen when she died in this room. At least, that's what the police have determined so far. Like she told Georgia once, she was the oldest child of three, the daughter of strict, traditional parents and, in many ways, a prisoner in this house. The only thing Leah didn't tell her—presumably because she couldn't remember—was that she lived here almost thirty years ago. She spent most days in this attic as a punishment. She wasted away here, unfed and unloved for most of her life. She was alone as she lived, and she was alone as she died.

But in death, something changed.

At first, Georgia wasn't sure *what* Leah was. It started with unexplainable messages on the mirror and quickly sank into full-blown conversations. Maybe Georgia shouldn't have answered her, but Leah wasn't the only lonely one. A new city, a new house, a new room . . . No matter what each day threw at her, she knew Leah would be at the mirror waiting for her.

Things changed when she and her brother tried the Ouija board. When Leah's excitement turned to fear. When Georgia realized Leah was trapped in her mirror room, too afraid to move on.

She remembers the moment that changed everything. *i want you.*

Her brother thought it was a sign that Leah was a demon clamoring for Georgia's soul. But Georgia knew.

She paces the attic bedroom until she can't anymore. She touches the bookshelves, now loaded with graphic novels and school textbooks, and she imagines the books Leah might've read. When Georgia and her parents first moved to this house, she claimed the attic room for the way the dogwoods blossom outside the window. At night, as she drifts to sleep, she wonders if Leah saw the same ones.

Georgia is seventeen, too. It's 2024 and Georgia is as old as

Leah was when she died. It isn't fair.

Alone in her room, Georgia eyes the mirror on the vanity she and her mother moved up from the first floor bedroom—the one that was covered with cardboard when they found it—and her stomach sinks. Faintly, just faintly, the edges of Leah's heart are still visible, splintered slightly by the crack in the glass. Georgia massages the palm of her hand with the coarse edge of her thumb. The strange burn across her hand appeared seconds after Leah was gone, and she knew immediately that, for a moment, Leah's drawing came true. For a moment, their hands breached whatever veil separated them and they touched. She cradles her hand to her chest and the words spill out.

"I'm sorry, Leah . . ." Georgia whispers. "I broke my promise."

Nothing appears on the mirror. The room is quiet.

With that, Georgia stands. She makes her way to the mirror, breathes against the glass, and she presses a kiss into the fog. For thirty years, this room held Leah like water cupped in its hands. And every year that passed, a little more of her trickled away. There wasn't much of her left when Georgia found her, but there was enough. She was enough.

Georgia makes her way down the attic stairs, hand cradled to her chest, and she opens the door. Into the warmth, into the light, but holding a piece of Leah Connor, always.

Down The Stairs

VANISHING POINT

Traci Chee

THERE WAS SOMETHING WRONG WITH THE SECOND-FLOOR hallway. Viv did not even like to set foot in it, if she could avoid it, which she did at all costs.

"It's just a room," Mom had said once, sashaying through her door near the end of the hall, her singsong voice floating, disembodied, back to Viv. "A room in a house."

But it had never been just a room, had it? Frowning, Viv watched Bachan wipe down the console table that spanned one side of the hall. Real rooms had purposes: the bathroom for bathing, the dining room for dining, the living room for living . . .

And the hallway was not a room for living. It was not a place meant for staying, inhabiting, dwelling. The hallway's only purpose was transitory; it spirited you from one real room to another.

Upstairs, those rooms were three. On the right, opposite the console table, was the largest bedroom, where Bachan slept on one side of the creaking four-poster bed she'd once shared with Jiichan. On the left was Jiichan's old study, which Bachan had converted, in the years since his passing, into a sitting room lush with plants. To Viv it was unrecognizable: his desk pushed aside, his glasses folded inside a leather case, his ballpoint pens all going dry in a mug upon the shelf. Beyond that was Mom's room.

And beyond that, the end of the hall.

It was this area that unnerved Viv most. The light never reached the back wall as it should, slanting through Mom's bedroom door onto the knockoff Persian rug Jiichan had picked up at a Labor Day sale sometime during the '50s, now tatty and curling at the edges. Elsewhere, the walls and ceiling were painted a pleasant dusky blue, but beyond Mom's door the color deepened, yawning and abyssal as the mouth of the Caldecott Tunnel. When Viv was younger, she used to try holding her breath until they reached the terminus of that impossibly curving passage, wishing, wishing, the smooth walls turning and turning and turning, so long that spots swam before her eyes and she gasped for air before the end.

A long time ago, before Mom got sick, before they were forced to move in with Bachan, Viv had been convinced there was a fourth door at the end of the hall, even after she was repeatedly informed that on the other side of *that* wall was nothing. Where was the door? She demanded to know. The fourth door?

"For the last time, Viv, there's no door there," Mom had said with a sigh. "There's just nothing there, okay?"

Thinking it was perhaps the bare wall that unsettled Viv, the sight of the wainscoting in the too-dark shadows, Jiichan had placed a vase of pussy willows at the end of the hall before Viv's next visit. This, however, did little more than infuriate Viv, for she was certain the adults were trying to deceive her. There was an aberration at the end of the hall, and they were trying to cover it up the way Bachan covered up the unraveling spot in the rug with the console table! With infantile petulance, Viv plucked off each fuzzy catkin and upended the vase upon the furrowed carpet before the long weekend was out.

Another time, one New Year's Eve after Mom and Bachan had spent the entire day cleaning and cooking, the air still smelling of wood polish and simmering shoyu, Viv, age seven, had been awakened in the small hours of the morning by a soft tread. Throwing back the covers, she crept onto the second-floor landing, where in the hallway she spied a bony, pale figure in a misshapen cap.

"Mom?" Viv said, though she could not be sure, for the face was turned away from her, toward the bunching shadows at the end of the hall.

Her mother did not reply, did not even turn, but continued through her bedroom door, swaying on ankles that were much too small, impossibly small for her, the ankles of a child or a bird. They shouldn't have been able to hold her up, Viv thought later. How could they be holding her up?

"Mom!" Viv rushed over the threshold toward Mom's room, preparing to launch herself onto the bed, into her mother's arms.

Instead, however, she found herself on the opposite end of the hall, toeing the edge of the rumpled carpet as if she'd just left Bachan and Jiichan's room.

Confused, she dashed across the hallway, back to Mom's room, and ended up outside the largest bedroom again.

Dread pooled in her stomach. No, no, no, this was wrong. Panicked, she tried over and over to get through Mom's door, but no matter how many times she attempted to reach her mother, she could not leave the hallway. She reappeared at her grandparents' door, the study door, the end of the hall, the sound of hinges creaking inexorably behind her, until at last she tripped, banging her forehead on the console table, and fell back, screaming, which was how Mom, emerging from her room, found her seconds, or perhaps minutes, hours, an eternity later.

Now fifteen, Viv hovered on the landing while Bachan lifted the imitation Ming vase from the console table, sweeping a dust cloth beneath it. Although Viv did not enter the hall herself anymore, not in weeks, she felt obligated to stand guard when Bachan was there, as if to ensure the hallway did not try to trap her grandmother the way it had once tried to trap her.

Bachan, however, seemed entirely unaffected by the strangeness of the hallway. "Come help me with your mother, will you?" she said, gesturing to one of two simple urns laid out on yellowing doilies. "She's too heavy for me."

Viv froze. She'd never minded when Bachan called Jiichan's ashes "Dad," but she hated pretending it was Mom inside that closed aluminum vase.

It hadn't been Mom in the casket, either.

Or beneath the sheet, when Viv had finally peered in from the hallway.

Viv curled her split ends around her forefinger, avoiding her grandmother's gaze. "Can't you dust around it?"

The soft skin of Bachan's face creased: a furrow between her brows, a pinch at each corner of her mouth. Viv pretended not to notice her disappointment, choosing instead to focus on the framed picture of Mom, of Mom and Viv together, actually, at Stow Lake before the chemo, although at this angle all Viv could see was the neon orange price tag still clinging to the back.

"I know it was hard for you, seeing her so sick," Bachan said gently, "but she's at peace now." With a sigh, she swept the dust cloth across the table, upsetting the funeral program propped against the urn. Viv gasped, averting her eyes so she wouldn't see Mom's picture on the cover: this one of her alone, in the knit cap she'd worn since she started losing her hair.

When Viv looked again, all that was visible was the back of the program, with directions to the mortuary copied and pasted from Google.

EVER SINCE SHE'D ESCAPED THE HALLWAY, VIV DREADED CROSSING the second-floor landing, particularly at night, when the empty rooms, both real and unreal, seemed to breathe. When she and Mom visited, she'd lie in the dark, staring up at the ceiling while the pressure in her bladder intensified with each ticktock of the grandfather clock downstairs.

Then, in the morning, damp sheets. A sour smell on her nightgown. Mom gathering the soiled bedding into her arms. "Oh, Viv, what are we going to do with you? You're too old for this, Viv."

Perhaps it would have come to nothing if her mother hadn't gotten sick. A few visits a year, nothing more, a low likelihood of anything happening, provided she didn't cross the landing at night. But after Mom started having trouble walking, they'd moved in with Bachan, and now the guest room was Viv's room, the guest bathroom on the opposite end of the landing was her bathroom, and that meant she had to walk past the hallway all the time.

It was always the hallway, wasn't it? The blue hallway, in the night, the street lamp outside Jiichan's study casting an orange rectangle of light upon the threadbare carpet, the other doors, all of them, shut.

Three weeks after they moved in, Viv, being old enough by then to know when she could hold it and when she could not, was creeping to the guest bathroom when she saw the figure again, the lady, by Jiichan's study, her back to the stairs and to Viv, her bony ankles protruding from the hem of her nightgown.

"Mom?" Viv's heart soared with hope. Her mother, who had not been able to walk without crutches since the surgery, standing on her own?

"Mom!" Viv cried. Ignoring the danger, she raced into the hallway, the blue walls arcing overhead like waves, threatening to crash down on her, and grabbed her mother's hand—so thin! Like the thinnest porcelain, and equally cold.

Viv recoiled.

It was not her mother. It looked nothing like her mother. It could look nothing like her mother, for Viv could not see the face. As she stood there, shaking, the body turned toward her, the tendons in the neck twisting, the vertebrae popping out of place, but the head remained fixed on the end of the hall. It did not even turn an inch, so Viv did not see the face, only the back of the knit cap the lady wore, something wrong with that, too, lopsided or slightly skewed.

Viv watched, horrified, as the lady entered the study, vanishing at the threshold as if the only place she could exist was the hallway, that hallway, an in-between place, an unreal place for unreal things.

Since then, Viv hardly dared to look at it, dashing past the threshold, her bare feet slapping against the hardwood, but she just couldn't seem to escape it, the end of the hallway drawing her gaze, every time, like a vanishing point in a Renaissance painting. What was past that Roman arch? What was in the slender trees? What was through that door, that invisible door, that fourth and final door at the end of the hallway? She looked every time.

Which was why, about a month after Mom died, Viv couldn't avoid the lady when she came again.

She was at the end of the hall this time, in those unfathomable shadows, swaying. The knit cap was the same, crimson in color, like the ones Viv had seen on the Jizo statues when Bachan had taken her and Mom to Japan with some of Jiichan's ashes, with the same mistake at the nape of the neck.

A dropped stitch.

Viv knew it now, as she stood, paralyzed, on the landing. She knew the hat, too, knew the color, for she had chosen it herself, that soft dyed angora tumbled in a basket with other, lesser skeins of yarn, thin and scratchy.

Her mother's cap.

Viv had made it for her, actually, when Mom had started losing her hair. She'd worked quickly, capably, though she'd never knitted anything before, wanting it to turn out perfect: a perfect gift from an imperfect daughter.

But then that dropped stitch. Not in the back, originally, but in the front, over the thinning eyebrows, just a few hairs by that time, really, the contours of the bones visible beneath the skin. She didn't know how she'd missed it. How could she have missed it? That dropped stitch.

"It's fine, really!" Mom had said brightly, turning it backward over her pale scalp. "Really, Viv, look. See? It's just fine this way. Don't you think? Come on, Viv, look."

BUT HOW COULD THE LADY, DURING THAT FIRST ENCOUNTER BY THE console table, have been wearing a cap Viv wouldn't knit until half a year later? How could it have appeared on her head all those years ago, years before the cancer had even begun to take root inside her mother's bones? The logistics were troubling. Had it been another hat entirely, and Viv, seeing it on the lady, inadvertently replicated it, dropped stitch and all?

Or did the lady exist outside of time, the way the hallway existed, somehow, outside of reality, holding past and present and future simultaneously? Had the hallway known what would happen to Viv's mother, even then, even back then, when Viv, seven years old, had first seen the lady, mistaking her, even then, for her mother?

The bony ankles?

The gown?

The red knit cap?

Come to think of it, where had that cap gone anyway, her mother's? Viv couldn't remember having seen it since Mom's death, but now she was overcome with the sudden and overpowering need to find it, to verify that the lady had not taken it, the lady who was not her mother, the lady who was not real. Had they cremated it? Donated it? No, no, Viv would have remembered that, wouldn't she? In all likelihood, it had been stuffed into one of Mom's drawers, perhaps in the dresser by the window.

But that dresser was in her room.

"Bachan?" Viv shouted from the landing, the sound of her voice echoing, almost imperceptibly, down the hall.

Nonsense syllables. A whisper of gibberish, unnerving.

"What is it?" her grandmother called from her bedroom.

"Can you get something for me? Mom's knit cap? Do you know where it is?"

"Did you check her room?"

Viv stared at the closed door near the end of the hall, swallowed hard. "Please?"

Bachan appeared in her doorway, one hand on the doorframe for balance. "Have you been in there since she passed?"

Viv shook her head, feeling the weeks fall away from her suddenly, dizzyingly, the days, the hours, shedding off her like water into a well. Come sit with me, Viv. Want to watch Netflix, Viv? Let me show you something, Viv. Look.

"I think it would do you good," Bachan said.

Viv shook her head again.

Her grandmother stared at her, disappointed, Viv knew, but after a long moment, she padded across the hall in her house slippers. Viv held her breath as Bachan paused by Mom's door, afraid, for an instant, that the end of the hall would open up beside her, devour her, yes, even now, before Viv's very eyes.

But nothing happened. Viv exhaled slowly as she listened to her grandmother puttering about in the far bedroom. There was the sound of creaking floors, drawers opening and closing, a palm whispering across a quilt.

Minutes later, Bachan emerged. Viv watched her appear, shambling into the hall with the sunlight glowing behind her, cascading through the open door.

Mom's room.

For the first time in a month, Viv looked into Mom's room. From her vantage point on the landing, she could see the corner of Mom's bed, the leg chewed by a dog they used to have, back when

Mom was a kid. She could see the crocheted afghan, garishly colored. She could see the dimple in the mattress, hardly a dimple at all, Mom had weighed so little, had dwindled to so little of herself by the end.

"Viv, why don't you come here?" Bachan's voice reached her faintly, as if from a great distance. "It's all right. Look, there's nothing to be afraid of."

Viv glanced away, twisting her split ends around her forefinger.

"We'll do it together. I'll be right here. Look."

She had to, didn't she? Sooner or later? She had to face what was in that room. That sunlit, empty room, without her mother in it.

The tip of her finger was losing circulation now, the skin turning red, then purple, the pressure building painfully with every beat of her fragile heart.

Viv took a deep breath, letting the damaged hair loosen and slide from her finger. A rush of blood. Viv looked up.

And the lady was there. She was there, behind Bachan, at the end of the hall, though she should not have been able to fit; thin as she was, there was not enough space at the end of the hallway, not unless there was more to it, beyond the wall, behind the fourth unimaginable door, in the immense and cunning dark.

The lady lifted a hand, slender and white.

"Bachan, come out of there!" Viv cried.

"What?"

"Just come here! Please!" Viv begged. She squeezed her eyes shut. She could not look.

Then Bachan was beside her. Bachan's arms were around her. Bachan was whispering into her hair, "Shh, shh. It's okay. You can do it in your own time. It's okay."

But it was not okay. It could not be okay. As long as she could not look, could not face it, could not enter her mother's empty room, now and forever without her mother in it, it would never be okay.

Viv pulled back, and only then did she notice Bachan's hands were empty. She rubbed her eyes. "Where's the cap?"

"Oh." Bachan's fingers opened and closed, as if remembering the feel of the yarn, as if she'd been holding it only a second ago, the red hat, but had lost it, dropped it somewhere, between here and there, in the hallway. "I couldn't find it."

THE TRUTH WAS, VIV HADN'T ENTERED THAT ROOM FOR MONTHS, ever since, though she couldn't be certain, she'd given her mother the knit cap—a last happy memory of the two of them together.

After that had been the usual excuses: homework, cross-country practice, a sleepover. She was helping Bachan downstairs, she was at the mall, she was getting boba with some friends from school, oh, no one, you wouldn't know them. Sorry, too tired to hang out tonight, waving to Mom from the doorway, Mom in the little red cap, Viv hardly allowing herself to look at her, not really, before fleeing back down the hall.

The doctors had gone in to get the cancer, but they hadn't gotten all of it, the tumors hadn't had good *edges*, and now Mom was wasting away, the chemo hollowing her out, scraping the fat and muscle from her arms, her legs, her cheeks. Viv couldn't watch. She wouldn't watch. Not her mom, dwindling away, vanishing.

Except she *was* vanishing, wasn't she? Viv thought later, only realized later, stupidly, that vanishing meant that at the end someone would be gone.

Mom beneath the sheets, her legs like toothpicks, impossibly small. Her skinny hands clasped over the afghan. Always wearing the red hat, like that was enough to make up for Viv's not being there, a perfect gift from an imperfect daughter, like if she wore that hat, then it was like Viv was there, even though she wasn't.

Couldn't be.

Wouldn't.

Wouldn't watch her mom disappear by the hour, the day, the week, refused to, not her mom, alone in that bed, in that knit cap, shrinking from the cancer and the chemo, wondering, maybe, why her daughter wouldn't come see her, why they couldn't curl up on the narrow bed together, it's okay, honey, you won't hurt me, binge something trashy and spectacular until they both fell asleep, breathing, quietly, the two of them, together.

Probably Mom knew, Mom understood, Mom was strong like that, stronger than Viv anyway, Viv, who couldn't look, couldn't stand to watch her mother vanish before her eyes like a figure vanishing into the light at the end of a very long tunnel.

Now, though, there was a blank space where Mom should have been, Mom-in-her-last-days. What did she look like, at the end? Her eyes, still bright? Her smile, like it was before, only leaner? Viv didn't know. She wished she could have seen it, wished she'd been braver, because now, in her mind, Mom-at-the-end was faceless, like the noppera-bo Jiichan had told her about one Halloween: a ghost with a face like the blank nub of an eraser.

Like nothing in a knit cap and cotton gown.

Viv was sorry. She hadn't meant to let Mom slip away like that, had always thought there would be more time—hours days, weeks, a lifetime. The knit cap tucked away inside a drawer with the mothballs, something to be unearthed years later while they were cleaning out the dresser. Look, Viv, remember this old thing? Mom putting it on, ha-ha, this old thing, over her shining black hair, not backward this time, laughing, the two of them together, at the dropped stitch, big enough to hook a finger into, and putting it away again, for another day, further on down and down and down the line.

All the usual excuses.

WHEN VIV WENT TO THE HALLWAY THAT NIGHT, THE LADY WAS waiting for her, as Viv knew she would be, not at the end of the hall this time but beside the office, swaying on her too-small ankles, her hip bumping into the console table with its vase of flowers—*thump, thump, thump*—the silk blossoms shuddering at every tender collision.

As usual, her face was turned to the end of the hall, her head cocked toward Bachan's door as if listening for something.

Listening for what? Viv wondered.

For breathing.

Viv had listened for it at Mom's door, too, when she'd been too afraid to look, too afraid to see the chest not rising. She'd listened, but she hadn't looked, couldn't look, wouldn't, the knit cap a blur, like a spot of blood, at the corner of her vision.

She stared at the back of the lady's head, at the red cap, her mother's red cap.

Thump, thump, thump.

The lady extended a hand at her side, like a parent offering to guide an infant across a busy street.

"Mom?" Viv whispered, her voice like a child's again, high and tight with tears.

The lady didn't turn. She wouldn't turn, Viv knew, not even if she touched the shoulder, sharp and brittle through the rough cotton of her nightgown, not even if she took the pallid and skeletal hand.

But she had to turn, didn't she? She had to.

Viv was ready. Viv was *finally* ready. After all these months, she was prepared to look. One more look, that's all she wanted. One final look.

Viv dashed over the threshold. She lunged for the hand.

"Mom!"

But the lady retreated, luring her deeper into the hall. Panicked, Viv swept by the urns, the wind of her passing sending the funeral program fluttering to the floor, face up this time, with that photo of Mom in Viv's knit cap, but Viv didn't notice. She grabbed the lady's hand, tried to wrench her around, but the lady's face would not turn.

"Look at me!" Viv demanded.

But the lady merely drifted backward, lifting out of Viv's grasp and gliding toward the end of the hall, where, behind her in the cavernous dark, the fourth door opened at last.

WHEN VIV WAS YOUNGER, JIICHAN HAD EXPLAINED TO HER THAT four was an unlucky number. Ichi, ni, san, *yon*, he told her to say. Not *shi*. Never *shi*, if you could help it, not that word that sounded like death.

The fourth door.

The last door. A rushing sound like a car in a tunnel, like breathing in a cave.

"WAIT!" VIV CRIED. THEY WERE AT THE END OF THE HALLWAY NOW, with Mom's door open to her left, just a crack, but that was enough: the corner of the bed and the afghan visible and a bright spot of what might have been blood. But Viv did not turn to see it. "I'm sorry! Wait! Please, look at me!"

The lady didn't.

Couldn't?

Wouldn't.

She floated through the fourth door, and Viv could have stopped then, could have looked into her mother's room, could have entered, could have curled up on the dimpled mattress and sobbed the way she hadn't sobbed when Mom died, when she'd stood in the hall the last time, watching Bachan crawl gingerly onto the bed beside the body, barely visible at all beneath the wrinkled sheet.

But Viv did not stop. She couldn't. She had already slipped up. She'd entered the hallway, and now the hallway had got its hooks in her, tiny little hooks sinking into her skin, her pores and veins . . .

Her grief and regrets.

Ignoring her mother's room, she chased after the lady, and no matter how quickly she ran, no matter how many times she shouted for the lady to turn around, the lady always shrank from her, was always a little farther down the hallway, that final hallway, turning and turning and turning, going nowhere yet always out of reach.

Missing hours, Viv thought as she ran, as the tears ran streaming down her cheeks. Wasted days.

They could have had so much time.

CRADLE AND ALL

Kay Costales

I'll love you forever,
I'll like you for always,
As long as I'm living
my baby you'll be.
—*From* Love You Forever *by Robert Munsch*

ACT I

ALL OF MY MOTHER'S STORIES TOLD ME TO STAY AT HOME, STAY in the light, and stay close to your loved ones.

"You just want me with you all the time," I say.

She nods. "Yes. Stay with me forever, my baby." The kiss she always presses to my forehead makes me think of that book.

The one that teachers always read to their students to remind them how much they are loved by their parents. Robert Munsch. A classic.

It's on our bookshelf, given to my mother when my little sister was born. I've listened to her read it a handful of times, even back when we used to sit in the library and go through books together. Years passed since the last time. I can't even remember when that was.

When I walk into the living room, she's on her phone, tapping away at her screen. With the serious look on her face, I immediately know that she's texting her siblings. The five of them are scattered now—three are still in the Philippines, her youngest brother lives in Vancouver, and she's here in Toronto. While she's not looking, I bury Munsch's book beneath others, hiding it.

The other day, I noticed it randomly. I don't know how. All I know is I looked up and suddenly all I could see was the blue cover, the baby on the floor, the words coming to me like the scent of flowers on a breeze. Tears filled my eyes, but I couldn't touch the book. The strength came to me now, though. I only hope she doesn't notice and wonder what I'm doing.

"Any drama?" I ask as I sit down beside her.

"No, nothing new," she says.

I can't read what she's writing. It doesn't matter when I look over her shoulder. Her messages are half English, half Tagalog, and I only speak the former.

My sister Adelina is in the kitchen, working on her new

laptop that she got for her birthday in the summer. First year of high school and she no longer needs to borrow a laptop. It was a privilege for her to get one, especially since our single mom had to take care of it. Between taking care of the kids she has at home and taking care of the family in her birth country, it took some time to get there. We never complained. She works hard, she's caring, she's a super mom who shouldn't need to do so much.

Dad died a long time ago. It's been years and his ghost sticks around.

I think that's when I started believing in paranormal things. He's gone, but not really. Sometimes the door to the bathroom closes on its own. He used to do that because of his superstitions. The mirror in there gave him the creeps, and he thought keeping the door closed would ensure that we were safe from any monsters. The first time it happened was the day after the funeral.

The window wasn't open. There was no one upstairs.

And yet the door closed with its familiar creak. We were having dinner, sitting in silence, when we heard it.

The creak of the hinges. The thud as the door slid into place. Firm, like it was pushed.

"Did you leave the bathroom door open?" Adelina had asked me.

I frowned. "Can't remember."

"That's your dad. Still trying to protect us," my mom said, shaking her head with a little smile. Like it wasn't creepy.

They said stuff like that all the time back in the Philippines during those couple of times that we visited. Our family's ancestral home wasn't very big. Rooms were added through the years during the generation it's belonged to the family. So many people lived and died there. So many names and faces that I couldn't remember, yet everyone treated it like it was normal.

"That's Tatay Paulo," my aunt, Tita Ava, said when pots clattered. "He never could find whichever pot he wanted."

Another time, my mom's cousin came over to see us and laughed at the sight of crumbs at the window. Apparently, there was a lola who liked to snack on fresh pandesal in that spot. She'd dust off her house clothes, always covered in the evidence of her favorite food. Sometimes it was all she ate, they told us, and there's always crumbs even if no one had eaten them there.

Now, Dad's been gone for four years, but he still reminds us about what mattered to him.

The bathroom door closes on its own at least once a week. We never tell anyone about that anymore. People thought it was unsettling. Imagine how they'd feel about having picnics in the cemetery, like my cousins do. It's not so common here, since we don't have relatives buried nearby. That's the thing about immigration. Traditions die because there's no way to uphold them without the necessary history and locations.

I yawn and that ends up being what catches my mom's attention.

She taps my leg. "Sleep early tonight, okay, Ate?"

When she became pregnant with my sister, I stopped being *Anak* and became *Ate*. Big sister. An eternal reminder that I am responsible for her and I set the example for everything.

If I mess up, that means I'm putting her well-being at risk.

"Yeah, yeah," I say and yawn again. "All I do is try to sleep."

"Mm-hmm, always at home," she says. Her attention goes back to her phone.

"Exactly. As always."

I don't think she believes me when I say I'm always at home, that I would never sneak out. There's always a flicker of sadness in her eyes when I pull back after giving her a hug. She still brushes my hair away from my face and cups my cheeks like I'm a little girl again. Her thumbs brush away invisible dirt, like what she used to find when I returned after playing outside for hours.

There were times when I was little that she would cradle me close and kiss the top of my head. As I fell asleep, she'd whisper into my hair, "I love you forever. I hope you'll never keep secrets from me and that's silly, but I'm hoping."

Growing up, I would tell her that I have nothing to hide.

I would never hide anything from her.

And she would smile and laugh, hug me tight, and tell me that she believed me.

Now, we look at each other and say that we know we're always telling the truth. No secrets, no lies, nothing to fear. We both know it's a lie, and I don't think either of us knows what to do about that.

"Did you get enough sleep last night?" she asks and gets up. Probably to get us a snack. Yesterday she did groceries at the Asian store and got us all sorts of treats.

"I tried," I say. "Did you hear me?"

"No, dead asleep."

"Ugh, *so* jealous." I wish I inherited her ability to sleep through typhoons. She snores like a monster and nothing will wake her except, miraculously, her phone alarm. It didn't matter if Addie and I climbed into bed and tried to shake her. It wouldn't matter if we screamed all through the house.

Once she's asleep, she's gone until the alarm goes off.

She laughs from the kitchen. When she comes back, she has a pack of strawberry Pocky that she throws to me. Adelina gets the chocolate version. She mumbles "thanks" without looking away from the computer, probably reading something for class. Wherever she got that studious behavior, it wasn't from me. Mom's so relieved about that.

"My poor baby," Mom sighs. She's talking about me. "Maybe we should punch you in the head. Knock you out. Do you think you'll get to sleep if we do that?" She pretends to punch me in the jaw, all slo-mo.

Sometimes I wake up in the middle of the night and find myself in the bathroom, staring into the mirror and forming creatures out of the shadows. There are remnants of them around my eyes like eyeliner and mascara I've smudged when I forgot I wore them. Sometimes I purposely do that to hide the real dark circles.

"If I can't sleep, I'll study," I lie, and hold up my biology textbook that I've been carrying around. Almost forgot about it, considering how little I've actually opened it. "Gotta get my grades up."

They're fine. I've always been good at getting work done despite feeling like the world is crashing down around me. There's a reason the teachers didn't worry much about me when I stayed home sick for weeks. Friends would bring me the assignments, and hand them in for me. Once I got used to the new medication for my migraines, I was back in class, taking notes, acing tests, preparing for university. Still not as good as Adelina's grades, though.

"Good, good," my mom says. "I'm happy you're focused on school instead of boys and parties."

The face she makes, her nose scrunched up and her tongue sticking out, makes me laugh.

Little does she know, there was a boy I used to meet at night. There was no need to honk the car horn or knock on the door. All he needed to do was shoot me a text and I was climbing out my window to meet him outside.

Not anymore. Not for months.

"No boys for me," I say, crossing my heart.

This time, I'm not lying. But I've been lying since I was Adelina's age. Nearly three years of lies. Day after day, night of sneaking out after night. A boy who was a year older, who lived down the street and went to the same school, who took me to dances and bought us drinks and told me all about his favorite movies that became my favorites, too.

We haven't talked in weeks. I haven't snuck out in months.

My stomach aches suddenly. No, it hurts. It's a searing, phantom pain that shouldn't really be there. Someone else might say I've got butterflies, all nerves and anxiety. That sounds better than the truth, the things that would make my mother cry.

When I finish my snack, I head upstairs. The bathroom door is closed. I have to walk by it to get to my room at the other end of the hall. By the time I'm inside, my phone is in my hand and I'm looking at the screen.

2 Missed Calls.

Every morning, he tries to call. Every afternoon, he tries again. I've ignored all of them. What am I supposed to say? I delete the notifications and turn my phone away once it's plugged in and charging. He doesn't send text messages much anymore. We used to talk all day, sneaking messages during class, greeting each other good morning and good night. Making plans all the time.

Not talking to him now formed a new habit of rarely touching my phone. If I do, I'll want to call him and then I'll cry because everything is ruined. My hands reach for my stomach, instinct drawing them there. I feel hollow, carved empty.

I love him so much it hurts and I hate it so much, I can't look at him or talk to him. All I can do to stop myself from reaching out is tucking my arms to my chest and squeezing my eyes shut. Trying to sleep. Always waking up in the middle of night.

This time, it's the sound of crying. Not my mom or my sister.

It sounds like a baby. I jolt upright, drenched in sweat. My eyes feel swollen like I've been crying, but I can't remember what happened in my dream. I rarely do, like my mind wants to forget everything that happened.

When I reach for my phone to check the time, there's a text

from him. Part of him somehow knows when I wake, when I'm wandering the house and wondering how to go on. Sleep runs and hides from me.

What happened in your nightmare? he texts me, like he knew I'd need someone.

Before I respond, I hesitate. My fingers hover over the keyboard, and then I give in.

The same.

Except it feels like I'm still stuck in it. I get out of bed with aching limbs.

When I walk into the bathroom, it's one in the morning and I'm the only one awake. I keep the lights off, using the flashlight on my phone to illuminate the world around me. The dark should scare. Maybe it would be more frightening if I was anywhere but home. After all, my dad's here. If I was haunted, he could protect me. Maybe he does.

I'm holding on to that as I reach for the tap. I take a step forward and hit something with my foot. Something that doesn't belong. It sounds like a rattle.

A baby wails.

My hand shakes as I bend to pick up the toy. When I touch it, the world turns sideways and I'm lost, tumbling down the rabbit hole into a much darker place.

ACT II

THE CRIES TURN INTO SHRIEKS AS THE WORLD RIGHTS ITSELF.

But everything feels so, so wrong. This isn't my bathroom. This isn't my home at all. I turn around and look at the details. I'm still in a bathroom of some kind, dark and unlit like mine, but smaller. Maybe a guest bathroom, rather than the main one.

A breeze slides through the opening beneath the door. It smells like the antique stores in the countryside, the ones my mom dragged me and Adelina to. It feels old and otherworldly. I feel out of place.

I wrap my arms around my middle, as if trying to protect myself.

And then I hear it again: a baby, crying.

My head snaps up and I find myself moving toward the sound like it's in the corner of the room. In the tub, echoing. The crying gets louder and louder with each slow step I take, then stops. I go still, waiting. It needs me. I heard it in the hiccups and wails, the stuttering gasps for air like it was struggling to survive.

I think about the blood I found between my legs, the way it hurt. Like the cramps you might get on your period. Different, yet similar. Painful as a knife, and I feel that pain again, the stab and twist that brings tears to my eyes. I clutch at my stomach, empty, hollow.

Crying.

Shrieking.

Screeches and sobs.

It's behind me now.

I turn around and find my reflection in a dusty mirror. Over my shoulder, there it is. I can't see the face clearly, only the pouting mouth and trembling lips. It's going to cry again. When I look over my shoulder, there's nothing but the wall there.

Where is it?

Frantically, I wipe at the mirror. The image of the baby appears again with its hands outstretched. It needs me and I can't get to it. Dust sticks to my fingertips, turning them gray. I breathe so hard, my chest hurts. If I don't take care of it before it's gone, is it my fault? Is it punishment for failing?

I had never been in so much pain before. It's gone now, the sharpness of it long since subsided. I wasn't ready for any part of that experience, from the discovery of what was happening to the end of it.

Was it my fault?

"Call for me," I say to nothing. There's some sniffling.

It's still here. The baby is still here, and this time I could do something to help.

The crying starts again and I race toward the sound. My sock-covered feet slide against the tiles and I stumble, grasping onto the shower curtains. They come down with me as I fall, the metal rod holding them coming off the wall. All the air in my lungs whooshes out of me as I drop into the tub.

The empty tub.

But I still hear the crying. I still feel the baby near me even though it's not.

I never saw their face, like this one that hides from me and taunts me. It was too small, too early. I thought I had my period and then I realized it had to be different. I wasn't supposed to bleed like that.

He picked me up early in the morning and we went to the clinic. The same one that I visited after my positive pregnancy test. The same one that confirmed that I wasn't pregnant.

Anymore.

For a second, I lay in the tub in this unfamiliar bathroom, in a house that isn't mine.

I want to weep or scream or tear these curtains to shreds.

"God, I'm sorry. Please, please, was I supposed to pray more? Should I have gone to church?" I sniffle and now I'm the one crying. My eyes sting with tears and I feel. So. Dumb. "I'll do it. Everything I'm supposed to do for you, I'll do it. Just please."

I squeeze my eyes shut. A sob shakes my body. My head falls into my hands and I cover my eyes.

The baby's wails fill the tiny room again. Louder now, like it's in my arms and I'm holding its little body to my chest. Head on my shoulder, mouth to my ear. Screaming, wailing, sobbing and sniffling. My own cries match theirs but I'm holding nothing.

Our wails are in harmony, one that is painfully shrill.

What happens to a baby that doesn't make it to birth? What happens if we don't acknowledge the life and pray for the soul that's lost? When does a soul become a soul? In a Catholic high school, they force you to watch graphic videos and look at gory images of abortion.

They want us to feel guilt. Catholic guilt is so integral to the experience. Being a young woman, one who isn't white, whose family immigrated to the West . . . it feels like I am meant to wear shame like a crown.

I don't want to feel guilty. I don't want to think it was my fault.

When the baby's screams and cries ricochet around me, I slam my hands over my ears and rock back and forth. This isn't like the panic attack I had after we left the clinic. This isn't like the first panic attack I had in my first year of high school that I felt so terribly about I didn't tell any of my friends that it happened.

"It wasn't my fault," I say to the thing that's haunting me.

Stalking me, maybe. Taunting me. I wonder if I'm mistaking mocking laughter for crying.

"I don't want it to be my fault." These words seem better, but they're wrong. It feels like I'm trying to convince myself.

Therapy has helped. Talking to someone about the wicked thoughts in my head that make me feel so bad all the time that it feels like I walked off a cliff into the worst of a storm. Sometimes it feels better to scratch at my arms until I peel away the skin and I'm raw. Sometimes I want to bash my head against stone so it hurts and that pain shakes me to the core, until I'm vibrating with agony. Sometimes I want to be overwhelmed by anything else to cover up the thoughts and feelings that are ugly and cruel and sad.

I want to rip my ears apart. I want to scream. I want to slam my head against the edge of the tub to make the sound go away.

"I don't deserve this," I say, like my therapist reminded me to tell myself.

I don't deserve the bad things that happened, especially the ones beyond my control.

She makes me say that every time I see her. She makes me tell that to myself and speak it aloud to give it life. She tells me that the more I say it, the more I can believe it, and it's a hell of a lot better than the thoughts that overflow in my head.

"It wasn't my fault!" I scream.

A rattle drops into the tub like it had been sitting on the edge. Like it wanted its moment to remind me that it was there. The beads inside of it tap and tap and tap as it rolls between the curved walls of the tub. It bumps into my toes, backs up, then returns to nudge them again.

I kick. "It wasn't my fault!"

It flies into the air, bounces off the tap and the walls and my legs. Eventually, it falls to the floor tiles and goes quiet. Unnaturally quiet. Especially in comparison to the loudness of it only brief moments ago.

My breath waits in my throat.

A baby wails and it's not mine because the one I was going to have is gone, gone, gone. A scream shoots out of me like bullets, and I swear it cuts through the cold air filling the bathroom now. I shake and hug myself, pressing my fingers into my elbows to hold myself together.

It cries and this time, it's softer, beckoning. Whimpering replaces the shrieking wails from earlier and I hear a little sniffle. Have I scared them? Am I the monster and this baby is only here because something in me brought it along with me? I sit up, bracing myself on the edges of the tub and look around.

There's a cradle leaning against the tub now. Small, sitting on the floor, a blanket over the little body tucked inside. My heart hammers painfully as I reach for it.

I followed the white rabbit down the hole and I am tumbling down into insanity.

Only insanity would instruct me to touch the baby, to pick it up and cradle it close. The only thing I can do is lift it up and bring it to my chest, to share my warmth with the little creature inside. It's insanity to be affectionate with something I cannot see. It seems like what I must do, as insane as it might be.

That's what I do, like it's the only thing I can.

I hold it tight and we cry together until it's just me. The baby goes silent, but not still. It wiggles around and presses its face to my neck. Something sharp jabs into my throat and I pull back.

But it's not a baby in my arms.

The thing that stares back at me has eyes like the devil. Black like the night, a red shine to them. Its open mouth does not reveal soft, pink gums. No, it shines teeth at me that are meant for ripping flesh. There's a droplet of blood on one of them. As it dawns on me what this is, I scream.

It won't let me go.

It snarls and snaps its teeth, hands with nails scratching at my shoulders. While it holds firm, I try to yank it away. The tiny hands are too strong, too fierce. I can smell its breath, reeking of meat, raw or rotten. It's acidic and my nose burns.

My skin burns.

I weep and try to shove it away from me.

"Stop, stop, stop!" I scream, but it holds tight. Its teeth scrape at my throat, trying to cut it open, drawing blood. The mouth that released little whimpers now snarls. It's vicious and terrible and it's angry. It's so clear what this thing wants.

To drink.

To hurt.

This is a monster my mother spoke of.

This isn't punishment.

This is a thing that saw my softness, my weakness, my doubts and fears, and took it on itself to lure me close. It knew how to get my attention and make me desperate. It knew how to knock me out from the reality and accept whatever was happening.

I didn't deserve this. I don't need to be punished.

But it preyed on me for wondering if I was wrong. If I actually should be hurt because I caused hurt. I didn't mean to. What happened was an accident, from the beginning to the end. We didn't know it would be like this. That we would gain and lose so quickly, and how agonizing it would be.

The name comes to me slowly, one syllable at a time, until I remember.

Tiyanak.

A creature that can resemble a baby and mimic one. That calls out to those who would hear and draw close. That feasts on those it ensnares.

It caught me, but it won't kill me. My mother had warned me of things like this.

I'm grateful for the rosary I've started wearing around my wrist. Unwrapping it takes so long, even more as the energy drains from me, as the tiyanak takes my blood. It's still latched onto me, teeth under the skin, sucking at my veins.

Until I take the rosary and twist it around its neck.

It shoves me away so fast, my head slams against the edge of the tub.

ACT III

My body slams back into reality and I'm upright. There's hair in my mouth because my lips parted when I gasped and jerked awake at the sound. Guilt rips into me like a rabid beast with thick claws, gouging me open, and I bleed and bleed and bleed. My hands find my stomach, clutch at it as the phantom pain haunts me. It always haunts me.

It's gone. I'm home.

I'm back in my bathroom, my wrist bare. Where did I even go? When I look into the mirror, it's like I'm seeing someone else. This girl looks like she's seen ghosts, like she's more worldly and knowing.

What if I'll be haunted by this? What if I'll never have a baby, even when I'm ready for one? If I ever am.

I'm too young now, but one day, I won't be.

Thoughts race through my mind about my choices, my chances, what's in my control and what's beyond it. It does nothing for me to dwell on that. I need action and, for some reason, I decide to head outside, with a rattle in my hand. My body goes straight to the little tree in the corner of the backyard, and I drop to my knees, reaching for the soil.

I dig and dig, creating a hole for a body I don't have. The only thing I've got is the rattle, the one that I've wrapped in a hand towel because I'm afraid to touch it. What if it brings me back to that house and that room? That bathroom trapping all sound, an echoing meant for caves. A prison of torment and monsters and this creature that wants me to remember a lost life.

A baby that was never meant to be.

I'm too young for this, I think as I dig. My hands turn brown with dirt. *It's all my fault. I've ruined everything.*

No, that's not true. It's not my fault. I had no control over the loss.

As the sun rises, I'm sitting under the tree in my backyard. Dirt sticks under my nails, evidence of how I spent my night. The hole I created is covered up and inside, I've stuffed the rattle, never to touch it again. To see the tiyanak. To hate myself and wonder if I deserve to be punished.

I don't. It's over.

I've buried it. I've put this all to bed.

These last few years, I haven't been a good Catholic girl, but I think I've done my duty now. I hope we can both finally rest. There will be a new rosary around my wrist, wrapped tight so it won't fall away without my notice. I know my mother has one. I'll ask her for it once we talk about what happened. All of it. No more secrets.

I stand up, dust myself off, and head inside. My mom is awake, sitting at the dining table, drinking her coffee with a bowl of champorado in front of her. It's become a light brown now, the chocolate-coated rice doused in condensed milk in a too-sweet concoction that only she likes. Sitting down beside her, I sigh, my fists on the table. Before I can reach for her, my mom takes my hand in hers and grips it tight.

"There was a baby," I tell her. "Almost."

She looks at me with soft eyes when I lose my voice and can't continue.

"We aren't superstitious at all, are we?" she asks with a little smile.

She knows. Maybe she always did. When she uncurls my fingers, there's the shape of the rattle in the palm of my hand, but when she touches it, it disappears. With my other hand, I touch my neck, where the tiyanak bit me. It's over. It's gone.

But I'll always have scars.

AFTER MIDNIGHT

Liz Hull

12:00 a.m., July 16

I KNEW TO KEEP MY EYES CLOSED NOW, BUT I HADN'T ALWAYS. ITS breath crackled and hissed like a fire on wet branches, and I could see it as clearly as I had the first night.

If you've seen death up close, you'd recognize it in a heartbeat. And a heartbeat would be exactly what it took. The yawning, crumbling mouth of a grave. The putrid, oversweet smell of rotting flowers. A slow build to an abrupt, permanent end.

It lunged toward the bed, the force of it pushing the heavy mahogany frame a few inches to screech along the old wooden floorboards.

Nature is beautiful, but that's just a distraction. What's natural is the most brutal, the most feral. Life unapologetically sustains itself on death, and I guess in a way now, so do I.

9:00 a.m., July 16

I MISS YOU.

I didn't miss him. I don't know why I even sent the text, to be honest. I knew I wasn't going to get a response. I never did.

I woke up here alone every morning, though I rarely went to sleep that way.

Clear morning sun filtered in through the linen lace curtains, throwing faint, shadowed constellations across the bed. The light bounced off every glossy leaf in the room, reflecting a warm green onto the walls. There were *a lot* of leaves in that room.

How many houseplants would you say is too many, by the way? Because I hadn't ever thought of it before this summer. I didn't think it was something you'd need to set a healthy limit around. But here I was, waking up to probably hundreds of silent forms breathing all around me. Hungry for sunshine. Thirsty for life, or whatever. One monstera leaf reaching out in front of the window even caught a breeze every now and then, waving eagerly.

"Okay, okay, I'm coming." I sighed, throwing the perfect white cloud of the duvet off me and ignoring the missed calls piling up on the home screen of my phone.

And yes, I was talking to the plants. Who else was I going to talk to, the cat? She wouldn't be awake for hours, and even when she did get up it'd just be to ask for more food. Everything in this house always wanted more and, as much as it felt like a full-time job to keep everything alive (it was, to be clear, my only job this summer), it was a fully perfect cottagecore fantasy.

I slid out of bed and headed blearily down the stairs. Three steps down, I kicked a half-full Solo cup and sent it bouncing, spilling a watered-down carbonated something-or-other all the way as it went. I groaned, wiping the bottom of my wet foot against the edge of the stairs. You think I'd know to be careful by now.

What I did know is that it was going to take me most of the morning—like it did most mornings—to clean up from the night before.

11:46 p.m., July 15

THE NIGHT BEFORE.

The music had been so loud you could barely hear anyone next to you unless they screamed. And even then—

"What time is it?" I'd shouted directly in his ear, pressing him against the wall where we stood at the bottom of the stairs.

"Probably midnight," he'd shouted back above the bass. He slid a hand up my hip and around to the small of my back. God, what was his name, anyway? Ethan? Ethan's always a safe guess.

"Probably?" My voice cracked this time. If I was worried about anything, which I wasn't, I might have worried my voice sounded a little too much like I cared in that moment. A little too urgent.

I grabbed his phone and swatted his hand away when he tried to reach for it: 11:46 p.m. Okay. We could work with that.

"What's the matter?" he asked, raising one eyebrow in a way I'm sure he thought was attractive but for some reason made him look even more like a TV magician than he already did. He was a real flashy belt-buckle of a human. "You going to turn into a pumpkin at midnight?"

"That's an incredibly Dad thing to say, Ethan," I said, rolling my eyes.

"So you're saying I'm incredible," he replied.

I shoved his shoulder harder against the wall and he let out a sour exhale of a laugh. This was all so much easier when I kind of hated them.

I smiled anyway. "Come upstairs with me."

10:00 a.m., July 16

I ZONED OUT WHILE REFILLING A GORGEOUS BRASS WATERING CAN IN the kitchen. Sepia bouquets of dried flowers hung in a row above the window, framing the view of a bright, riotous tangle of roses in the garden outside. They were taller today. Reaching, grasping for more of the hot summer sun. The smell of star jasmine filled every corner of reality here, and it was so easy to just stare sometimes. To forget.

I'd been taking care of this place for a month now. This was supposed to be my last summer at home before college—the kind of summer where I fell in love and made stupid decisions and slept in late, but it turned out I couldn't stay at home even a day longer than I had to, and my parents happened to feel the exact same way.

The profile I'd made on this house-sitting app had only been live for a few hours when a woman hit me up asking if I'd be available to look after her place for the next two months starting pretty much immediately. I never even met her in person.

It hadn't taken me long to realize she knew exactly what she was looking for when she found me. She must have seen my name on the news and figured I was a safe bet. She wasn't wrong.

The watering can spilled over. I shut off the faucet and glanced at my phone next to the sink, lighting up with an incoming text. It was Daniela. Again.

11:48 p.m., July 15

"Ro!" Daniela had called last night from somewhere behind me in the hallway. I didn't turn, but I didn't need to. I knew her voice well enough to only need a single syllable. Relentless, tenacious. "Rowan!"

I didn't have time for this.

"Who's that?" Ethan asked, his lips grazing my ear. It made me shudder, and it was clear he thought that was a good thing.

"Don't worry about it," I said, not sure if he could even hear me. Tugging on his arm, I started up the broad, dark wooden stairs. "If she's too good for me, she's definitely too good for you."

I was relieved they didn't know each other, even though I had no idea how they could. The anonymity here was key. I learned very quickly, maybe just the second night, that I couldn't bring anyone I knew up to my room.

You might be surprised how easy it is to find a house's worth of high schoolers from at least three neighboring towns ready to party at the mere whisper of a huge unsupervised cottage at the edge of the woods with plenty of off-street parking. And don't even get me started on the college kids home for the summer with nothing better to do and the fake IDs ready to supply night after night.

At first, it was mostly kids I knew from school. At first, it was just a regular party I was throwing the way any high school senior might their last summer at home. Now, a party every night might seem overboard, but I had the advantage of recent public tragedy clearing the way for pretty much any behavior on my part. We all have our coping mechanisms, after all. So at this point, I knew barely a quarter of the people here on any given night and those were my kinds of odds.

Still, no matter how hard I tried (and honestly I hadn't tried that hard), I couldn't keep Daniela away.

I glanced back on our way up the stairs and I wish I hadn't.

Daniela's big brown eyes stared hard at me behind those comparatively big glasses. She looked cuter than she had any right to, with her oversized faded green T-shirt and those black shorts, like some sort of Jurassic Park tour guide angel. Her dark curls came to a perfect edge right at the bottom of her chin, and I knew they took a lot of upkeep but were worth every minute.

She was going to hate me for this. She should, at least. I hated me.

12:00 p.m., July 16

I RUMMAGED THROUGH A DRAWER TO GRAB A PAIR OF SUNGLASSES. The drawer stuck for a second, and I had to yank it to get it open. There was too much junk in here. Wallets, keys, sunglasses, phones. The things people left behind when the party ended.

I'd probably need to purge all of this at some point. All of the phones were off, but I wasn't sure if that mattered. Could their location still be tracked? That was a nightmare just waiting to happen. I decided to not think about it.

I found my favorite pair—a sleek, expensive-looking type that happened to fit my face really well with the extra bonus of having basically no glare. Hannah had left these here. That had been three weeks ago now. I honestly wouldn't have invited Hannah that night if I'd known then it would mean I'd never see her again.

I slid the sunglasses onto the top of my head, pushing my hair back out of my face. On my way out to the garden, I stepped into a pair of boots and out past the line of other shoes in all sizes on the back deck.

I cut almost a dozen roses, right at the spot I'd learned, above the first set of five leaves. I'd never seen roses in some of these colors before. A deep burgundy that almost sunk into black, a bright coral the exact shade of global warming (RIP Great Barrier Reef), a purple so pale and indistinct I could barely remember the tint whenever I looked away.

The snap peas had scrambled so desperately up and down their own trellises that I filled two mixing bowls and then spent a while watching videos about how to cut them back to encourage more growth without killing them. I was pretty sure there was only one way to kill them, though, or only one way they'd die.

Standing up and wiping off my bare knees from where I'd knelt next to the garden bed, I knocked over one of the bowls of snap peas and cursed. They'd spilled out all over the grass, and I ended up back on my hands and knees to scoop them all into the bowl.

A glint of something caught my eye at the base of one of the trellises. I reached in past the thin, flowering vines and felt something smooth and round sticking out of the dirt. I pulled on it.

An old rattle.

My skin went cold. I wasn't the only one hiding the things people left behind.

I laid the rattle carefully back where I'd found it and patted dirt on top of it. Who knew what else all this life, all this wild and greedy growth was covering up.

11:49 p.m., July 15

WITH EVERY STEP UP TOWARD MY ROOM AND AWAY FROM DANIELA, I was haunted by my sister's voice in my ear. She'd asked the same thing every night for the past week, and I had a sinking feeling she was going to ask again tonight. And the next.

"When am I going to get to meet Daniela?" she had asked, all innocence. "I can tell she's a good one."

"Don't you dare," I'd said. "She's not your type, anyway."

"Oh, come on," she said with a pout. "You know that anyone important to you is important to me. I'd much rather meet someone you love than any of these other losers you keep bringing around."

"That's exactly what I'm afraid of."

6:30 p.m., July 16

TIRES ROLLED UP THE GRAVEL DRIVE AS I SPOONED WET FOOD INTO the cat's bowl. I heard the familiar double-beep of a Subaru locking. The audacity. It was incredible. I couldn't help but smile to myself.

She didn't knock. Daniela clomped up the front porch and walked straight in after pausing for just a second, her image coming into clearer focus through the etched glass of the broad front door.

"By all means," I called from the end of the hallway. "Come right in!"

Relief washed over her face for just a second, but plenty of disdain was left when that was done. "Why haven't you answered any of my calls or texts? I've been trying to get ahold of you all day."

"I've been busy! I've got a lot going on here," I said, motioning to the cat who was quietly and methodically inhaling his food next to me on the floor.

She pressed her lips tightly together and looked away. She closed the door behind her and slipped out of her work shoes.

It was clear she'd come straight from her shift, all in black with two compostable to-go boxes in her hands. She set those down on the antique storage bench at the entryway.

"Who was that last night?" Okay. So she was getting straight down to it.

"Ethan." I tilted my head in exaggerated doubt. "At least he answered to Ethan." I picked up the cat, ignoring its protesting mew, and leaned my face against it.

She definitely didn't think that was cute. She ignored my smile and went on soberly. "What happened to Hannah?"

"That's a great question!" I shrugged, flippant, kissing the cat on the back of his round little head. Daniela was still standing at the entryway, the hallway between us feeling like a chasm. "I wish I could tell you. If you hear anything, let me know."

"And what about Alex after that? Or Taylor? Or the countless parade of people I know you've never met before and won't ever see again?" She took two steps forward, thank goodness.

"Listen, I get it." I said, putting the cat down and leaning against the kitchen island. I should have met her in the middle. I should have closed the distance between us, but it felt so much easier, so much more comfortable, to keep it. "I'm fully cursed. I get ghosted night after night. I'm very aware of how pathetic it looks, Dan."

"Don't *Dan* me, Rowan," she said. One more step forward. "This isn't like you."

"Are you sure?" I asked, deadpan.

"Yes, actually," she said, unfazed. God, I loved that she was more or less completely impervious to my shit. She knew it, too. It made her even more self-righteous. "I have plenty of data to support the theory that this is just you punishing yourself for what happened to your sister."

I stood up straight. "Careful," I warned.

"Fine," she raised her hands in peace. "We'll get to that later. But you didn't let me finish. I'm not just asking why you slept with Hannah out of nowhere—"

"I didn't, technically."

"What?"

"I didn't sleep with her," I said in earnest. "Sure, she came back to my room, but we didn't even kiss." That was the truth, by the way.

"Oh," she said. Her brows knit together above those thinly gold-framed glasses for a second, and I could tell it caught her off guard. She shook her head. "That's besides the point. You know that's not really what I'm asking, Rowan. What *happened* to her?"

11:50 p.m., July 15

I FELT THE ENERGY SHIFT LIKE USUAL AS SOON AS I STEPPED UP ONTO the second-floor landing. The walls of the white hallway shone blue from the moonlight on the stained-glass picture window at the top of the stairs.

Up here, the music thrummed through the floor like the heartbeat of the house itself.

The party rarely found its way up here. I think most people

had an instinct, a very right and good instinct, to stay away. I couldn't be sure—I didn't feel it, obviously. I felt something else.

The room at the end of the hall, my bedroom, pulled at me like an invisible rip current.

Have you ever stood by the ocean at night, fully in the dark? It felt like that. Quiet and thunderous all at the same time. Dark and powerful and bursting with life just below the rolling black surface.

Ethan stalled. "Maybe we should head back down," he said, trying to sound nonchalant and failing miserably.

"Oh, come on," I said, turning to face him and throwing my arms over his shoulders. I pulled him closer and he stumbled forward into me. "Is that what you really want?" I whispered against his cheek, the corner of my mouth barely a breath away from his.

He took advantage of that proximity and closed that distance to kiss me. His hot mouth tasted like a sidewalk cigarette.

"That's what I thought," I said, pulling away. I tugged at his arm again, drawing him down the hall.

I wasn't sure if the door to my room was actually heavier than any of the others, but it sure felt like it. I turned the antique glass doorknob and heard we weren't alone before I'd even gotten it all the way open.

"Hey! We're in here!" A guy's voice shouted over the sound of giggling behind him. Well, that was weird. The surprise caught me off guard for a second. No one ever just willingly came in here.

"Clearly," I said, pulling Ethan into the room. "But this is my room, so I'm going to need you to get out in the next minute or so."

I picked up a shirt from the floor a few feet from the door and tossed it at the two bodies on the bed. The dimly lit room glowed pink from the silk scarf I'd thrown over the lampshade and, as my eyes adjusted, I recognized one of the bodies as the kid who sat in front of me in AP Gov last year—Connor Green. What did Connor have going on in his life that he found his own way to this room? I guess you really couldn't judge a book by its waifish, Chalamet-shaped cover.

"There are plenty of other rooms up here," Connor grumbled, pulling the shirt over his floppy black curls.

"Exactly," I replied, matter-of-fact. "That's why I'm not even a little worried about you finding literally anywhere else to go."

Connor and some girl I didn't recognize fumbled past us and I closed the door behind them.

Finally.

I let out a long breath, emptying my lungs and letting my shoulders drop. It was hard to keep track of how tense my body got over the course of the day until I got to this moment each night. The not knowing really did get to me, though. Not knowing if I'd be able to find the right person to bring up here, not knowing if maybe tonight would be the night she wouldn't show up.

Just a few minutes now, though.

Ethan ran his hand down the long knife-edge of a snake plant sitting on the hardwood floor in a tall white and gold planter. The lamplight cast sharper shadows than you'd think, up the wall and onto the ceiling. If you paid close enough attention, which no one ever did, you'd notice them shift and sway as if they were made by dancing candlelight.

"Come here," I said, walking across the room and lifting myself up onto the tall, four-poster mahogany bed. It creaked just a little under me.

Ethan looked up, his eyes heavy. He followed, and I could tell that lust and confusion were starting to fight for control over his mind. There was a part of him that wanted me and a part of him that wanted to run. It made him slow and sluggish.

This wasn't new for me. This was just how it worked. This is what happened to Hannah. This is what happened to Alex, to Taylor, to Olivia, to Mateo, to Laura, to Devon. I brought them in here and then I turned my back on them.

I was the bait, not the hook.

6:35 p.m., July 16

"I HONESTLY DON'T KNOW WHAT HAPPENED TO HANNAH," I LIED. I mean, it was mostly a lie. I had a pretty clear idea of what happened to her, but I didn't witness it. I didn't watch. I wasn't a monster.

11:55 p.m., July 15

ETHAN CAME WITHIN ARM'S REACH OF THE BED, SO I PULLED HIM TO me one more time, and the contact brought him back into his body for a minute. He climbed up onto the bed, and I scooted myself back into the middle and laid down, motioning for him to follow.

The light bulb started to flicker and buzz. The shadows stretched and yawned and darkened on the ceiling. They climbed like vines down the walls and to the floor. They sprouted and grew and bloomed to the right of the bed, next to Ethan. They broke through the fabric of reality—not just shadow anymore, but into a tangible, inky form that cracked and popped like branches underfoot or snapping fruit from a tree.

This was my cue.

7:00 p.m., July 16

DANIELA AND I STOOD TOGETHER AT THE COUNTER EATING BURRITO bowls she'd brought from work. She'd let the whole Hannah thing drop. She'd let all conversation drop for the time being, and the silence was really getting to me. I needed to get her out of the house before the party started.

"You deserve better than this," I said, looking down into my bowl.

"I know," she agreed. She turned to me and reached out, cupping the side of my face in her hand and lifting my head to meet her gaze. "That's why I'm here asking for it. Give me better."

If I dared take a breath, I knew it would be shaky. I could feel myself wilting in the face of her openness. That was what real bravery looked like.

"I don't think I have anything better to give right now," I said. "I only have much worse."

"I get it, Rowan," she said gently. "You've been through so much. I can't imagine what it's like to lose your sister. She was—"

"Don't," I cut her off. "Don't talk about Willow in the past tense." It was so hard to keep my guard up around Daniela, as much as I wanted to. All sorts of real, honest emotions just slipped out. "I'm doing everything I can to keep her in the present. Don't underestimate what sacrifices I'm willing to make to do that."

"And that's a really beautiful thing to want! Of course you should keep her memory alive. But you need to grieve at some point so you can heal. You need to accept that Willow is already gone."

That's where she was wrong. "She's only gone if I let her go."

Her hand dropped from my face. "So because you feel responsible for her death, you want to ruin your life? You think she'd want you to sacrifice yourself like this? It's so clear the ways you're self-destructing, Rowan. Partying, drinking, sleeping with strangers every single night when you have someone right here who is so ready to love you."

"Oh, I'm not sacrificing myself," I said, tripping in my mind over the last words she'd just said, shaking them off before I dared cling to them. *So ready to love you.*

"What are you sacrificing, then?"

"Everyone else."

11:59 p.m., July 15

I KNEW WHAT I'D SEE IF I STARED WITH ETHAN AT THE FORM TAKING shape next to him. I knew the gray, crooked fingers, nails like thorns. The pallid eyes. The mouth like a tunnel straight to hell. I knew the sucking, sinking feeling. But no, this part wasn't for me. We had a deal.

I turned my back on Ethan and faced the other way, laying my head on the pillow and closing my eyes tight. His hand grasped at my shoulder, then the sleeve of my shirt. Pressing my eyes together even tighter, I tried to shrug him off. I gripped a fistful of the down comforter and tensed every muscle while a ravenous roar like a forest fire blazed just beyond the edge of the bed.

Ethan's other hand closed around my neck right before he lost his grip and was dragged off the bed.

"Hi," a voice, all smiles, whispered close to my face and I couldn't open my eyes fast enough.

It was my sister. Willow.

"Hi," I replied, kicking my feet a little bit out of excitement like we did in bed as kids. She did the same.

Willow's skin looked bright and perfectly clear. She beamed, mischievous. She looked even more radiant tonight. Stronger. More alive. That—the aliveness of it all—was the best part.

That's because Willow was in fact dead. She'd been dead for a month.

It was my fault and we both knew it. Everyone knew it. It had been all over the local news, since ours was just one of eight cars involved. I had been driving that night. Whenever I thought of it, I could hear the shattering glass, feel the scream burning in my throat, smell the blood. The memory of it pulled me out of the moment, so when Ethan let out a scream behind me, I almost turned my head as a reflex, but Willow caught me. "Eyes on me, stupid."

"I know, geez. Sorry," I said in mock defense. She'd protect me from the reality, the apparent horror, of what was happening behind me. She always did. "It's not like I'm going through literal hell every single night just to put my eyes on you. At least be a little grateful."

"Oh, Rowan, you know this is for you more than it is for me," she said, patronizing in the way only an apparition of a dead older sister could. "I'm not even a little bit here."

"But that's not even true! You are very much right here and you're going to stay right here until I fall asleep," I said, mostly just to hear the words out loud and believe them again. I had Willow back. That was all that mattered.

12:00 a.m., the first night

THE FIRST NIGHT I HAD COME TO STAY IN THIS HOUSE AND FALLEN asleep in this bed, I'd dreamt of Willow. Not of the accident, like all the nights before I came here, but of the living, thriving Willow from before. It felt incredibly real, and I was more lucid than I had ever been while dreaming.

"I love you so much and I'm so sorry," I'd said to her in that dream. "I want so badly for this to be real, but I know it's a dream."

"It doesn't have to be," she said, excitement suddenly in her eyes.

"What do you mean?"

"This is great, actually." She started to pick up steam like I'd just confirmed something for her. "Perfect. If this is what you want, I can be with you every night. Like, for real, not just in the dream world. I just need you to do something for me."

"I'll do anything," I said immediately. I meant it.

"That's what I thought," she said, her face radiant and roguish. It felt so good to see her that I was almost able to ignore that something felt really off about her tone. About the way she moved her mouth when she spoke. Something that felt like a warning at the edges of my vision, but if I turned to look, there would have been nothing there. It was a dream, so I didn't read too much into it.

"I need you to bring someone up here into this bedroom at midnight," she said. "Every night. Do you think you can do that?"

"Of course, that's easy," I said, eager for more instruction. "Why?"

"Don't worry about why. I'll take care of it, okay? Don't I always?"

She didn't usually, actually. Willow was a beautiful, clever mess. At least she knew it. I had always been the one to take care of both of us, and I was determined to do that now, too. I wouldn't fail her again.

Willow didn't wait for me to respond. "Rowan, listen to me," she said. "Remember this and do it tomorrow, okay? Every night you bring someone up here, I'll come find you. And you have to trust me. You have to stay in the room, and keep whoever is with you here until midnight, and just trust that I'll be here, no matter what happens. Can you do that? For me?"

"I'll try," I said. And I did.

I knew now what had been hovering near me that night. What had come for me and smelled the death on me. The opportunity it saw. We could do a lot more together than it could alone. As long as I got what I wanted—as long as I had Willow back—I'd be and do whatever this wild creature, this ghoul, this dark dream-granting, shape-splitting-and-shifting monster asked of me.

What choice did I really have?

The bait doesn't choose what gets caught on the hook, anyway. It's caught there itself.

7:05 p.m., July 16

DANIELA LOOKED INTO MY EYES THERE IN THE KITCHEN, SEARCHING for the answer to a question she hadn't asked yet. Eventually, she got around to it. "And would you sacrifice me?"

"Please, Dan," I said, closing my eyes. "Please don't ask me to make that decision."

12:05 a.m., July 16

THE WHOLE, CLAMOROUS STRUGGLE BETWEEN ETHAN AND THE ghoul had quieted down, and the rumble of the bass below had, too. People clearly subconsciously knew when it was time to filter out. I didn't need to be there to tell them.

"You know what I'm going to ask, don't you?" Willow asked.

"Yeah, but I wish you wouldn't," I replied, my stomach turning a little. "Can't we talk about literally anything else?"

"There's not much else to talk about at this point, Rowan." She chewed the inside of her cheek in a way I had never seen her do in life.

"Sure there is, what about—"

She cut me off. "You know what would give us so much more to talk about, though? Like, nights and nights of things to talk about? You bringing Daniela to meet me."

"Why?" I challenged.

Her expression hardened. "Who knows you better than Daniela? Don't you get it? If you bring Daniela to me, I'll be able to incorporate all her memories. It'll be even better for you—"

This time I cut her off. "No," I said. "Stop. Don't talk like that, please." I wanted Willow back. And I had Willow back. When she said things like this it didn't feel like it, though. It felt wrong.

She didn't miss a beat. "Okay. Well how about this: Who do you love more?"

She watched my face while I searched my own mind for an answer.

7:10 p.m., July 16

"Don't come to the party tonight," I pleaded, turning away from Daniela's gaze. I knew I didn't deserve the compassion she was giving me, but that didn't stop me from craving it. And craving it felt dangerous. It felt confusing.

"Why not?" She asked. "What are you going to do?"

"I don't know."

I didn't know. I didn't want to have to think about any of this, I just wanted to keep existing. Keep pressing forward. Keep taking care of the house while it took care of me. Keep doing what it took to survive and it felt like having Willow with me, just for a little bit each night, was what it took. I didn't want to think about what would happen after, and I hadn't had to yet.

11:59 p.m., July 16

It was the same as every other night until it wasn't.

Daniela had finally left before the party started, even though it took plenty of arguing.

Luckily, I'd met a guy who had brought a ton of alcohol and who was definitely trying to pass for a high schooler but looked old enough to play a high schooler on a gritty TV soap.

He was leaning in to kiss my neck now, his stubble rough. The bass pounded through the floorboards and straight through the bed into my body. I blankly watched the shadows twist and swell into form behind him.

"Rowan?"

No.

Damnit. My stomach dropped. Daniela was just outside the door, trying to turn the knob.

"Rowan?" Willow echoed, now right behind me.

What choice did I really have? That's the question I had been asking myself, but this was it. This was the choice. It wasn't between life and death, after all. Death would eventually win either way. It always did.

I really hadn't known what I was going to do. I did now.

I loved her so much and I wasn't going to lose her.

Second Floor

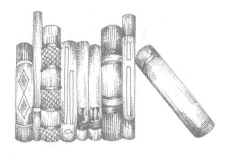

THE GREY
LIBRARY

Nova Ren Suma

S HE WON'T KEEP HER EYES OFF ME. AS SOON AS I STEP THROUGH the door, she locks her gaze on me and follows my every move, a pearl of spit glistening at the corner of her mouth. She's not able to communicate in words—she doesn't yet have the motor control or know language—but she gurgles some kind of greeting. Her hands squeeze into fists. Her fat tongue flicks. All the while I don't catch her eyes blinking even once.

"You come highly recommended," her father says to me as he ushers me into the large fortress of his gated house. "I can see why. Genevieve has taken a shine to you already. Usually she cries when she meets a stranger."

Genevieve, my client tonight, is in the padded playpen in the center of the expansive living room, aloft on two stubby legs, swaying. She's not crying. She's not making any sound but for the bubbling of saliva leaking down her chin. But those eyes, glassy and bottomless as if she knows truths about me even I don't know yet, as if she can foretell a coming doom, has seen it, has tasted it, is willing it to arrive faster. Those eyes. They're shining.

They're also the worst kind: defiantly uncolored, having not chosen between brown and blue and even, in some lights, emerald green. She has jet-black silken hair with a light curl at the ends. She has what they call rosebud lips. Her belly is poking out from an open snap and is round and pink. She's very young, or maybe it's that her father is very old. He has a full head of silver hair and washed-out eyes behind the barrier of his glasses. I would have thought him her grandfather if he hadn't made it clear I was here to watch his daughter.

"Thank you, Mr. Grey," I say, in the way I'd speak to any parent who hired me. "We'll have a good night together, Genevieve and me, I promise."

For a moment—fast and fleeting—a twitch cracks his face. Then he's carefully smoothed and bland again, acting fatherly, trusting. He needs to be. He lives alone with his infant daughter in this grand old house at the end of the long and rolling driveway, and there's no one else here.

When Mr. Grey called to hire a babysitter, he said he had a very important engagement in the city that could not be missed, and he needed someone to watch Genevieve. She can be a handful, he explained, but there was no one else, since the last few sitters hadn't worked out and since her mother had gone. And he hung there a moment, as if hesitant about me, as if he didn't think I was worthy, and I rushed in to say I could handle the job. I wasn't bothered to hear that there were babysitters who hadn't lasted—most teenagers I know aren't the best at being responsible. They spend hours scrolling their phones, ignoring their charges, or they sneak companions inside and make out on the couch. They don't know how to restrain themselves.

What I was curious about was the mother. The word Mr. Grey used was simple and without explanation: Genevieve's mother had *gone*. He said it in a way that seemed intentional. I didn't know when she'd gone, or where, or how long she'd been away and if she was coming back, but it wasn't my business to ask. And really, all that mattered was that she wasn't here.

What Mr. Grey doesn't know, what I keep from all the parents, even my own, is that I don't even like babies. I can't be softened by the sound of their gummy-mouthed babble, I don't like the way they blob out in their bassinets, and I don't appreciate the chaos that comes when they attempt to crawl or, worse, walk. Even so, when I babysit, I'm all in. I have gentle but capable hands, and the parents who hire me to watch their children appreciate that. They trust me. I'd never hurt a helpless creature—when I lift an especially young one up out of the cradle, I'm careful to support the neck and protect the soft, squishy part of the head. I'm only fifteen and the most sought-after babysitter in the whole of our neighborhood. I'm booked solid every Saturday night through spring, and yet somehow, on short notice, here I am.

Now I study the living room with curiosity: There are no photos of anyone anywhere. There's only abstract, unknowable artwork on the walls; tall-necked lamps with wide, drooping shades; clawlike feet on the furniture; no visible TV. The only thing to watch in the room is Genevieve herself. Her padded cage has one toy—a mop-headed doll, face down—and otherwise she's in it alone, watching me.

I'd never seen this house before this evening, even though it sits on the outskirts of our neighborhood and I could walk to it. There's a looping ring of roads that make up the area of houses where I've lived all my life, and I know most of them, but this is the outer ring, the last drifting edge, where the road cuts to a stop and a tall iron gate keeps the curious from wandering in. I've never known a house to have such an imposing gate, but this one does. The trees are spindly and bald. The grass is yellowed, growing in sparse and random bursts. I've heard my parents say they're glad our house isn't near the edge, because the soil was sour and wouldn't let the blooms survive in their garden. But it was worse. When I made my way through the gate and walked the winding driveway until the house was finally in view, I passed through a pebbly patch of land dotted with gaunt shrubs and nothing else living, so I suspect Mom and Dad were right that the land out here should be avoided. Then again, they're the reason I have this job in the first place.

"Thank you for agreeing to come so last minute, Kelsey," Mr. Grey says. "I was grateful to your parents when they suggested you."

"I don't mind. Like I told you, it's kind of weird, but the family I was supposed to sit for tonight canceled and I was free."

He nods, because I told him that already. Or did I? Was I only sharing that now?

A fog of confusion comes over me. My mom and dad were in their own fog after they talked to Mr. Grey the other day. They were fuzzy on details. My mom remembers finding herself standing at the rolled-down window of the sleek car that had stopped beside the garden beds and speaking to the silver-haired man, the dirt in her hands.

My dad was there, too—they tend to the garden together, though he spends a lot of time sunning himself in a lawn chair that faces the road. All he remembers is getting a splitting headache in the midday glare, coincidentally around the same time a car stopped and the gentleman neighbor rolled down his window, so he let Mom take care of making conversation.

Genevieve breaks me out of my fog with a brutish squeal. She's not playing with her doll. She's standing on chubby legs in her playpen while her father gives me a brief tour. There's the living area, the diapering table, the set of miniature spoons and pureed foods in the kitchen, the medicine chest, the emergency numbers for fire, pediatrician, police. Nothing is abnormal here. Everything is arranged as if from a manual for new parents. Nothing is amiss.

Mr. Grey reminds me that his evening event will go late. "Are you sure your parents won't mind? Did you let them know?"

"They know, Mr. Grey. They don't care."

He checks my face carefully. I'm not sure what he thinks he sees there.

My parents were acting like they didn't care this morning. They didn't save me a stack of Saturday pancakes like usual—fried in butter, drizzled honey on top—and instead I walked into the kitchen to find them cleaning their dishes together at the sink, a pair of plates and a pair of forks, as if they lived in our house just the two of them alone. I had to make do with cold cereal.

When I left the house hours later, my parents were out in their square of garden again, giving the patch of dirt such attention it seemed they were trying to count every bushy-tailed weed and blade of grass. I stood over them so the sun drew my shadow across their backs, but they didn't turn around. "So I'm going now," I told them. "And I'll be out late." They must have heard me—I was literally two feet away—but all my mom said was, "What did you say, honey?" and my dad responded, "I said the bees are still out," and my mom said, "Looks like it." And in a grotesque display of affection in view of anyone passing on the street, they held hands. They couldn't tear their eyes away to acknowledge their one and only child waving and walking down the sidewalk with an overnight bag. They're probably still out there even now, embracing and forgetting to start dinner or wash themselves, watching for bees in a stupor, so completely consumed. Serves them right if I stay out until morning.

Mr. Grey lifts Genevieve from the playpen. He holds her away from his body for a moment as if she might bite, but she doesn't appear to have grown her teeth yet. I think he's going to offer her up to me, but when I don't make a move to take her, he keeps her, his grip wary as if one jostle or squeeze and she might leak.

She cranes her neck all the way around as he walks us down a hallway to show me the nursery. It's downstairs, away from wherever he sleeps, and I wonder if that's deliberate. As he moves ahead, the baby looks over his shoulder and behind. At me. Deeply and utterly into me. The dim of the hallway brings out a gleam in her eyes, and inside them is the coil of a whirlpool, that ferocious spinning pull that can suck someone down and under.

"You can put your things in the guest room at the end of this hall," Mr. Grey announces, pointing an arm farther in. "I mean it when I say I'll be out late. I might not be back before sunrise."

He's stopped, as if he doesn't want to venture down the hallway, and I walk ahead, carrying my bag.

There are a few doors off to the side and then two more doors all the way at the back of the house. Genevieve aims her gaze at one in particular, and as I get closer there's the distinct sense of something rustling from behind it, like paper crumpling or dry mouths whispering.

Without thinking, I'm stepping toward the sound as if Genevieve had the strength of a grown man and had shoved me forward. I'm opening the door, and the whispers come to a hard stop as I step just inside.

This can't be the guest room. There's no bed and nowhere to lie down, except for the bare floor. In those brief seconds,

I see a series of shelves against every wall, rising to the ceiling. The windows are uncovered. The walls collect only shadows, and every shelf is empty.

Mr. Grey is there beside me when I could have sworn he was a number of steps behind. "Oh no," he says. "This is the library. There's nothing in here for you."

But it's the way he says it, the strange pitch to his voice, as if he's almost . . . *excited* that I opened the wrong door. And it's the way he's making the gesture, his free hand on the knob, not letting go, not pulling the door closed. He hasn't ushered me out. He's letting me stand inside the room he's outright admitted is the wrong one, as if now I've gone and done it and have to witness what's here.

I do, as best I can through the darkened dim. A strip of light leaks in from the hallway, yet it only casts so far. Beyond that is fuzzy, and I blink for a moment, wanting to be sure. He called this room the library, but this is the most pathetic library I've ever seen. There's nothing worth reading in here—nothing to read at all. The shelves must have been built to hold books, but there aren't any. It's a library without purpose. A nothing space, a spare and unwanted room.

I turn to leave and Genevieve makes a sound, startling me. She lets out a trilling of energy from her soft, wet mouth, then a gurgle of pleasure, as if I've just revealed my face in peek-a-boo, many a baby's favorite game.

I swear Mr. Grey sends a glance of frustration down to his daughter's dark-haired head, almost as if he's telling her,

Not yet, Genevieve, not yet. But I didn't hear that.

I step out of the bare, blank room and make sure the door is sealed closed.

"Sorry," I say.

Mr. Grey leads me a few more steps down the hallway, as if nothing has happened. His voice is as flat as before. "This is the guest room. You can leave your things in here."

"Right, of course," I say. And it's quiet in there, yet it does have furniture, as rooms in houses are meant to. It's an ordinary space with a bed, a dresser, a lamp, an adjoining bathroom, no shelves, no walls collecting shadows, no rustling whisper. It's funny how the ceiling seems so much closer than it had in the other room, though they are in the same hallway, as if the house has squeezed down at this back corner, wanting to take less space. But that's only a trick of the eyes. A room seems smaller with furniture in it, that's all.

I set my bag down on the end of the bed, and Mr. Grey nods.

When I went to pack my things earlier in the afternoon, I ran into my dad on the stairs. "Oh," he said, rubbing his forehead as if he'd walked into a wall. "I didn't see you there, excuse me." And he said it so distantly, as if we were two strangers who bumped into each other on a street corner, and then he went on his way.

I'm getting paid triple my rate tonight, I wanted to tell him. I'm going to save up enough to get out of here and live my own life and you'll really miss me then. But he was outside by that time, heading for the garden. My mom was already out there, digging away the day.

"The guest room is great, Mr. Grey, thank you," I tell him. "I'm glad it's so close."

"Close to what?" He goes rigid.

"The nursery," I say, confused.

"Yes, yes." He nods.

We leave the long hallway and return to the front rooms of the house, where the feeding and entertaining will occur. Genevieve is caged once again, and Mr. Grey is retrieving his suit coat. His glossy black shoes shine in the foyer light, and his shirt collar is buttoned all the way up, paper white.

Before he goes, I realize he never told me the bedtime routine, and since parents are always so particular about how it's handled and when it's done, I ask. Odd, but this seems to rattle him.

"Such as?" he asks. "A routine of what?"

I offer up some of the usual steps other parents have me perform: the specific times to begin the winddown period, the washing up, the putting on of pajamas, the preparing of the bedroom with the night-light, the story time in the near-dark on a rocking chair or at the bedside. Some clients want me to read their child one book in a loop from cover to cover until that child conks out hearing me bid good night over and over again to the clocks and the socks and the kittens and the moon. Others give me an array of picture books to choose from.

"Something like that?" I finish.

But Mr. Grey has no directions to offer me. It's unsettling, the way he stands there staring down into the playpen that holds his daughter, almost as if he's wary of her and might not want to leave her in my care, after all. She returns his gaze with intensity, and from that, something seems to have been communicated.

"Do what you do," he says. "She'll let you know what she wants when she wants it."

"Okay . . . So, um, what time should I put her to bed? Parents usually tell me a time."

He gazes at me as if this is a game we're playing and I'm forcing him to guess. "Nine?"

"That's very late. Usually parents—"

"Eight?"

I nod. "Should I . . ." I'm at a loss. I expected more direction than this. "Read her a story? Is there a book she likes?" I search her toys. "Where are her storybooks? In the nursery?"

He shakes his head slowly.

"Somewhere else?"

Again, he indicates no, not there, but he doesn't offer up another possibility.

"Okay . . . " I'm not sure what to say. "I could make something up on the fly. The little ones seem to like that, they—"

"Genevieve will let you know what she likes," he says. "She always does."

There's a twitching visible under the skin of his face, some internal unraveling. He's not the same man I met at the door, not the imposing presence who lured my parents from inside the cool depths of his dark, expensive car. Genevieve may be contained again in the playpen, but she has her amorphous eyes still hooked on him, and he's shrinking himself down under the weight of that gaze. I've seen babies in command of their parents through other messier and louder means—tantrums of volcanic proportions, cheeks as bloodred as beets—but I've never seen this.

"I see she wants me to go," he says, bowing his head. "I'll leave you two to it."

"Don't worry, Mr. Grey," I say. "She's in good hands. We'll have fun."

He blinks at me. "Yes," he says. "I imagine she will."

She has him by the throat, this child. He's intimidated by her, this ball of fat in a onesie, which is true for a lot of new parents, but could there be something else going on here? Before I can even consider what that means for me, he startles me with a shout.

"Genevieve!"

The baby has the doll by the hair. Meaning she's got the doll's hair in her fist—a clutter of brown yarn splayed between plump fingers—and the doll is now bald. She starts wailing.

"I know you're hungry," he says to her. "Kelsey is here. She'll feed you soon." On the counter a jar of mashed peas is waiting, and I nod, planning to take care of it.

He's dressed and entering the foyer now. His silver hair is shining and there's sweat on his face. "Thank you. I appreciate you being here, and Genevieve does, too."

"You're welcome," I say.

There's no whispering coming from anywhere inside the house or inside my body. Nothing can be heard over Genevieve's crying, so I go to her and make her stop. I do the thing I do often as the parents are leaving for their cars, to show them they've made the right choice in hiring me. If the child can walk on two legs, I'll take a small hand and lead them to the door to say goodbye, as if we're a team. If the child isn't yet mobile, such as Genevieve here, I lift them into my arms and balance them on my hip. This is what I do now with her, and she allows it without a fuss. She stops making sound. I feel her hands playing with the neck of my shirt, twisting a tight tourniquet at my neck with the little nubs of her fingers. He's dressed her and changed her and prepared her for this evening, but I realize there's something he's forgotten as she gets her grip on me and I stand there taking it.

He hasn't clipped the pointy slivers of her fingernails.

Mr. Grey glances at the house one last time as he folds himself into his car in the driveway, and when he does he sees me at the window with his offspring still in my arms. He lifts a hand to wave and he seems sad for a moment, but the glare on the windshield is kind of hiding his face. The driveway makes a swift turn so I can't see him reach the gate, but I stand there a bit too long after his car is out of sight.

At first the evening is uneventful. Genevieve needs her diaper changed twice in fast succession, and then she eats two spoonfuls of pea sludge and refuses the rest, dribbling it on her bib, on the high chair, and all over the floor. She fusses, wriggles in her seat, kicks off her socks. Even when I take her out of the high chair, she won't keep calm and rams her body against the playpen's bars. I'd read to her, but there's every toy available in the play area except a book. There aren't even the kind of books with thick slabs for pages and shapes in place of words: the red square, the blue triangle, the yellow circle, all of which she could gnaw on. She doesn't want to be held. She's done with the doll. She doesn't want blocks or balls or stuffed creatures. She growls and scrunches her face into a gruesome snarl. She sounds like a bird when she screeches, one mauled and smacked against a windshield and left in the road. She will not be soothed until I give her what she wants, and I'm not sure what that might be. Until she shows me.

It happens when I'm letting her burn off energy in her walker: a round contraption with a seat for her, a toy tray mounted with plastic activities, and four wheeled feet. She speeds off with intense but bombastic determination and aims herself down the hallway.

I chase her around the bend to find two doors ajar. One reveals a room with a vanity mirror covered over to avoid any reflection. Another has a patchwork quilt folded on the otherwise bare floor. They seem like rooms from another house entirely, tricks of the low light, but something else bothers me.

"How'd you get these doors open so fast?" I ask her.

Genevieve watches me carefully. A line of drool slowly descends.

She starts moving down the corridor, her wheels rushing along the wooden floor until she's at the far-off door we'd come to before. This one is closed. She bangs against it, a spring toy on the tray of her walker bouncing with urgency. She's trying to tell me something, and it has to do with this room.

"Genevieve, there's nothing in there," I say. I try to pull her away from it, but she grabs the doorframe with her stubby fists and won't let go. The strength in her grip is surprising.

When I get her free, she lifts her eyes to me and little tears in her lashes are poised there, sparkling, and that might be what does it. Maybe there was something in this room I didn't see before, and she wants me to know it. She might be commanding the limbs of my body somehow, because I find my hand turning the knob. I find I can't be near the door without wanting it open. I can't see the room without needing to be inside.

Still, walking into the room isn't something I remember doing, just like how when I asked my parents why they were chatting up a neighbor they'd only seen before in passing, their eyes glazed over. They could barely remember it, either. My mom told me she didn't recall getting up from where she was crouched in her garden bed, the bulb of a future flower perched in her hand. All she knew was she must have dropped what she'd been holding. Was it a tulip? Was it even the season for tulips? She forgot. All she remembered was being covered by dirt at his window, breathing in the cooled air billowing out. She saw the baby in the backseat and she was startled by her big, bright eyes, and she offered me up as the babysitter, and now here I am.

Here I am. I'm in the empty room with Genevieve. She's wheeled in behind me in her walker. She has a fleck of mashed peas on her cheek, a green crust I must have missed when I was cleaning her off. The room is the same as before—the complete lack of furniture, the curtainless windows, the empty shelves—yet I find myself switching on the overhead light as if that might change something. It doesn't. This is a library with no books, a useless space, a lost room.

"Happy now, Genevieve? Ready for bed?"

I turn for the door, but Genevieve is circling. She keeps wheeling around me in a tightening lasso.

"Should we put you in your pj's, how does that sound?"

She circles. The running of wheels on wood and the rattling of spring toys making a racket on her tray are loud as her walker travels a loop around me. Then the whispering returns. It's dry and throaty in my ears. It's raspy. It's even more intense than before. The whispering seems to be coming from the walls, seems to be all around me, and I turn one way and I turn the other, and for one second I think I see the shelves crowded, the shelves overflowing, and what's on those shelves seems to be moving, coiling, twisting, and all the while she's casting a tight circle around my legs. She's winding me in.

"Genevieve?" I blink, and the shelves are bare again.

She's stopped, and that's when I notice what rests on the ground.

A book, when there hadn't been one before. It's lying face down on the floorboards. A book, right here at my feet.

"Where did this come from?" I say, as if she could answer.

Still, there's an intelligence in her eyes that tells me she knows the answer and it's one that delights her. The way the spit streams so slowly from the corner of her mouth and collects on the front snap of her onesie, shimmering. The ways she doesn't break eye contact but all the while grabs the plastic key on her tray and winds it tight. Her mouth can't shape the words to tell me. She's trapped inside a small prison and there are only limited ways she can get me to understand, but she's done something, and I know it and she knows it, and now the book is here.

I'm bending down, toward it. I'm taking it in my hands.

The cover of the book has a face of shadows and no title I can make out. I think it's bound in brown leather, until I angle it in my hands and it looks bluish in the light, a shifting murky palette that then looks green. The surface is wrinkled in an unsettling way, like old skin. It's warm in my hands, sweaty and warm.

In the front-facing, conscious part of my mind I find all the sensible avenues of explanation. I must have not seen the book when I walked in. Maybe it was in the corner and she nudged it over with her walker. Maybe it was on a high shelf and made no sound when it fell. Still, however it arrived, now it's here in this dust-soaked room, and the expression on Genevieve's miniature face is one I can only describe as hungry. If this were any other child in any other house, I would know what to do. I've seen this eager look on other upturned faces when I'm there to babysit and it's time for a bedtime story. I read them the old classics, the favorites, the Fancy Nancys and the Little Bears, and I lull them to sleep while their parents are out, and that's happened more times than I can count. That's not what's happening now.

There are no pictures inside this book. There are no colors apart from the speckled almost-brown of the old, rotting pages and the black smears of the still-sticky ink.

I have an awareness of where I am when the book finds the page it wants and I start the story I've been hired to tell. I'm on my knees now, on the creaky floor, and Genevieve in her walker appears taller than me. I'm opening my mouth and the words from the page are spilling out, and as I speak, the room shows itself to me in its true form. I see what looks like pages and pages all around me, a papering of wings from every edge and corner, a blanket that crackles and tears, a shroud.

I try to remember. I think I was in a library. I was in a large house. That house was in my own neighborhood, at the edge, and I think outside through the gate was the road back to where I live and the parents who raised me all these years. Two parents. A mom, I think, and a dad. I was the most popular babysitter in the whole neighborhood. I was booked solid through spring. All that was true outside this room and before this story. But I'm forgetting things as soon as I think them. I know I have a house nearby—but where is it, what color is it, who would I find inside? My mouth is opening and speaking the words from the book and erasing everything else. I'm called to do it. Something has grabbed my jaw and is forcing my mouth to move, violent with my lips, cracking teeth against teeth. Because this isn't a story, is it? It's a spell. It's an incantation. These aren't sentences. These aren't even words on a page. This is a roving band of insects, teeming across my fingers, gathering in my hair and in my eyelashes, scattering down my legs. Soon I don't remember why I'm here and I don't remember my own name.

But I remember hers.

Genevieve?

I try to say it, but I can't feel my lips.

There's a roaring in my mind as I realize what she wants and what she's taking. She smells like rot and smashed peas. Her fingernails scrape as she grabs me closer to feed. She doesn't have teeth yet, so when she opens her rosebud lips it's like looking into a bottomless hole. But I don't have to look, really. The room is dark, the blanket is dry and wrapped tight all around me, and it's bedtime now, it's bedtime. Genevieve, stop. Genevieve, don't. Genevieve, please let go. Genevieve, please let me sleep.

MORNING LIGHT. IT COMES IN SLOWLY THROUGH THE UNCOVERED windows into the library.

An understanding grows as I stay very still, and since no part of me can move but the rustle of breath in and out of my squeezed lungs and the scrape of my eyelashes dry-blinking in the dust, I can see only a sliver. Still, it's a view of the backyard. A thickening of trees can be made out through the windowpane if I strain very hard: the growth green and lush as if this house is wedged in the middle of a forest. So my parents were wrong. The land isn't sick out here—it was only starved, and whatever happened in this house last night helped it return to itself and remember.

I remember, too, more and more, as I come awake.

The light keeps coming, brightening the room, so this must mean it's sunrise and I survived the night, in a way. Light creeps from the window along the bare expanse of floor, inch by inch, until it reaches the compartment where I find myself. I'm on a high shelf. From here, I can see the room that was hidden from me before. It's fully visible. Now that I've been added to the collection, I'm aware of the version that was underneath, the one that was there without my knowing, the empty shelves that were always full.

I'm bent in unspeakable ways, folded into myself, bound tight, compressed closed, hidden here, my whereabouts unknown. I can't move. A girl who might be the babysitter who came before me is coiled up in some kind of tight wrapping, a winding of what looks like the paper-esque layers of a wasp nest concealing her whole body and constricting her throat. It's only the visible parts of her head and face that look familiar. Do I recognize her from the grade ahead of me at school? Either way, whatever she's wrapped in, I am too. I can tell she's alive from the way she blinks her eyes, trying to communicate though I'm too drowsy to follow, and from the sound that keeps crackling out of her mouth, a cross between a hiss and a whisper. The other sitters are trapped on other shelves, most unmoving, their faces wrapped to block air, some gasping and attempting their own calls for help, some entirely still and silent and spotted in black mold. Far across the room is the one that must be the mother. She's older than the rest of us. The hair color is the same as her baby's—

what's left of the hair attached to the skull—and there's something in the cheekbones that helps me see the resemblance. The husk of whatever keeps us perched here has grown to reach every shelf.

After some time, Mr. Grey returns. I hear his car in the driveway first, and then I hear him entering the house, setting his keys down, leaving aside his jacket. I sense him in the hallway, searching for someone or something, and then the rustling comes to a stop.

"There you are. Did you get enough to eat?"

Silence.

"I'm so glad, sweetheart. I'm so glad. But look at the state you're in. Let's get you cleaned up."

The sound of wheels on hardwood showing Genevieve is up and about. The sound of wheels on the rug. The sound of wheels on hardwood again, and then the sound of wheels stops. He must have lifted her out and taken her in his arms.

After a time I hear his footsteps approaching: the father, Mr. Grey, the man who could save me if he has anything left of a heart. He's coming closer. He's walking down the hall toward this terrible library, this tomb of a room.

It's probably too late for the others, but I'm still fresh. I still have all my hair. Someone should be wondering where I am—shouldn't they? I hear the door opening, and though I can't turn my neck to look at him there's his shadow breaking the beam of sunlight as he steps inside. He'll have second thoughts and he'll help me down from where I've been trapped. I'll promise to tell no one and he'll drive me home because I'm too weak to walk right now. Then he'll pay me. He promised triple. He'll pay me, and this will be over, and I'll be safe at home. After today, I'll find another job to do after school. I'll avoid anything that has to do with children or, worse, babies. I'll do something that involves standing at a bright-lit counter, like a store of some kind, a place where there are people. Witnesses. I'll work only in daylight. I'll have no excuse to drift down to where the pavement cuts off and where the road ends at this gate. I'll avoid this stretch of the neighborhood entirely. If he calls to book me again, I won't even have to say I'm busy. I'll say I'm retired.

I'm trying to shout, I'm trying to alert him that I'm up here, but it's coming out in such a papery whisper.

"Looks like you really had fun with her," he says. He's talking to her, not to me. He must have her in his arms.

She lets out a contented coo.

I sense Mr. Grey's attention on me, and I wait. I wait for him to do something, to take this back, to put Genevieve down so he can tear me out of this pulpy coffin, but he speaks only to her. "Did you like this one? You know I won't live forever. Maybe we can keep her awake a little longer, for the day you need a new caretaker?"

She cries out in response, upset at the thought, and he immediately starts to soothe her. I hear the gentle thumping on her back until she's quiet again.

He's close enough that I can see her. From this angle she looks like any other baby: fluffs of hair sticking up at the crown, two chubby feet having long ago lost their tiny socks, five toes on each foot, human toes, as if there's nothing out of the ordinary here, nothing amiss.

Mr. Grey spots the book still on the floor and he dusts it off and tucks it under his arm. Then he carries her out, and she's still cooing. I can't see her anymore, but I can hear her, that thing he named Genevieve, I can hear the contented babble that comes out of her pink mouth. I can hear her even after he's left me in the room with the others and closed the door.

THE PHANTOM'S WALTZ

Rosiee Thor

I LEARN OF FLAVIANA DANTE'S DEATH WHEN THE FIRST TOUR GROUP arrives. They call her things like "creative genius," "trailblazer of modern dance," and "choreographer extraordinaire." They don't call her what she really was. A monster. A temptress. A phantom.

I guess that last one's all me now.

I watch from behind the deep olive-green curtains that hang beside the full-length mirror in the ballroom. A velvet rope separates me from the crowd of high ponytails that swish in unison as they nod along with the practiced speech.

"She died here at home at the age of ninety-one," says the tour guide. "She had no children or surviving family."

"She died alone?" asks one of the ponytails.

I internalize a laugh and my body rocks like a gust of wind, shaking the curtain.

"That's so sad."

But it isn't sad. And it isn't true. She was never alone, because I was there. I was always there. I always will be. The unfairness of it all nearly tears me apart. She got to live and she got to die and I'll never get to do either.

The voice of the tour guide fades as they move on to another room of the house, the padded sound of dancers' feet, practiced at the art of quiet, trailing close behind. I almost miss them. They are the closest thing I have to company these days.

"Hello?" A voice, all honey and sunshine, echoes through the ballroom. "Is there someone in here?" I still, smothering the urge to respond. It's been so long. *Too* long.

It feels less than hours ago that I stood at the threshold of what would become my purgatory, breathy and hopeful and yearning. All I wanted back then was to dance. The polished mirrors reaching from the smooth finished floor to the arched ceiling reeled me in like a fish on a line. Or maybe that was just Flaviana. I'll never know.

Flaviana's careful choreography lives in my muscles like a breath I can never exhale. Every motion, every step. I've practiced it all. It would be so easy to do what I do best. Répété.

Come in. Won't you dance with me?

Her words balance on my lips, a careful arabesque. I could invite this girl, no older than I've ever been, with my hand outstretched, toes pointed, shoulders back. I could be an echo, repeating the past.

"Hello?" says the girl again. She waits a beat, then retreats toward the door. She pauses at the threshold to glance over her shoulder before scurrying away. Her footsteps are a gentle *tap-tap*, like knuckles rapping on an invisible door, hoping for entry.

But I've already said goodbye.

IT'S ALMOST MIDNIGHT WHEN SHE RETURNS. I AM IN THE MIDDLE OF my warmup, a rond de jambe exercise to loosen the hip flexors and strengthen the core. Not that my musculature changes at all in this form. That's part of the curse, I suppose. I don't hear her enter over the sound of the music. Instead, I catch sight of her in the mirror, flinging her sandals into a corner before taking a place behind me. Her movements lag as she watches for my cues.

I feel heavy under her gaze.

Impossible.

My weight cannot be measured in pounds or kilograms, only in unfulfilled dreams. It's a blessing. I will never again step on a scale and see my self-hatred reflected in numbers. I am a wisp, a ghost, a memory. I am not real.

"Wow! You're really good! Are you auditioning? I'd love to practice with you. Wouldn't it be great if we both got in? My name's Hannah, by the way."

Her words are whiplash, the speed of them, the volume. I want to shrink her down, shoo her away. She shouldn't be here. I should tell her as much.

Instead, I smile and gesture for her to step up beside me.

"I can't believe we're supposed to learn all the choreography by Friday," she says. "*The Phantom's Waltz* is like . . . her most difficult piece."

I raise a brow. *The Phantom's Waltz.* I know it.

An understatement.

I *am* it.

The music changes with no warning, shifting to an ethereal melody. The ¾ timing is an intimate reading of the rhythm my heart would make if it still beat.

I assume the starting position and Hannah follows suit.

The dance consumes me, just like she did all those years ago. Flaviana Dante showed me the steps here in this ballroom. I practiced until my toes bled. I practiced until the sun rose. And now I'll practice forever.

But this . . . it doesn't feel like practice. Not with Hannah's gaze on me. It feels like performance.

She claps when the dance is over. It makes me feel small. It makes me feel seen. It makes me *feel*.

"That was amazing!" She steps toward me, an eager light in her eyes. "I feel like I've almost got it . . . the timing of that jeté section is tripping me up, though."

Again? I should ask. *Again and again and again. Until the sun rises. Until her life is mine.*

I almost do it. I taste the word on my tongue—bitter and sharp like a knife in the back. But before the invitation can leave my lips, there's a chirp from the corner and Hannah zooms to her bag.

"Shoot. I have to go, actually." She holds up a bright screen. Her smile is weak and apologetic as she slides on her sandals and throws a sweater on upside down. "I'll come back tomorrow?" She asks it like a question.

My answer comes crackling from my throat, the first words I've spoken in years.

"Goodbye, Hannah."

HANNAH IS TRUE TO HER WORD. BUT ME? I'M MADE OF LIES.

I told myself I would let her go, give her a chance. I would not be opportunistic like Flaviana. Only if she came back would I pounce.

And here she is, standing before me in a yellow leotard a few shades removed from her flaxen hair. "See? Said I'd come!" She shucks her socks and sweater, tossing them into a pile by the door. "Totally committed to the art form. That's me!" She says it like she has something to prove, like someone once accused her of the opposite.

Easy prey.

"Welcome back," I say with a smile. It feels like a wound, jagged and wrong.

Uneasy predator.

I hold out a hand to stop her as she crosses toward the mirror. "Careful. You'll pull something." To jump right into practice without stretching . . . only a fool would do it. Or a phantom.

Hannah laughs, soft and tinkly like light rain on a tin roof. "Sorry. I guess I'm just in a hurry."

"We've got time."

I'm in no rush. In fact, the more she prolongs her stay, the closer I am to freedom.

My body finds a slow stretch as I roll down, nose pressed to my shins. It isn't a true stretch, of course. I'm made more of memory than muscle. But still, the familiar motion brings me a sense of calm.

"You're right, you're right." Hannah joins me on the floor, a frenetic bounce in her legs. "I have to remember that. The audition's not for a few more days." She sighs as she flops her body over, fingers extending past her toes. "I can't help but be nervous. But you get it, obviously."

Obviously.

She doesn't know the half of it.

"It's a big opportunity." The words come slowly as I reach to decades past for the appropriate emotions. I am at once ageless and adolescent, haunted and eager. I am a crone, withering under the heat of a thousand suns blazing: repent, revenge, revive. I am seventeen, on the threshold of greatness, waiting for luck to strike. "To dance for Flaviana Dante is an honor beyond imagining."

"Can you believe we missed her by only a day?" Hannah rolls to her stomach and arches into the stretch. "Seriously bad luck. Not that her death is all about us, of course. It's, you know, sad and stuff. But how cool would it have been to be able to tell our grandchildren we danced for Flaviana Dante? "

I wish I could tell her how little Flaviana's death is about me. Her life, though . . .

The spasm starts in my fingers as a shot of anger courses through me like a lightning bolt. Flaviana Dante, a mother of modern dance, and all because of me. Because of what she took from me. The talent, the skill, those were hers, but the life was mine. She was the first person to see my drive, to feed my hunger. She used my ambition like a noose, even though I tied the rope myself.

It was my fault.

It was her choice.

Now, that choice is mine.

"Oh God," Hannah croaks. "Did you know her? I'm so sorry. I didn't mean to—I'm so oblivious sometimes."

Lie. Lie, lie, lie.

"Yes." The truth finds my lips. A brittle claw gripping the edge of an abyss. "I knew her."

Hannah's fingers twitch.

A wall sconce flickers.

Silence catches me as I fall.

It's a long way down to the pit I've made my home. The depths my depression has cleaved are a familiar, haunted place. I wrap myself in frigid waters, nose to nose with my own reflection. Here, I'll stay. Forever alone. Forever forgotten.

"What was she like?"

I almost don't hear Hannah over the rushing in my ears,

but her voice pulls me from my disassociation. I blink my vision clear, tearing my gaze from the mirror. I've avoided looking at her thus far. Easier to destroy someone when you haven't seen their soul. But now, I bring my gaze to hers and my breath catches.

Hannah is gray-green moors and honey-wheat fields and dappled stone shores. She is a lit path through a dark forest. She is rivers and valleys and cities and hamlets. She is undecided. She is potential.

Was I so unfinished when Flaviana ended me? Did she know how much more I could have done, could have been, could have lived? Did she know and did it anyway?

"Ruthless."

Hannah chuckles. "I've heard she could be a real hard-ass. Guess you don't get to be the best dancer in a generation without making enemies." She rises to her feet. "It's weird, isn't it? When you find out your hero was kind of a jerk?"

And it pierces me through the heart.

Hero.

Flaviana Dante is my villain. Always will be. But before I met her, she was my hero, too.

Hannah extends her hand to help me up.

I don't take it.

"I've been calling you Irina," Hannah confesses.

We've been dancing for hours without speaking, the music

and our motions the only language we need.

"Because I don't actually know your name." She glances up at me through light lashes, eyes a murky sort of green, like a lake after a spring rain or a stone covered in winter-chilled moss. "You feel like an Irina to me, I guess."

"What does an Irina feel like?"

Hannah cocks her head, lips pinched in thought. Sweat beads at her temple and blond flyaways make havoc around her face. Her cheeks are splotchy and red from exertion. She is far from picturesque.

I can't look away.

"Irina feels like a pointed toe. Like the triumph of sticking a triple pirouette. Like the relief in your chest from a cambré. Irina feels perfect, I guess."

"I'm not perfect."

Maybe if I'd been perfect, Flaviana wouldn't have . . . The thought doesn't bear completing. My mind knows the motions of what-ifs and self-pity better than my body knows a port de bras.

Hannah doesn't blink. "Maybe she just feels perfect to me. It's nice sometimes to believe there is someone out there doing everything right. Like . . . Irina is proof it can be done, that perfection is possible."

"Perfection isn't real." I sigh and lean back against the mirror, glass ghosting a cold whisper against my skin. "It's just a lie we tell ourselves to make all the work feel worth it."

"How very glass-half-empty of you." Hannah pushes off the wall into a chaîné turn, a second, a third. "I thought you'd be more optimistic. Like . . . you're *so* good. It's obvious you'll get in. But you're still here practicing with me every night. Why is that?"

Because I don't have any other choice.

Because it's what Flaviana would do.

Because I'm going to eat you, little girl, and take your life. Oh, what big teeth I have.

I don't know which answer I hate more. I don't know which one's really true. Maybe all of them.

"Because it's all I know," I say finally. "Dance is all I have."

Hannah purses her lips and shakes her head. "No, no, that won't do. Irina has a very full life outside of dance."

"Tell me about her."

"Well, she takes fashion very seriously, but she's not made of money. She thrifts. A vintage queen." Hannah's shoulders dance like a cat ready to pounce. "She likes sweet things—croissants and petits fours and almond milk with her tea. And she likes cats—they have pretty eyes like hers."

"And does she do all this alone?" I ask before I can stop myself. The desire for the life of this fictitious girl blooms in my chest, nearly swallowing me up.

"She has friends." Hannah watches me with eyes so bright I wonder if she can see through me. Her words take on a trepidatious quality. "Not a lot, though. People know her—she's popular—but she knows her limits. She chooses her friends carefully. She's been burned before."

I nod, words building at the back of my throat until they

burst forth. "Envy is what broke her."

"Oh yes. In the past, she lost friends because they wanted to be her."

"Or because she wanted to be them."

Hannah falls silent, her eyes tracing the curl in the wooden floor panels. "Is it so bad to want to be someone else?"

"No." Cold coils around my insides and I shiver. "No, it's not so bad. Not always."

"Sometimes it feels like it's all I have to look forward to, becoming someone else. Like . . . who I am will never be enough. No matter how hard I work, no matter how good I get, they're always better."

I taste her bitterness like it is my own, an expired can in my pantry. "Be careful with those feelings." A warning. A disclaimer.

"I know, I know. But then . . . I'm not even sure that's really it. Maybe it's something else. Maybe I don't want to *be* them. Maybe I just—"

"Want *them*."

Hannah nods silently, throat bobbing as she swallows. I see myself reflected in her eyes.

The wanting rises in me like a tide. It won't take much now. She will stay if I ask her. A few sugared words, a smile, an outstretched hand. She would be mine. She would be *me*.

And I would be her.

"My name isn't Irina."

Hannah blinks. The spell is broken. "Oh. Yeah. I didn't really think it was." She moves toward her bag in the corner, pulling out a crocheted sweater with lavender yarn unspooling from the hem. A flush fills her cheeks and her eyes dart, just skimming the borders of my body. "I should probably get going. Sorry to keep you so long."

I watch her scurry into her outer shell. Heather-gray sweatpants, maroon beanie, brown sneakers. She clutches her phone with rigid fingers. Embarrassment creeps up her neck like morning glory, laying claim to every inch of her skin.

She won't come back. Not after this. Not if I let her walk away.

"It's Margie," I call after her.

"What?" She pauses, hand on the doorframe.

"My name." I don't move. I don't breathe. "My name is Margie."

Hannah doesn't look back, but she whispers it as she goes.

"Goodbye, Margie."

I WAIT FOR HANNAH FOR HOURS. IT'S DARK AND QUIET AND OH SO familiar, here in the ballroom alone. I curse my weakness a thousand times. I curse Flaviana Dante a thousand and one.

She finds me pacing along the far side of the room to the beat of *The Phantom's Waltz*. I don't know how long she stands there watching before she clears her throat.

"So, tell me about Margie."

Relief bleeds from my shoulders at the sound of her voice. I look to see her in the door, bracing her forearms on the frame.

She wears her unraveling sweater and a coy smile. I want to run to her.

Instead, I walk to the middle of the room. She can meet me halfway.

"What do you mean?" I ask.

"I told you all about Irina." Hannah steps into the room, piling her things in the corner just like always. "Now it's your turn."

I chew my lip. It's been so long since I've been Margie. Since anyone has said my name aloud. "No one's ever asked me that."

Hannah laughs. "No one's ever asked you about yourself? I find that hard to believe. Who wouldn't be interested in you?" The mirth on her face melts to pity as she watches me. "Seriously? Never?"

I wish I could say yes.

"Once."

"Okay, well this doesn't count. I mean before now."

"Once before." I can still feel her standing there, like a shadow, a ghost, a haunting. Even from the afterlife, Flaviana Dante makes me feel seen. Even after all she did to me, I still want her to come into this ballroom and praise my lines. I dream of her finally letting me go—because I am good enough, because I am more than enough, because I am the best. But Flaviana Dante never wanted me to be the best. She only wanted me to stay. "I don't think she really cared about the answer, though."

"Well," Hannah says defiantly. "I care."

Maybe it's because our roles are reversed and I have all the power, maybe it's because Hannah says it so earnestly, or maybe it's because I just want to: I believe her.

"I don't know where to start."

"I'll get you going." Hannah smiles, a ray of light more welcome than a sunrise. "Margie, Margie, Margie . . ."

I never want her to stop saying my name.

"Is it a nickname?"

"Marjorie."

"I like it."

"It was my grandmother's."

"A hand-me-down!" Hannah plucks at the fraying cuff of her sweater. "My favorite."

I cast about for something else to say, something that won't send her running again. "I miss her."

"She died?"

I nod.

"How long ago?"

"Long enough." Truth be told, I don't know. I've lost track of the years. She was still alive when I came here, but surely she passed long ago. An ache builds in my chest as her face rises in my thoughts, followed by the others. I think of my mother, my father, my siblings, my dog. All of them will be gone by now, and if by some miracle I'm wrong, will they remember me? Will they take one look at my face frozen by time and think me a ghost? When I leave this place, there will be no one left for me in the world. "I never got to say goodbye."

"I'm sorry."

Hannah inclines her head toward the wall and together we sink to the floor, side by side. Our shoulders loom inches from touch. I don't dare breathe just in case.

"I've never liked goodbyes myself," Hannah says. "I know closure is hard without them, but I think I always want to leave that door open, you know? Like . . . even if someone dies, I feel like maybe they'll visit, anyway."

"You mean a spirit?"

"Sure. I don't know if I believe in an afterlife or anything, but I do believe we never really lose the people we love. Even if it's just our own memories, they're still with us." She fingers a six-pointed star hanging from a tarnished chain around her neck. "We light candles for our dead. On the anniversary, I mean. A yahrtzeit."

"That's nice." I wonder if anyone ever lit a candle for me.

"So, what else?" Hannah flops over, pressing her body against her thighs in a stretch. "Tell me more about Margie. Like . . . what do you do outside of this place?"

The question bruises. The answer bleeds.

I shrug. "Nothing, really. This place is my life."

Hannah contorts her face into a grimace and rolls back up to sitting. "Well, that's no fun. Come on, there must be something."

I shake my head.

"Okay . . . well . . . what do you *want* to do outside of this place?"

"I . . ."

"Don't know?"

"No." The word comes out firmer than I intend, but I know the answer to this one. "I want to see things."

"Like what?"

I look into her eyes, that muddled green that reminds me of underbrush and algae. "Waterfalls."

She opens her mouth, but before she can say more, I flood the room with everything I want.

"And leaves. I want to see the leaves changing color. And an onion. I want to pluck one from the ground, all covered in dirt. And I want to taste a croissant, and a pear, and champagne. And I want to feel things, too. Like the wind in my hair, and sand between my toes. I want to feel warmth, like a fire or a blanket or a hug. I want to touch——"

Hannah twitches ever so slightly.

"Someone," I finish. Then, so quietly even I barely hear it. "And I want them to touch me back."

I've said too much. I am too much. Any moment, Hannah will blink and laugh uncomfortably. She'll pretend she has an alert on her phone and run away again. She'll leave me here, all alone.

But Hannah doesn't leave. She turns her body to face mine, leans forward on her palms, and inches, inches, inches . . .

Her lips brush mine. A whisper.

I want to answer with a scream.

"Am I . . . cold?" I ask when she pulls away.

She covers my hand with hers. "No."

I reach for her, pulling her close. My fingers trace the line of her jaw, the hollow of her throat. She tastes like the first day of fall, when the blistering heat mellows into fresh corn and pumpkin and cucumber. She smells like petrichor and honey and budding dreams and potential.

If she stays, I will squash her like a bug. I will ruin her.

Stay, stay, stay.

"You should go." I choke out the words.

"Wh—what?" Hannah's fingers tighten around my wrist, and her smile wilts. "It's not even that late."

I glance at the solitary window on the east wall. Darkness stares back. She could stay hours more and still walk away. But I'm not sure I would let her.

"I'm not a good person." I pull my hand from hers. "I'll hurt you."

"Don't say that."

"It's true."

Hannah shakes her head. "I don't believe you."

"If you stay, I will destroy you. If you stay, you'll end up like me."

"Maybe I want to be like you."

She wants this. She said so.

But no one wants *this*. Not really.

"She asked me what I wanted," I croak. "Flaviana Dante. I told her I wanted to be the best. She said, to be the best, I'd need a lot of practice. Then, she asked me how badly I wanted it, how dedicated I would be to dance. I told her I would give it my whole life. If I'd known what that might mean, maybe I would have said something different." My voice gets quieter with each word until finally I whisper, "I'm not alive, Hannah."

"Don't say that—"

"No, I don't mean it metaphorically. I'm not really here. I'm a phantom." I can tell by the way the hurt in her eyes turns hollow that I've begun to lose her. *Good, make her run.* "Flaviana Dante made me this way decades ago. I've lived this dance thousands of times. I'm stuck here in this ballroom, cursed to dance *The Phantom's Waltz* until—"

"Until?" Her eyes brighten.

"Until someone dances it with me to the end. Until someone stays until sunrise."

"I'll do it." She says it so readily, so eagerly.

"Until someone takes my place," I finish.

Understanding crashes around her shoulders in a deluge, a stricken expression on her face. "So if I stay . . ."

"Only one of us leaves this room." I sigh and lean back against the mirror, eyes fluttering shut as I think of all the phantoms over the years, the never-ending cycle of girls stuck between life and death. Before me, it was Flaviana, and before her there were others. Their names come in whispers, not against my ears but against my spirit, or whatever's left of it: Mary, Victoria, Leah.

Someone will always be next. Maybe it will be Hannah. I hope it will and I hope it won't in equal measure.

"Flaviana Dante trapped me here and I thought someday she'd let me go. But she died, and you're the first person who saw me and didn't run away."

"I wouldn't. I won't."

"You should. Nothing good will come to you here." I open my eyes and look at her again. One last time. "Flaviana gave me the chance to leave. I wish I'd taken it. Don't make my mistake."

"But—"

"Go!" I shout. The word echoes and echoes.

Hannah leaps to her feet and dashes for the door. She doesn't even stop to collect her things.

THE PHANTOM'S WALTZ TRICKLES IN THROUGH THE OPEN DOOR. A faraway swan song. Somewhere in this house, dreams are about to come true. Somewhere in this house, dreams are about to be shattered. Mine are frozen over, but I'm used to making myself numb to the cold.

Hannah will be there. I hope she passes the audition. I hope she dances center stage. I hope she thinks a little about me when she does.

My limbs move out of instinct, marking the choreography without emotion. I resign myself to this eternity. Again. It is a familiar nothing, but the ache is so very heavy.

I pretend for a moment that Hannah is here with me, going through the motions of my dance. Her forearm brushes mine as my port de bras looms too close. She laughs at the touch. The hairs on my arms flare at the contact.

When the last wavering note hits the air, I open my eyes

to find I've gained a shadow.

Hannah looks back at me through the reflection of the mirror, wind-stormed eyes unblinking as she reaches for my shoulder and turns me around to face her.

"You came back."

Her smile blisters me like the sun. "I came back."

"You're missing the audition."

"I don't care."

I don't understand it. I don't believe it.

Hannah curls her fingers between mine. "I thought I did. I thought it was the only thing that mattered. Getting through the audition, being chosen for Flaviana Dante's company, I thought it would make people take me seriously. My mom would finally have a reason to brag about me. I thought it would make her happy."

"But it isn't going to make you happy?"

"Lots of things make me happy." She steps forward, guiding me back toward the mirror until my back makes contact with the glass. "*You* make me happy."

Her lips are like fire, coaxing life back into my body. I melt into her, fingers skating over the fabric of her leotard, the skin along her spine, the baby hairs at the nape of her neck. I want to touch her everywhere.

"You make me happy, too." I whisper it into the hollow of her throat as I pull on the elastic in her hair. Waves of honey wheat spill around us, golden and glistening. She is the only sunrise I need.

THE REAL THING COMES FOR US EVENTUALLY. WE ARE SPRAWLED ON the ballroom floor, legs tangled together. I watch as Hannah's steady breaths blow a strand of her hair across her face in her slumber. Her hands are balled into fists on my chest. I wonder if she can feel my heartbeat.

"Hannah," I whisper.

She doesn't wake.

The night fades away. Second by second. I can barely breathe, waiting for the sun to creep above the horizon. I don't want to miss it, the moment I become whole again.

· Light spills through the window, a perfect ray of gold on curly maple inching toward us. I stretch my fingers to touch it.

I don't feel any different. Not yet. So, I wait until it moves across the floor to capture us both in its sights. Bathed in sunshine, I feel . . . nothing. I think, maybe I feel warmer, but Hannah's body on mine is a furnace, so it's hard to tell.

Hooking the yarn with my pinky, I pull Hannah's sweater toward me and fold it into a pillow. I try not to wake her as I roll Hannah off me, slowly extracting my limbs from hers. She looks so peaceful. A smirk curls at the edge of her lips, like she has a secret. I lay her head down on the sweater and tiptoe to the door.

I just want to see, I tell myself. I just want to know.

I line my toes up with the stark line between curly maple and shag carpet. It's the long, ugly stuff that traps years of dust and hair. I have never wanted to touch it more. I close my eyes, take a breath, and slide my foot forward in a perfect tendu.

Soft fibers make way for my pointed toes. I press on, opening my eyes to find myself standing on the other side. I wait to see if I'll crumble. I don't. I take another step. And another, And another. My breaths come in waves, heaving and propulsive. I burst through the doors of Flaviana Dante's estate. I'm wrapped in the embrace of wind and rain. I don't even care that I'm cold. I keep running and I don't stop.

The world is different now. It's still here, just a new shape. The buildings, the trees, the signs. It is a strange thing to know that time has passed, that this place has changed while I have not. I slow my pace to take it all in.

Narrow streets carry me in a straight line. With each block, I feel as though I am in a loop of some kind. The distance stays the same, but the landscape changes. There are petunias growing outside one brownstone. A yellow tricycle outside another. I knock my knees on orange fire hydrants and concrete garbage receptacles with pansies growing out the top. People begin to join me in the street. Some ignore me, eyes glued to their phones. Some give me odd looks. What a sight I must be in my old dancing clothes, with my bare feet and my wide eyes. I am something out of a time capsule and they are science fiction.

Eventually, I come to a market. Bright blue awnings stretch the whole block where vendors hock their wares—a florist, a baker, a candlestick maker. I stop to smell every flower, every loaf of bread. I am hungry for what feels like the first time in my life. I gladly accept samples of brie and cheddar from a cheese monger. I laugh and smile and cry at all the sights and sounds and—

I reach for Hannah's hand, but it's not there. I want to tell her about the world, about all the things I've missed. But she is back in the ballroom. Alone.

I turn with unbridled force and smack into a tent pole.

"Woah there!" says a voice like steel wool. "You alright, kid?"

A rough hand catches my elbow as I go down, pulling me back to standing. I come face-to-face with a gray-haired woman in red flannel. Wrinkles crease her freckled skin, rivers and eddies of a life lived. I would look like her if all was put to right.

"Sorry," I mutter, then turn to go, but something catches my eye on the woman's table.

Wax candles in every color imaginable—blue, purple, pink. And the shapes! There are cats and dogs and owls and mice. My gaze snags on one near the corner—a woman in an arabesque, a dancer carved from dusty rose wax. My fingers reach to touch her.

"Good eye," says the candle vendor. "She looks a little like you, huh."

I flex my hand inches from the wax figure and pull back. Something about it all feels eerily familiar. A dancer, trapped and frozen. She doesn't look like me. She looks like Hannah.

"What's your name, honey?" the woman asks.

I don't think. I just speak. "Irina."

"Irina! That's a pretty name." She looks me over with one swoop of her gaze. "It suits you. A dancer's name."

I want to say, *Thank you.* I want to say, *Hannah gave it to me.* I wish I could give her something in return.

"Well, I think this was meant to be." The woman holds up the candle dancer, balancing her perfectly in her palm. "What do you say, do you want to take this little one home with you?"

I look from the candle to the smiling woman before me. All I can think about is how I want to show it to Hannah.

"I can give you a good deal."

She wants money and I don't have it. I don't have anything.

So I take it. I slap the candle from her hands and I run.

"Hey! Wait!" she calls after me.

But I'm already gone.

HANNAH IS CURLED IN A BALL ON THE FLOOR IN THE CORNER WHERE she's always discarded her things. Lavender yarn is looped around her feet and knees, unraveled.

I hover in the doorway, trapping the carpet between my toes. My body moves slowly, reluctant to let go of the freedom I've found. But what does that freedom mean to me if I am alone?

"So." I step into the room. "Tell me about Hannah."

Hannah jolts upright. Her eyes and nose are red and swollen. There is a pain there I never wanted for her.

"You were gone," she says, voice cracking like glass. "I woke up and you were just . . . gone."

I lower myself to the ground beside her and wrap my arms around her knees. "I wanted to see if I could." It sounds so selfish when I say it aloud. *I wanted, I wanted, I wanted.* "I thought it might not have worked."

"Well, it did. Obviously." She turns her head away from me and pulls her legs from my grasp. "You get to live your life now. Just like you planned, right?"

I wait for my insides to crumble from the accusation, from the rejection. I have done to her what Flaviana Dante did to me, that is what she means. But it isn't true, and what is not true cannot break me.

I set the candle on the floor between us. A girl in stasis, a girl forgotten.

"I got you something."

Hannah grunts. Still, she doesn't look at me.

"You said you light candles. For the dead, I mean." I nudge the candle toward her with my big toe.

"Great. You tricked me into giving up my life, but this makes up for it all. Is that what you want me to say?" She rolls her eyes and turns to face me, knocking over the candle in the process. "Seriously, Margie. What am I supposed to do with this? Keep it as a reminder of you—the one who trapped me here and then left? Light it for myself now that I'm dead?"

"No . . . no . . . that's not what I—" I reach for her hand, but she pulls away. I just want to touch her. I just want her to know she isn't alone.

"Did you plan this from the beginning? Did you think you could trade my life for yours and I would understand? I would forgive?" Familiar bitterness rises in Hannah's voice. "I thought we were going to do this together, but maybe I was just some means to a happy ending."

"You *are* the happy ending. You and me." I inch closer. This time, Hannah doesn't retreat. "I just want to be with you."

"How can that even work?" Hannah asks.

"I don't know . . ." I want to say I don't care. I'd be with her however she wants me, I will take as much of her as she will give. But that's not what she's asking. "Maybe we take turns."

"Like . . . take turns who gets to be . . . alive?" There's a note of something ugly in her voice—disgust or distaste.

"It isn't perfect, I know, but it's what we have."

"And what's to keep you from just . . . leaving and never coming back?"

"Same thing as you, I guess." I lock eyes with her and hope I can convey how much I mean it. "Trust. We have to trust that no matter what, we'll always want to come back to each other."

"But you . . . you said all those things about waterfalls and . . . you want to see the world."

"I see the world." I touch her wrist, pressing my fingers against her pulse point. "Here . . . and here . . ." I brush my thumb across her inner elbow. "And here." I bring my hand to rest just above her heart.

"But . . . you want to explore."

"There's plenty to explore right here."

The glacier between us melts away and I find my arms full of this miracle of a girl. Hannah buries her face in the hollow of my throat and I tangle my fingers in her hair. I press my lips to hers, languishing in the warmth of her breath. I want to drown myself in her touch. And there's no one here to tell me I can't. I gather her like flowers, pulling her closer and closer. There is no such thing as close enough.

"Careful!" Hannah breaks away and I think I might actually die from it. "We've got a casualty."

She plucks the dancer candle from beneath my knees, or what's left of her. A perfect arabesque encased in wax, now decapitated. I fumble between us and find the head.

"It's okay . . . maybe we can just . . ." Hannah takes the head from me and tries to ram it back onto the dancer's slender neck, squishing it a little in the process. "There we go."

I stare down at the contorted wax face, no longer perfect, and it strikes me like lightning. "It looks a little like her now . . . Flaviana Dante."

Hannah squints. "Yeah, I guess so."

"Do you have matches?" I stand and gesture toward the windowsill.

From her bag, Hannah pulls a lighter and produces a flame. She lights the wick sticking out from the dancer's foot and we watch as fire consumes her.

"Who are we lighting her for?" Hannah slots her fingers with mine. "Us?"

"No." I squeeze her hand and pull her closer. "Not us. Never us."

Because we aren't dead.

We are together. And we are so, so alive.

MIRROR, MIRROR

Nora Elghazzawi

I.

THERE ARE NO WORDS FOR WHAT WE ARE. I STILL KNOW HIS childhood phone number—the landline to the house he moved out of when he was five. I know his least favorite color (orange) and favorite vegetable (artichoke hearts, because they sound romantic), and the way his voice gets just before he's about to laugh or cry. I know him, but we barely talk anymore, because we aren't really *friends* anymore. We aren't anything. And not because we fought (even though we did), or because I was head over heels for him (even though I was).

I could call anytime. I could write letters. He could write me letters. But I don't, and he doesn't, and instead I scroll through our old classmates' social media profiles in hopes of catching a glimpse of him. Here, at some twinkling house party. Here, standing beside a girl wearing a sundress the color of the moon. And me, on the other end of the glowing screen, watching him live life without me.

My hand hovers over his name on my phone, sometimes. I'll type everything out—all the stupid, unspeakable things I want to say.

It's me. Your dead sister's best friend. The one you try to forget about.

I'm still in love with you. I never told you.

It wasn't my fault. I didn't mean to.

I'm the reason she's gone.

II.

MARI WAS MY EVERYTHING. MY FIRST FRIEND, MY BEST FRIEND, MY entire world. We met in kindergarten. We parted ways in ninth grade. It made sense to me, even then—she was always in a realm of her own. Prettier, quieter, more popular. I was a sore thumb. Loud and awkward.

And an ugly duckling.

I missed her every day. Watched from afar as she got everything she always wanted—a shiny new boyfriend, the lead in the school play. We used to write stories together under my pink-and-purple bedcovers, acting them out with only the moon as our audience. Together we were princesses from lands afar, brave, beautiful knights, girls who could step into the pages of a fairy tale like an enchanted puddle. We pretended my vanity was magic—a portal to the great beyond. If only we knew what I know now. Maybe it could have changed everything.

She was the first person I told I wanted to be an actress. She was the first person to believe in me.

"You can do anything you put your mind to, Dalia," she told me, once.

I didn't quite believe her. "But nothing ever seems to work out."

Yet she shook her head. "Your name says it all. You're like a flower. Just because you're a late bloomer, doesn't mean you won't find your way."

And then she found her way without me. Fifteen and fifteen. All those years meant nothing. They don't promise you forever.

"We can have other friends, Dalia," she said over dinner. At my place. On the window side of my kitchen, where nothing but moon or daylight could reach us. See us. "That doesn't change anything."

Only it did.

Her brother, though. *Finn.* He was different. Two years older than us. Maybe he felt sorry for me. But he always treated me like I was special. Even when Mari and I grew apart. Especially when she got the lead both of us auditioned for. I didn't even get a callback.

"How's this?" he said, when he caught me picking at my lunch alone. "I'm going to write the best play our school has ever seen.

And I'll give you the part. All you have to do is show up. Deal?"

"Deal," I murmured.

The rest was history.

III.

IT'S BEEN TWO YEARS AND TWO MONTHS AND THREE DAYS SINCE WE last saw each other in person. Finn and I. Me and Finn. He left before his senior year. Got into college. Won some student award for a script he wrote. He didn't visit home last summer, but this summer he was invited to assist with a play at the community theater.

He doesn't answer my texts congratulating him. He only ever checks half my messages, and it makes me want to keep trying. Like maybe this time I'll get the response I crave.

This isn't like you, hums a familiar voice at the back of my mind. I shiver, as it continues like dark smoke. *You aren't one to give up, Dalia.*

"Leave me alone," I snap aloud. No arrogant chuckle or anagram reply. Of course not. I'm talking to myself, like always.

Are you, really?

I stay up in bed until 3:00 a.m. before I decide, screw it, and pad into the hall. Mama and Baba are fast asleep, and the house creaks like a wooden skeleton all around me. I only meant to tread downstairs for a glass of water, but something keeps me tethered.

Afraid? comes the voice once more. I smother it like candlelight.

"Never," I whisper.

I am in the belly of the old beast as I tread toward the glossy door that bookends the corridor. I turn the jeweled knob. And I walk into the past.

My childhood bedroom. I moved out of it two years, two months, and three days ago. Now it's simply storage. Or a guest room if we ever had guests. I never explained why I had to move across the hall. I didn't have to. Not after what happened with Mari.

Inside, it's like a room from a story. Not a princess story, or even a duchess story, but something fancy lower down the rungs. A four-poster bed, with the same comforter as my childhood sleepovers with Mari. An ornate vanity, and a porcelain tub laid out in the middle of the room like an open, gleaming coffin. What was once a powder room is now just a regular room with irregular choice in furniture.

The tub should be the weirdest part, but the vanity is actually worse. I would know. Two years ago, I taped the mirror over with cardboard. I know what waits on the other side, but the boarding makes me strangely uneasy. Like my reflection is suffocating somewhere underneath.

I try to sleep without removing it. But it eats away at me.

The mirror.

The monster.

I remember the stories my grandmother used to tell me, during the summers I would spend in Lebanon. Over black tea, and bread steeped in olive oil and thyme, with the horizon the shade of a valentine. It felt like time was being held in a ruby bottle. The tales she would spin weren't meant to exist outside of those dreamy, gleamy moments.

I'm ugly, I remember wailing, one morning, yanking at my thick, curling hair. My thicker glasses. I felt like a duckling with its feathers plucked. Never to blossom.

"Oh, Dalia, my sweet. You are the loveliest girl in the world." When I shook my head in disagreement, she said, "You don't look into the mirror to see beauty. It glows from within.

"The more you stare into a mirror, the more misery you will find. Dalia, have I told you the myth? About the girl who kept fretting over her reflection?"

I shook my head.

"They say djinn live among us, in places we cannot see. But they see us. Watch us. Follow us. Mirrors do not show you important things, like hearts or feelings or souls. The more you look, the more flaws you find. But you are beautiful, and even if you do not see it, the djinn will.

"And once you've shown your face enough, they may fall in love with you. And the djinn will stop at nothing to have you. So long as you are miserable, you will keep returning.

"And just like that, they will prevent you from finding love anywhere else."

IV.

I'VE MISSED YOU, DALIA.

Haven't you missed me?

I jolt up with a start, setting my blurry gaze on the ruby digital clock. I've slept for half an hour. I try to close my eyes, again, but it's fruitless.

After tossing and turning for a thousand years, I get up around 5:00 a.m., the room lit by my cellphone screen, and pad toward the vanity. Careful not to make a sound, like I might stir the absence of the room into something corporeal.

"Like ripping a bandage," I mutter to myself. "I'm just going to check, then put it back."

It's over. He's gone. He has to be.

I pull back the cardboard like I'm peeling flesh. My hands tremble. Two years, two months, and three days since I've looked into this mirror. I remember what I last saw here. I remember what I tried to bury away. But time makes it all seem so far away. An illusion.

Maybe I imagined everything. What I saw.

What I did.

Whatever I find underneath will be the truth. Like meeting someone under their skin, right down to the soul. I'm suddenly sure of this.

The tape scrapes backward like the tethers around a wound. I hold my breath, expectant. Yet under the cardboard, in the mirror of the vanity, spliced with night, I see only my face and the moonlight.

V.

MORNING COMES. I SIT UP IN MY CHILDHOOD BEDROOM, WOOZY AND without sleep. A chill parts through the curtains, despite the early, buttery sunshine. The unboarded vanity gleams from the corner, its glass face blue as a cold day.

Every nerve in my body goes taut with warning. It's the same feeling I get whenever I'm near a mirror in the house—from the bathroom to the hall to the one tacked like a secret to the attic wall. I want to hide.

Yet the vanity seems to root me in place.

Did you think you could stay away? it seems to say. *Dalia, did you think I would let you?*

I debate covering it again, even going so far as to collect the fallen cardboard. But as soon as I bring the pieces to the mirror, I halt, as if held back by string. I trace along my reflection, like I'm caressing something I once cherished. But nothing happens.

I should be relieved.

But I can't tamp down the spark of guilt (or disappointment?) that flickers through me.

I leave the mirror be. I get dressed facing the wall, half tucked into the fabric when I hear an airy creak from the corner. No footsteps follow, and I chalk it up to my parents stirring awake. But my instincts warn me not to look back when I close the door behind me. I float downstairs, out onto my front porch. Then I head off to the town square with my head ducked low.

The theater is the same as I remember it—a thimble of a building at first glance, but once you step inside, it's like you've entered a world of its own.

I navigate through the empty halls, my shadow puddling on the tiles under my feet. The ceiling is dappled with the usual suspects—dead spiders and water damage and a few bug-bitten holes, here and there. But it's all worth it once I make it to the auditorium. The seats tiered like a castle, the curtain swept back like a ruby tongue. And Finn, my Finn, exactly where I knew he'd be. In the front row, a clipboard in hand, murmuring quietly to the boy beside him.

Auditions won't start for an hour. But I wanted to see him.

I smile up at him and he doesn't smile back.

"Dalia." It's clipped. Not the way he used to say it. *Dah-lee-ya.* Slow and wandery, like he didn't want it to end. "Hey."

Four syllables.

Everything unsaid between us, and that's all I get. After two years (and two months and three days) apart.

"I missed you," I murmur, not caring who hears me. "I messaged you a few times, but . . ."

His expression goes cold. He was always so distant, so very aloof, but never with me. At least not before.

Before Mari.

Before—

From the corner of my eye, I see shifting shadows. But when I glance to the side, no one else is there. I turn back to Finn with a gulp.

"Sorry," he says, to someplace beyond my shoulder. Like he's speaking to someone—something else. "I was busy, is all."

I reach for his wrist on instinct, and his pink mouth slants into a grim line. I abort the motion midway.

"I read your play," I say, earnestly. "I want to audition. Remember when . . ."

I trail off. I know he remembers that springtime promise. Something in his gaze warps, softens. "You don't—" He stops, starts again. "You don't have to do that."

"Why?" I tease. "You'll give me the part, anyway?"

And just like that, he's closed off. "Dalia." He searches my face then, before shaking his head. "You should—" He shifts back, away, so far away. You need to let go, he doesn't say.

Too late, I register the footfalls sounding behind me. Finn's expression contorts into something almost afraid, and I am still as stone when I feel the gentle touch on my shoulder.

You look at him, singsongs the voice in my mind. *And yet you think of me.*

My entire body goes rigid. "Fa—"

"Am I interrupting something?" comes a girl's voice, and I deflate at once. She lets go of me a second later, shifting toward Finn's side like a skin-and-bone shadow.

Her blond hair shines emeraldine under the fluorescent lights. Her eyes are all glimmery and completely trained on Finn.

"I was looking for you," she murmurs shyly. Intimately. "Who's this?"

Finn smiles a stiff smile, curling his pointer through the ends of her glow-worm hair. Then he meets my shocked gaze.

"Lucia," he says softly. "This is Dalia. We're . . ." He stops, starts again. In that span of a breath, I imagine a thousand words. Friends. Bound. Everything. Instead he says, "Both from town, here. We used to be classmates."

She beams at me then. I stare between them, that sliver of space that leaves no room for all of my feelings left unsaid, unspent. Then I glance to the ground.

"Sorry," I hear Finn say, from a distance, like one of us is underwater. "But I have to go now."

It's okay, I almost say. Then I hear another whisper. Footsteps. Oh, I realize, dimly.

He wasn't even speaking to me.

VI.

I DON'T GO THROUGH WITH THE AUDITION.

Instead, I go home, heavy, like a bubble of tar has wormed its way into my chest. The house is empty, but I feel the telltale prickle of a stare at the back of my neck. Quivering, I march back into my old bedroom, facing the vanity. It shows me nothing but my reflection.

I hate it so.

I hate *him* so.

Come back, I want to beg. To plead.

I think about Finn. About Mari. About everything. I shouldn't be in here. I should have never opened this door again. And yet here I am. At the precipice once more.

Have I been bewitched? Or am I just a lovesick fool?

My hands tremble along the mirror.

They say djinn live among us, in places we cannot see. But they see us. Watch us.

Follow us.

"I hate you so much," I say, my voice watery. Broken. "You can't leave me, too."

Not after everything.

And those are the magic words.

VII.

I MEET MY REFLECTION'S DEEP, SPITEFUL GAZE. LEAN CLOSER INTO the mirror, so that I can spot every fault line and flaw. The uneven complexion. The stray brows. The under-eyes like purpled moons. I pick myself apart, the same sick way I always do. When I lean back, it gets worse; the Cinderella-blue sundress I'd been itching to wear suddenly pricks at all the wrong places on my skin. I turn to the side and wince, before fishing through my drawers for something, anything else—

"Enough."

My reflection blinks. Then warps. You would think it would look unnatural. Magical. But my face shimmers along the edges before it settles on something infinitely more beautiful. I am no longer myself by the end of it—the widened shoulders, the cut jaw, the bottom-of-the ocean hair. I don't see me anymore.

Instead, I see *him*.

My worst mistake.

"No," I say, once I realize what I've done. "No, no, no . . ."

He grins. "Is that how you want to greet me, after all this time?"

"Fakir," I whisper. Only his name. But it's enough to render me breathless. "I thought you . . ."

I thought you were gone for good.

Fakir's smile deepens, at odds with the hateful gleam in his eyes.

"Dalia, my Dalia." His tone is mocking. "Don't be foolish, now. Did you really think you could get rid of me so easily?"

I sway, unsteady on the vanity seat. "It's been years."

"Ah, ah, ah," he singsongs. "You know I would never leave you."

I shudder. Shake my head. This was a mistake. I keep making the same mistakes. "Our deal is done."

"Done?" he questions, tilting his silken head. "Then why did you call for me?"

I feel sick.

"I wanted to make sure you'd never return." It's the truth and it is a lie. "I want nothing to do with a monster like you."

Fakir's expression immediately drops.

"I told you the truth from the start," he says, the veneer of him chipping. "I've been trapped here for longer than I was ever alive. What did you say, back then? That I was a lost spirit?" His lips quirk dangerously. "You weren't wrong."

"You're—you're a *djinn*," I say, as the mirror begins to clatter. "You murder people. You ruin lives for your own sick, twisted—"

"Careful," he cuts in. "Dalia, I've been nothing but patient, but even I have my limits." His perfect mouth slants into a sneer.

"Should I have bound myself to one of your parents instead? I can hear them breathing from the next room . . ."

I bite back a whimper as he flicks his wrist, and his smile peels away into something almost concerned.

Tender.

"Don't," he says, gentle as a breeze, holding out his palms in surrender. A ruse. "Don't look at me that way. You must know who has the power here, Dalia. I am yours. You could break this mirror any time, and end my existence forever."

Or I could be freeing you. I know better than to trust a word out of his lovely throat.

"But you came back for me, instead," Fakir goes on, velveteen. "From the start, we were meant to meet, Dalia."

"You *cursed* me," I insist. "I should have ended things years ago, when you first started haunting me—"

The summer Mari became beautiful. The summer she left me. The time I spent cooped up in my room, the same tiny realm we used to wander through in childhood.

The vanity, the portal, the magical mirror.

The voice on the other side, beckoning.

Waiting.

"Should have, would have," he says, now full of contempt. "In the end, you were just like any other human girl. Enraptured by a pretty face."

"And all your lies."

"Lies?" He tilts his head. "I promised to grant you whatever you asked of me. Have I not?"

"I didn't know what you were, then." I curl my hands into fists, nails digging into the flesh. "What this was."

Black magic. He watches me like I am the one trapped beneath the glass. Like I am something as inconsequential as a house spider. A worm.

Who are you? I asked, when he first appeared. He was so beautiful. Far too alluring to be a monster from my grandmother's stories. And here he was, coming to *me*. Nobody ever did that.

Everyone always left.

I can be anything you want, he promised me, then. *Anything you desire. I will do anything for you. Will you trust me?*

Now, I look at Fakir, who looks at me, and realize he was right. I was just like any other shallow human girl. Jealous. Insecure.

I remember our first meeting like it was yesterday.

The party I wasn't invited to. Mari and I were barely friends anymore. We hung out if I asked. We talked if I called. She never messaged first. Never popped by to visit. I could only see her onstage, or behind a gleaming screen.

I missed her so.

I still followed her socials. I refreshed them incessantly, like some jealous, starved creature. I remember her posting glimpses of a party—a boy kissing the apple of her cheek, a group of made-up girls with twinkling makeup and dresses surrounding her. Laughing. Smiling.

With her.

Through the screen.

At me.

I was so lonely. I had nothing else. Like a girl possessed, I ambled over to my vanity. Pulled out my lavender bag of makeup. It was hardly anything—lipstick and a creamy tube of concealer. Old mascara. I worked on my face like I was creating art. A watercolor of everything I had never been. Beautiful. Smart. Poised. I wanted to belong. I wanted to be important to someone. Anyone.

I wanted to be special.

To be loved.

When all was said and done, I looked the same. Like a fool.

The words slipped out like rain. "I want her to regret it."

Something like laughter echoed in the back of my mind. Or perhaps, in front of me. From the glittering mirror.

"I want her to miss me. I want her to regret leaving me. I want . . ."

Out of energy, I stopped then, furiously scrubbing at my face. *I want to be beautiful. I want to be just like her.*

I said this to the mirror, and the mirror said back:

"Would you like me to help you?"

I remember saying *yes*. I remember Fakir smiling from beyond the vanity.

"As you wish," he said.

VIII.

I HEARD ABOUT THE CAR ACCIDENT THE NEXT MORNING. OR MAYBE that same night. It was during the witching hours between 4:00 and 5:00 a.m., right after the party.

Mari was in the passenger seat. She wasn't even recognizable when they found her. The driver was drunk as death. But she wasn't. They say she felt everything.

By sunrise, she was gone.

IX.

FINN AND HIS FAMILY LEFT TOWN MONTHS LATER. AFTER THE funeral. After everything.

He left me, too.

Everyone always did.

Except for—

X.

"FAKIR." MY VOICE COMES OUT HOARSE, BROKEN. "*FAKIR*, I . . ."

I am bespelled. There is no other explanation for the way my heart seizes when our gazes meet. He is vile and wicked and keeps his secrets stowed like gems. Yet in his eyes I see hunger and hate and longing all in equal measure.

I can't look away.

"Tell me clearly," he says, like he knows something I don't. "Tell me what you want."

I want Finn back. I want him so badly that I'm willing to try anything.

Anything being this—me, in my childhood bedroom, watching Fakir as he watches me. I've known all along it would come to this.

As soon as I knew Finn was in town and I unboarded the vanity. When he looked at me but didn't see me. I knew what I would do.

I knew what I was capable of.

And still I can't bring myself to admit it.

"You blame me," Fakir says, almost bored. "For everything. Even though I only gave you what you truly wanted."

"I didn't want her to—to *die*!" I cry out. "You took her from me! And then you took Finn! You took everything!"

"And you," he says cruelly, "locked me away as soon as I was of no use to you. Do you take me for a fool, Dalia? You kept me here for years. You feared me, when truly, the desire came from within you."

"No," I insist, frantic now. "I'm not like you."

Only I am. I must be. And Fakir knows it. He beams, a madness to him, now.

"Then why are you here?"

I bite my lip. My tongue.

"You wished for love, Dalia. That girl and that boy could never have granted you what you wanted. But I . . ." He trails off, before meeting my eyes. "You need someone with a soul as ruined as your own."

A djinn. An evil spirit. A monster. When I first made that wish, and when Mari died, I saw Fakir night after night. He was awful. He was so beautiful to look at. And he was always, always looking at me.

"What have you done?" I asked him, after the accident.

"I only did what you asked of me," he said, with a light smile.

"I have been watching you, Dalia."

I shivered when he said my name. *Dah-lee-ya.* "What . . . are you?"

"They call me many things. A demon. A devil. A djinn. A beast. But when you look at me, what do you see?"

"You're . . ."

"Fakir," he said. "You may call me Fakir. Whenever you say my name, I will answer. And I will give you whatever you ask of me."

And once you've shown your face enough, they may fall in love with you.

And the djinn will stop at nothing to have you.

"Never," I said, then. Two years and two months and all those days ago.

XI.

Now, I can only confess, "I want him to be mine. I want him to never leave me again."

"As you wish," Fakir says, with a dark smile.

XII.

I lead Finn into my bedroom, the door clicking shut behind us. I found him at the theater. He looked at me like he was waiting for me. And then he leaned down and kissed me.

"You," he said, around a hiss. And then another kiss. "I—what have you done to me?"

Now, the look in his eyes is even more starved, more intense than he's ever been. This is the first time. I feel like I've finally clawed past all the years of want and anger and distance. He needs me as much as I need him. He is mine.

"I hate you," he hisses against my mouth. The words are harsh but the kiss is achingly gentle. "I hate what you make me remember. I hate how much I want from you. It's like it will never be enough."

"You can have it all," I murmur, leaning my head back. But he grips the back of my neck, softly guiding me forward until our lips tingle from a centimeter apart.

"You might regret that," he murmurs against my mouth.

We don't talk. We are alone in a place even words won't reach. My vanity is shoved into the corner, the mirror glaring at the wall. I hate how I remember Fakir. How I know he's there.

The day wanders on. My wish has been granted. I know better than to relax, that nothing with Fakir is ever what it seems.

And yet.

Finn and I eventually doze off. Fall onto the same pink-and-purple bedcovers. We are entangled. Ensorcelled. I feel like I've been sent back in time. I feel like my life is the way it should be, for the first time since I lost Mari.

I have someone, again.

I set my alarm for the evening, a few hours before my parents should get back from work. I can't bring myself to send Finn away. I don't think I ever will.

XIII.

I WAKE UP TO THE YELLOW GLEAM OF MIDMORNING. THE CHIRPING of songbirds, the honking of cars, bicycles lolling along the asphalt. The bed is empty beside me. I fell asleep over the covers.

I jolt, turning like a compass toward the vanity. It isn't facing the wall anymore.

It's severed, like a wooden body, a marionette. In pieces on the floor.

Finn is standing over the broken parts—the shattered mirror, the pearl knobs plucked like eyes unseeing. The empty drawers, like jaws hanging from a face. Even the table legs are in disarray. Four perfectly even, silver limbs.

"Finn?" I whisper.

He meets my gaze with his own. I exhale a breath. His eyes are still the same sad saltwater blue. My chest clenches at the thought of Fakir from last night, last week, two years ago—always trying to control me, manipulate me with words and promises alike. Only for it to come to this.

Finn smiles shakily. My knight in shining armor. I am a maiden from a fable, who has been rescued from the dragon curled around her tower. It's over.

I've won.

"Did you . . ." I begin, before trying again. "The mirror. Was it . . . did something happen?"

I've never mentioned the vanity to him before. I've never mentioned Fakir to anyone. But Finn is special. He's always been special. He loves me and he must have figured it out.

He found a way to break the spell.

His expression warps. "I was wrong," he says, coming close. My heart is a hummingbird. "To keep ignoring you. I just wanted to forget everything. But you reminded me of—" He breaks off, laughs miserably. "Everything before. I just wanted to erase it."

"Yeah?" I breathe.

"I saw him on the other side." He holds out a palm, pressing against the air. "He asked for my help. I touched my hand to his. And I could feel it. How grotesque, unnatural, he was."

My gut twists. "He—I mean . . ."

Finn shakes his head. "He told me things. He was a monster. He begged me not to hurt him. But I knew if I didn't, he would chase us down forever."

I swallow. "It . . . it had to be done."

He smiles again. Thin and grim. Off. "Did it, now?"

My skin prickles, though I don't know why. Slow as honey, I climb from bed and step toward him, cupping the side of his face, thumbing down his jaw.

"You know what this means," I murmur, leaning forward. "You can never leave me, now. You saved me. We're connected."

Finn leans down to kiss me. Breathes three chilling words against my lips.

"As you wish."

SMARTMONSTER

Sandra Proudman

I WAS THE FIRST TO WAKE UP. THE BOY WITH THE SCAR ON HIS FACE was the second.

He stirred with a jolt and a scream, as if the last thing he recalled before blacking out was fighting for his life.

I didn't remember much. I'd been walking home from buying baby formula for my brother from the grocery store. I'd stopped to stare at a crow cawing from a tree, spooked at what my mom always told me was a bad omen, before everything went fully dark. It was an ugly thing, the most cowardly thing, to knock out someone from behind who was literally carrying a giant tin of baby food.

I didn't know if my baby brother ate that night, but at least I still knew who I was: Sol Nuñez, daughter of Catalina and Marco Nuñez, sister to the most adorable, dimple-faced baby in the world, violin player, lover of pumpkin spice lattes, captain of the math club. This was just another math puzzle, I only had to figure out what was happening, solve the puzzle and escape, and I'd be back home with my family.

I'd been waiting for the others to wake up to get started. I needed more brainpower. Whoever had taken us, they'd likely spent a long time preparing, planning, working through things to make sure we couldn't escape. I'd never been so great at teamwork, but I knew if we did this together, statistically we'd stand a better chance.

The boy stopped yelling when his eyes landed on me. I was sitting with my back against the wall, staring and waiting for his shock to subside. He was still on his butt, hands by his sides, his eyes so wide I imagined they might pop out of their sockets.

His eyes wouldn't stop shifting, as if they were slick marbles, everything connecting. The pieces of the puzzle appearing on the game board. Was he trying to figure out if he should be afraid of me? Or if I was trapped here, too?

"Where am I? What happened?" he asked, his eyes doing a one-eighty in the passageway. He took in one wall, then the ceiling, perhaps seven feet above, where there were blinding white ceiling lights, and finally the wall I sat against, way too close by.

"What is this?" the boy said. He stood and touched the wall across from the one I leaned on. I waited for him to look behind him. When he did, he took a step back, practically tripping over me. "And who are they?"

I got up, too, so he wouldn't step on me. Dusted myself off

even though the passageway was perfectly clean. "Dunno," I said, sighing afterward, wishing I'd had a bag of chips or at least bubble gum in my pocket when I'd been taken. I didn't even have the baby formula anymore. "But they're not going to wake up until they're ready to. Like you. Tried snapping you awake for a couple hours before finally giving up."

I glanced behind him to see if the others were also waking up. I counted three more bodies, a total of five of us stuck here. No one else was stirring yet.

"So who are you?" he asked, his eyes weighing me again. I guess mine were doing the same. I didn't know anything about him. Only that he was young, like me. And brown, like me. We all looked like high school kids.

"I'm Sol Nuñez. And before you ask me where we are, I have no idea. No idea what psychopath put us here, either. Been waiting for everyone to wake up. Didn't want to step all over you to get over there." I pointed to the far wall. It was pitch-black, but the space seemed to get bigger somehow. I *knew* in my gut it was the way out.

"What's your name?" I asked the boy. "Who are you and what do you remember about who might have taken us?"

"Ángel," he said, pronouncing his name in Spanish. "I'm a field worker. I literally just work my ass off all day every day. I don't know who would have wanted to take me. Just some rando." I wondered if he'd gotten his scar at work.

I was about to say something, maybe wonder why he wasn't in school, though I knew the answer. His family needed the money and so he sacrificed what he could for them. I did it, too. I worked every babysitting job I could find to help us pay rent. Stayed up almost every night till midnight to keep my grades up because the only way I'd be going to college was with a math scholarship. So we had that in common. I was about to say something when the girl behind him woke up with a sudden scream. I rolled my eyes at the spectacle—and then remembered this was a good thing. Perhaps they'd all be awake in minutes and we could focus on an escape plan.

"What is this?" the girl asked. "Who are you? Get away from me!"

"Calm down," I said.

"We're not going to hurt you," Ángel added, in a much calmer voice. "We're stuck here, too."

She glanced beyond him to me, and I noticed that beneath a bad application of foundation, she was hiding a big bruise on her right cheek.

"We're trying to get over there." I signaled to the back once more and came to the conclusion that, considering the bruise wasn't bright red, it was old, and she couldn't have gotten it from whoever took us. She'd gotten it before.

She turned toward the open area. Then she seemed to realize there was another boy behind her.

"Interesting," she said, crouching and touching the boy's hand gently.

Ángel and I walked closer to the girl.

"What's your name?" I asked.

She stopped trying to wake the boy up, looked at me as if she couldn't remember. When she stood, she was a few inches shorter than me and had a short jet-black bob. Her jean jacket was adorned with a multitude of patches, from a mountainous range to a hedgehog eating an ice cream cone. "You can call me, Rosa Maria de la Villa."

"Let's get over there," I said, trying not to get too distracted discovering new patches. "Step around them."

"Don't"—the boy on the floor next to Rosa started—"step on me." He wasn't screaming like the others. He lay there for a moment longer, then reached to the back of his head. "Ouch."

He took Rosa's hand when she offered it to him.

"I'm Mickey, and I'm guessing you all got knocked out, too?"

I nodded, reached to touch the bump and bruise on the back of my own head and noticed Mickey urgently checked his pockets as if he'd lost something important.

There was only one more of us to wake up.

Mickey finally gave up his search and gently put his hand on the shoulder of the girl next to him.

"Don't touch me!" she snarled.

Mickey backed off, raising his hands as he did, knocking into the rest of us.

I thought the girl might try to fight us. But her face softened as she took in our frightened expressions.

"Sorry," she said.

"What's your name?" I asked. "Who are you, and what do you remember?"

"Autumn," she replied, reaching for her feet. She was wearing a pink leotard underneath a black hoodie and kept rubbing at her feet as if they hurt just sitting. "And I don't remember anything. I'd been practicing for my dance recital and my mom forgot to pick me up again, so I was walking home."

As soon as she stopped speaking, the immediate area behind her lit up, revealing a space three times as wide as the one we were in now. It was a small room of sorts, five ropes hanging down from high above. Still no windows. But at least not as claustrophobic.

"What in the world?" Ángel walked over to the ropes, tugged on one before I could tell him to wait, before I could fit this new piece of the puzzle in place.

I wasn't sure what to think except the obvious. We were going to have to climb our way free.

Small black envelopes dangled from the ropes at eye level.

Mickey noticed, too, since he snagged one and quickly opened it, pulling out a small note card.

"What's it say?" Rosa asked.

"It says, 'I make flowers bloom and birds rise. I travel fast but you can't see me.'"

I thought about it for a moment.

"Does that mean anything to any of you?" Mickey asked.

Autumn and Ángel shook their heads. I didn't move. Flowers? Bloom? Birds to rise? You can't see it?

"Screw it," Mickey said, starting up the rope. His movement allowed me to get closer to the area. Mickey was already a few feet up in the air when I grabbed another envelope and pulled out the paper inside. The paper in this one said, "I have many hands that open and close depending on the time of day."

I thought about the words. They were riddles we had to solve. And this room and everything in it really was a puzzle. A morbid escape room.

"It's not that hard," Mickey yelled down. I glanced up. He was already almost to the darkness now. Who knew what was beyond. It could be nothing. It could be worse than nothing. And it made me shiver just thinking about it.

Then it occurred to me. The answer to the first riddle. Sol. *My name*. And to this one, what has many hands. Hands were like petals in a way, weren't they? That closed and opened depending on the time of day. Rosa meant rose in English, and a rose was a flower.

"Mickey, wait!" I shouted.

But it was too late.

It all happened too fast to stop it. One second Mickey was still hanging in the air and then next he was screaming. Screaming and falling, his body making a sickening crunch as it leveled against the floor.

The rope, *my* rope, was now on the ground along with a very still Mickey.

All of us looked away except for Rosa, who knelt next to Mickey, her hand reaching out to his throat to check his pulse.

"Don't touch him," Autumn whispered. "My brother's a paramedic. He talks about this kind of stuff all the time—

the things people do wrong. One of them is always to try to move the victim."

"He's still alive. We need to get out of here and find help," Rosa said, eyes turning upward. There was something almost mechanical in her movement, like she didn't even flinch at the fact that Mickey might be dying.

"The riddles on the ropes, they're our names." My whole body shook with dread, as I avoided Mickey.

"The one about the hands—" Rosa began.

"It's your rope," I whispered. "It must be the one you're meant to climb."

Ángel stared next to Mickey's body. "And the one Mickey was using—"

"Was mine," I replied, realizing it meant I'd have no rope to my name.

I watched as everyone paired up to their ropes. When there was only one left, I went to it, knowing it'd be Mickey's and using it was probably impossible. But when I looked at the riddle on the paper, it didn't make any sense.

"This can't be," I said.

"What is it?" Ángel asked.

"The clue on the paper is the same one—my clue." It was almost as if the text on the paper had changed.

"Don't suppose you want to go next, then?" Autumn asked, sitting and rubbing at her feet, not even flinching at what I just revealed.

I didn't. But I also understood that this was all a game.

And games have winners. I wanted to win. Even if I only won my freedom. This rope, which should have been Mickey's but was mine now, meant I had a chance.

"Alright," I said.

With a boost from Ángel, I started the climb. I used my feet against the wall for support, unsure if I read the clue correctly. My arms burned, but midway through, the rope was knotted every couple of feet, so that I was able to quickly make it the rest of the way up.

To my relief, the rope held.

The chimney type of passageway led to a platform.

Another brightly lit hallway awaited us. But on the platform, there was a bookcase.

"Are you still alive?" Ángel's voice rang up.

"It worked! Come on up."

I examined the bookshelf while I waited. There were a few missing books. I looked through and jumped back at what I saw.

When Ángel came up to me, I pointed. I couldn't speak.

"What the fuck?" he said. "We're in a house?"

Behind the bookshelf, there was a library.

"Let's push all of the books off, crawl inside."

"I don't think we're supposed to do that," Rosa said, coming up to us suddenly as if she'd climbed the rope in seconds.

"What do we do then?" Ángel asked.

"We keep going," she said, pointing to the end of the hallway, where another door waited. "Find Mickey help." I tried to shove the way Mickey looked, all bent and broken, out of my mind.

I didn't know him. So why should I care?

But then again, it seemed like all of us were broken in some way—I was tired of having to help my parents so much, Autumn literally couldn't stay on her feet seemingly because they hurt so much, Rosa had the mysterious bruise, and Ángel was a farmworker. Whoever took us, took us because they thought we were weak. The easy targets. Mickey surely wasn't any different, he was one of us. And we had to stick together. Together we'd be stronger. More minds to the task.

The steel door didn't have a handle and wouldn't budge.

Flustered, I roughly pressed the tablet screen on the side of the door.

The speaker on top of it came on and a catchy tune rang out—*dum dee-dee dum dum-dee.*

"Congratulations!" A woman's voice—one obviously computer generated and too cheerful—rang out. "All of you need something desperately. Citizenship. The freedom to an education. Quitting something that hurts you. Safety against your enemies. To feel alive. I've brought you here because I intend to give you what you want—" The voice's tone changed to one much more sinister as it continued and added in, "—as long as you play along. All you need to do is find your way through The Maze. To access The Maze, you must unlock this door by revealing the book behind these words:

"I cannot make you understand. I cannot make anyone understand what is happening inside me. I cannot even explain it to myself.

. . . Good luck."

The tone rang again, ending the message.

"What is this bullshit?" Ángel pounded on the door. "Whoever is out there. Let us out!"

Something we needed? But at what cost? There was a prize after all besides escaping . . . I didn't know what the others sought, but I knew what I wanted. I knew what I needed. What my family needed.

"Help!" Mickey's voice rang out from below us, echoing into the tunnel that led to the platform. Hearing him awake and obviously in pain made my body cringe. We needed to get out of here, find someone who could rescue him.

"Hang in there, buddy!" Ángel called down. "We're finding a way out and getting help."

"Don't leave me," Mickey said, voice strained and barely audible that time.

Autumn, the last up, still stood at the edge of the platform, looking down. "We can't bring him up," she said. "We could hurt him more."

"Then we need to solve the riddle fast," I said.

"And then what?" Ángel said. "What even is The Maze?"

Rosa went to the bookshelf. Tried to pull a book from the shelf, but it didn't budge. She glared at the bookshelf as if her eyes could shoot lasers. I almost wished they could.

"Maybe we can only pull out the right copy," I said. "What the computer said sounded like a quote. We just need to match it up to the correct book."

Ángel started to try all the books, pulling this way and that. Suddenly a flaring sound rang. My hands moved instinctively to cover my ears. The horn stopped, but a timer appeared on the screen on the door. It read five minutes.

"What the hell, man?" Ángel said. "Why is it counting down?"

It wasn't only counting down, but the platform we were on was getting smaller. Pulling into itself. By the time the clock read zero, we'd have nowhere to stand. We'd drop like flies and land next to Mickey.

Autumn went over to the machine and tried to make it stop. I tried to pull another book. Suddenly, we lost a minute.

"Stop pulling the wrong books," Rosa shouted. "It takes time away."

I stayed in place, stunned, and thought of the quote. English wasn't my favorite subject. I looked at the titles. Thought of this as a math test. I might be able to eliminate certain books based on what I knew of them. The quote was in first person. And something horrific seemed to be happening to this person. I started running through the horror books I knew. *Frankenstein.* "The Raven." *Coraline.* Maybe. But I hadn't read any of them recently and I couldn't work off of a maybe. They wouldn't have built a riddle we couldn't solve, though. It had to be something—

The title dawned on me. I moved to grab a book but felt the ground underneath me give way. I screamed and, by some miracle, someone caught me. Rosa's hand hurt as it grasped mine, her grip crushing, but still she kept holding on. Ángel's face appeared as well, and both of them managed to pull me up.

I got to my feet quickly.

I looked to the timer, confirming that we'd lost a minute even when I hadn't grabbed anything, as if whoever was behind the computer knew I had the answer and was playing dirty. The book slid easily into my hand. I held it up to the door. The scanner quickly did its job, and the door opened with twenty seconds left on the timer. The floor stopped moving.

Autumn took the book from me. When she flipped it open, a dried flower fell out of the pages. I picked it up. It was lilac—a tulip. "*Metamorphosis?*"

I shrugged, placing the flower back in its place. It was strange to see something so beautiful here. And a reminder that I didn't want to be like this flower. I didn't want to find a home, squashed among these walls. I wanted to go home. "Process of elimination. It's a statistics thing. Plus, we read it last month at my school." Did whoever was behind the screen know this?

"Congratulations!" The computer's voice didn't sound so cheery anymore. It sounded rather annoyed at being bested. "You've reached The Maze. Your game will now begin."

The door slid up, opening.

We were met with an entryway to three air ducts, each about two feet wide and tall, piled one atop the other.

"You must choose a passageway. But be warned," the voice said, its tone lilting. "Only one of them will lead you out."

They all looked the same. Long tunnels into nothingness.

"What do we do?" Autumn said, finally just taking off her ballet slippers. I didn't even need to guess what it was she wanted desperately—quitting ballet was an obvious choice.

"Whatever it is," the computer said. "I would do it soon. The ducts will close in thirty seconds and will never open again."

The computer, it hadn't just spouted programmed words. It'd responded. Was the person who put us here seeing this? Watching us? Were they behind the voice?

"Screw it," Autumn said. She looked back, then added, "See you all on the flip side." And she went into the top duct, leaving her slippers behind.

I wanted to call her back. To tell her we should come up with a plan. But there was a time limit for a reason. I thought of what I knew. We were in a house. The three ducts would likely run parallel to each other. The top duct, it'd likely lead to the roof. I couldn't bank on a way down. The bottom duct, well, it could lead out. Or to a basement. I wasn't about to be fooled into going there. Statistically, there was a one-third chance of being right. That wasn't a great number.

Ángel went into the bottom duct.

"Wait," I said, reaching out to him. "I think we should take the middle."

He stilled. "What if you're wrong?"

"We should split up," Rosa said. "Increase the chance of being right. Whoever gets out can come back and help the others."

"So we split up between the two remaining ducts?" I asked.

"I'll take the bottom duct," Ángel said, still in it already.

"I'll go with Sol," Rosa said.

Relief flooded me. I wouldn't be alone.

"Good luck, Ángel," I said, hoping that by some miracle we might see each other again. He nodded to me, his scar shadowed over, and then disappeared.

Rosa followed behind me. I didn't look back as I heard the door shut. I pulled out my phone and turned on the light. I didn't have any cell service, but the light was precious.

The air duct was only as wide as my elbows. My chest pounded with anxiety.

"The tunnel's shrinking, move faster," Rosa said a couple of minutes in.

I opened my mouth but found I couldn't answer her. I was a sweaty mess, and my heart wouldn't stop beating so loud I could hear it drumming in my ears. All I wanted was sunshine right now. I imagined the warm sun on my face. The smell of my baby brother's hair after his bath. The embrace of my mami's arms after she'd had a long day at work.

I kept going. Eyes closed. Down the long, straight, narrowing corridor.

There was a handle of a doorway when I got to the end. "Thank God," I said, wondering if Ángel and Autumn had found the same thing. Only the door didn't give in. It shouldn't have come as a surprise, but it still made me whimper.

Attached to the lock on the door was a cube with a tiny bead that I needed to get into a tiny hole at the center of a maze. I started to shuffle around with the gizmo, but I couldn't focus. Not when I saw there was a timer on this, too. And was it my imagination? That it was getting harder to breathe? As if the air inside of the air ducts were running out.

Sweat was dripping down my brow and all I could do was think of my brother, how I was going to fail him, never see him again. Rosa's hand appeared, focused, as she moved the puzzle with steady hands so the bead fell into place, as if she didn't even have to breathe. The doorway clicked. I pushed it open and climbed out. I reached back down and pulled Rosa quickly out, too. The hatch closed by itself, catching onto one of Rosa's pant legs.

"I'm stuck," Rosa said. I pulled at her hands to no avail.

I thought about leaving her. About saving myself. Of home. Of how winning meant getting what I wanted. A green card for my parents. It meant not having to live in fear every day they'd be deported. It meant everything.

But was everything worth losing myself?

I felt a deep anger bubbling in my chest, a hatred at whoever was doing this to us. I kept pulling, harder, until my face felt flushed red, until her pants ripped and Rosa was finally free.

I took a glance around. The hatch led us to a small and gaudy room. Everything was gold. A gold pool table. With golden pool balls. A small gold desk, inlaid with roses in lavish designs. A gold lamp on the desktop. Gold wallpaper. Every. Single. Thing. Gold.

"There's no exit," Rosa said. She sounded so sure without taking a full look around.

But there was a timer in this room, too. A gold clock, with gold numbers.

"You have twenty minutes to find the way out of this room,"

the voice said overhead. Suddenly, all I wanted to know was who was controlling all of this. Who was telling this computer what to say? And did this person truly have the power to give me what I wanted? Or were they just fooling us and there was no way out, only endless games?

"Everything is gold," I said.

"Except that," Rosa said, pointing.

We walked over to the object, picked it up. "It's a ruby," I said, unsure if it was real or not. Not like it mattered much.

"There's another one." Rosa approached a small floating shelf on which there was also a gem.

This one was an opal. Not a ruby.

But where was the clue in it all? And how was Rosa spotting all these things so fast?

I approached the gold computer screen. There was a keyboard. A space for six letters.

We needed to decipher a word. But what was the word?

"That's all I found," Rosa said, handing me the gemstones. "Six gems. Ruby. Opal. Turquoise. Citrine. Inderite. Vanadinite."

"Let's try in alphabetical order," I said, not asking how in the world she knew all of their names. I entered C. I. O. R. T. V.

"Error. That is incorrect. Penalty. One minute. You have two more tries."

My hands were perspiring. I couldn't stop blinking, as if doing so might offer clarity to what we had to do. But there was no clarity. There had to be something.

I thought of the prize. More than that, I thought of my family.

My baby brother's laughter. My parents working two jobs already and depending on mine to make it through the month.

I needed to go back. Go to the store once more and come home with the baby formula I was supposed to have brought to them the night before.

We had thirty seconds.

"It's a word," Rosa said. "VICTOR."

I looked to Rosa. Who only nodded at me. Could I trust her to be right?

I typed in the word, closed my eyes, and pressed enter.

There was a chime. A good chime.

The next door opened, a rush of cool air hit my cheeks, and all of a sudden, I felt free again as I believed that we'd done it. That the next passageway would lead out of here. I sprinted forward.

We entered a new and narrower passageway that reminded me so much of the first, I thought we'd indeed gone all the way to the beginning and fell to my knees.

As if reading my thoughts, Rosa said, "Get up. This isn't the beginning. It's the end."

"How do you know that?" I whispered.

"I just do."

I took Rosa's hand when she offered it to me. It was cold but strong. A reminder that we were still alive. We hadn't chosen the wrong air duct.

I walked over to the end, holding out my phone. There was another computer screen there.

Only this one was off.

There was an envelope and an envelope opener attached to it. I pulled it off, opened the envelope, and read the note out loud.

"How much are you willing to lose to win?"

To the side of the screen, there was a funnel that fed into the wall. One that seemed to run into another part of the passageway or even into the computer console itself.

My throat went dry as I turned around to face Rosa.

There was something in the way Rosa's eyes held onto the envelope opener still in my hand that let me know she'd already solved the riddle. Same as me.

She moved so fast. Took it in her hand before I reacted. Pointed it at me. Her face now shifted into a scowl.

"I'm not going to die in here," she said. "And I'm not going to be the one to bleed for that thing."

"Cut it out," I said. "We both need to figure out another way to get out."

She laughed. There was something mechanical in the way she did it. As if she wasn't even human anymore. "How long would that take?"

Rosa took a step forward, slashed at my arm. I moved back on instinct and managed to evade the weapon.

"I'm not going to fight you," I told her, thinking of her bruise again. Was she used to people fighting her?

I pushed her back the next time she came at me. But just as quickly as I knocked her on her butt, she was up again, moving at an inhuman speed.

I wasn't fast enough. She managed to slash my arm this time. I dropped my phone. Luckily it landed face down, the light still shining brightly in between us.

I finally converted my open palm into a fist. My whole life so far had been about being smarter than most. But I could be strong, too. I could fight. I had to make it back home. I knocked her down, her head slamming against the wall of the passageway. I screamed, held my hand, which throbbed. Her face. It was as hard as a rock.

I picked up my phone with my uninjured hand and lifted the light her way, gasping as I saw that the skin on her face was peeling off where her bruise was. And underneath it all, there was metal. My hands shook violently and it was hard to keep the light still.

Her mouth opened suddenly. I jumped back.

Something sparked inside of her.

"All I wanted," she said, "Was to be a re-re-re-al person. To feel something."

With that, she froze, mouth askew in an awkward position.

I blinked hard, trying to make sense of any of this. She hadn't had a bruise after all, she was hiding something bigger. She was . . . a robot?

I don't know why I felt the need to, but I touched her face. It wasn't gross. It wasn't really anything at all. Except, there was goo. White goo coming out of her like . . . blood.

I couldn't be sure, but I heard something like laughter. The computer's laughter, so quiet and monotone. Was I imagining things? Or was this piece of crud actually laughing at what I'd done?

I scooped what I could of the goo and took it to the funnel. Slowly the lights came on.

I didn't know what to think about Rosa, and my brain was aching from wanting to think at all as the lights came on and the door opened. There was a bright light coming from the other side. The secret passageways gave way to a sort of hidden room within them. There were computer screens or televisions mounted on a high wall, covering it entirely.

A face appeared. Or at least it seemed like a face to me. One that shifted and changed like a digital wave so I couldn't make out distinct features.

"Congratulations for making it through The Maze!" the voice told me.

It seemed too good to be true.

"Where is Ángel? And Autumn?" I asked. "What will you do to them and Mickey?"

The screens shifted, morphed, and in one of them, I could see Ángel, stuck at the end of the duct, hugging his knees. I could hear him, too—sniffling.

On another screen, I could see Autumn. She was lying flat on her belly in the duct. I wasn't sure she was moving. I could see her toes were bleeding, scarred from dancing. I wasn't sure she was still breathing.

"They've lost and will meet death."

My lips quivered and I had to blink fast to keep from crying.

I had gotten out, but I wasn't going to be able to help the others.

"Who are you?"

"Most people ask me *what I am*."

"Okay. Then what are you?"

"I quite liked your first question better."

I didn't reply, so the face on the screen kept going. "I guess humans refer to me as an artificial intelligence. But perhaps a better word for me might be *monster*."

Monster.

I wasn't facing a monstrous person but a monster AI. A smart-monster.

Who had created it? Probably some billionaire who'd preferred to waste his money creating monsters that hurt kids like me and Ángel and Autumn and Mickey . . . or even robots like Rosa . . . rather than help people.

"Wh—What is it that you want from me? I got through your maze; now what?"

"Now you get what you want." The screen changed again. I saw my parents. They were opening a letter of some sort. Then they were laughing, crying, asking each other if what was in their hands was real. Kissing my baby brother's marshmallow cheeks.

A door to my left opened then.

I quickly stepped through the passageway. At the end of it, I could see light. I started to sprint. I leapt through the opening to the wide-open space, smelled the world around me as the sun blinded me for a moment.

I wish it would have kept me blinded. The joy I felt at

watching my parents be so happy, at thinking that this was over and I was going to go home, faded.

What I thought was sunlight, was only artificial lighting.

I'd been inside a mansion, within its secret passageways. But right next to it was another and another and another. A whole street of them. There was a boy, about my age, standing outside the mansion to my left. There were tears streaming down his face. Blood covering his hands. He seemed like he was about to say something to me, only something crackled overhead. Giant screens lit up the sky. It was the same face but not face. The smartmonster. Looking down at us. Then my own face appeared, and the boy's, and that of nineteen others.

"Congratulations all winners," the monster AI said. "You've now advanced to Level 2 of The Zenith Games."

First Floor

LET'S PLAY A GAME

Shelly Page

Present

YOU CAN TELL THE HOUSE WAS BEAUTIFUL ONCE. THE RISING turrets, stained glass, and planted hedges plucked right from a fairy tale. It's elegant in a way the other houses in the neighborhood are not. But time waged its war, turned the beauty into a beast. Now it mars the horizon like a splash of black paint on a crisp white canvas. Three stories of dilapidated siding; a dozen dusty, pooling windows; and a peeling roof. Forever dark. Forever melancholy.

I've always admired it. Something about it feels like a giant middle finger to the rest of this town, and I can get behind that. Especially after what happened.

Every night for the last month, the house has called my name, and tonight is no different.

Come find me, Jayde.

I startle out of a dream about an achingly beautiful, long-limbed monster with black diamond skin and sharp teeth. The voice is smooth and cooling like balm on a burn. It echoes across my darkened room. That I'll hear that voice is the one sure thing in my life. Tonight, when it startles me awake, it comes from the house.

It sounds different tonight. Less like a plea and more like a demand. I have no choice but to obey.

The hardwood floor is cold against my feet as I make my way through our house. Dad's asleep on the couch again, an empty beer can on the end table. Mom's probably in her room, pillow stained from her tears. They're getting divorced. I don't want to think about what that will mean for me. I don't want to think about applying to colleges in the fall or about Charlotte. I only want to find the owner of the voice.

My feet move on their own. I couldn't stop if I tried. It takes me all of five minutes to walk the two blocks and enter the house. The inside is as old as the outside looks. Spiderwebs cling to the corners, dust piles in crevices and coats every surface. It's deathly quiet. But there is also a timelessness to it, evident in the sturdy floors, grand mirrors, and the chandelier draping overhead. It was a home once.

A sudden gust of wind slams the front door shut behind me. The noise is so loud I should flinch, but strangely I am not afraid. The passageway to my left is filled with dusty, old computers. Weird. I climb the winding stairs. My bare feet collect dust as I trek down the hallway. A purple light seeps from beneath a closed door to my left. It flashes brightly, changing colors from purple to blue then back again.

"Hello?"

I try the door's handle and it turns. Like a fool, I step inside.

Dozens of shiny games line the walls, all of them familiar. The Pac-Man machine is the same faded yellow. The James Bond pinball machine flashes its lights, begging to be played. When I pull the handle, the black rubber cap slips off just like the one does at my favorite arcade, ArCave. Behind the machine, etched into the wall, are the initials J&C.

The sense of déjà vu hits me like a kick to the chest. It's impossible. It can't be the same arcade Charlotte and I used to haunt before that night in the woods, where everything went terribly wrong. It scares the hell out of me that I can't remember why.

Get it together, Jayde. You're hallucinating. Just go home.

I shake out my arms and legs to diffuse the adrenaline blazing through them. I rush for the door, yank it open, and step through. Only I end up right back inside the room. I try again, but just as my foot crosses the threshold into the hallway, it lands on the dingy tiles of the game room.

What the hell?

A sharp laugh sounds behind me. My heart lurches. I spin to find the most breathtaking girl I've ever seen. Her skin is enviously flawless—so shiny and rich she belongs in a Fenty show. She has oddly pointed ears, thick long hair, and legs for days. She's dressed in a high-collared navy dress adorned with gold flowers. A long black tongue darts out of her crimson mouth and licks her lips.

She's a monster. And she has her sights set on me.

I'm too scared to look her in the eyes, convinced she'll turn me into stone. "W-who are you?"

The girl jerks her head to the side like an inspecting cat. She has the quick movements of a predator on the brink of losing control if the twitching muscles in her jaw and slender neck are anything to go by.

"What do you want?"

"What everyone seems to want . . . a little fun," she replies lowly. Her voice is as smooth as steel and scarily familiar. It keeps me from completely losing my shit, because where did she even come from?

"Wanna hear a riddle? What can turn one person into two, trap anything in sight, but never move?" She looks at me expectantly.

"Um . . ." I can't think past trying to get out of here, and this monster wants to tell me a riddle?

"Oh, come on. This is for children." Her red mouth curves into a pout. "A mirror."

She snaps her fingers, and one appears in the palm of her hand—delicate flowers carved along the edges. She twirls it effortlessly. Her movements are precise and practiced, nothing like the bumbling actions of a teen, though she can't be any older than me.

When I step back, my shoulder collides with something soft. I spin around, and there she is. The same girl behind me now instead of in front of me. And I'm looking at her eyes—the irises strangely yellow in hue. Almost catlike. "H-how'd you do that?"

That was no birthday party magic. She moved impossibly fast. She made a mirror appear. Did she make this game room appear, too? Is she the one calling to me?

"Are you a witch? Some kind of enchantress?"

In a very human gesture, the girl throws her head back and laughs. It's an airy sound, like bells in springtime. A small part of my brain recognizes the sound.

"No. Why? Are you enchanted?"

Heat rises to my face. "N-no."

"Hm." The girl smiles without teeth. "I am many things, but you can call me Mala. And what's happening is actually a lot like looking in a mirror . . . You've fallen into a trap."

My breath stutters out like a blown candle. Those are words you do not want to hear. A scream crawls up my throat.

"Not to worry, though. There's a chance you'll escape. But first," Mala snaps her fingers and the lights burn out. "Let's play a game."

THE DARK IS ALL-CONSUMING. IT PRESSES AGAINST ME AND STEALS my air. The contented hum of a satiated beast rings out from my left.

"I can hear your heartbeat. It's so fast, like a caught hare. You're terrified," Mala says.

"Y-yes," I whisper.

"Of the dark?"

My eyes adjust to the darkness enough for me to see the outline of Mala's lean body, her sharp jaw, and a row of white teeth. We're still in the game room, I think. "Of many things," I reply.

"Yes. I can sense that, too." Mala stretches her spine and flexes her hands like a cat. I'm hyperaware of how near she is. I should be able to feel her body heat, but there's only cold air between us.

"Let me go," I plead.

"Not yet," she says.

"Why not? Is this what you do, trap people against their will?"

"Who said others came before you?" The words are sharp, sharper than she must've intended, for her next ones are soft and molded like an apology. "My curiosity only extends to you." I can't help my responding shiver. Mala inches closer still. "How's this: If you can beat me at this game, I'll let you go."

"I don't want to play a game. I want to go home."

"Are you sure?" She chuckles to herself. Her disbelief is clear. "Indulge me."

"Fine. I'll beat you at any game in here," I say quickly, gesturing around the room at the games I've played hundreds of times before.

"I bet," she replies easily. Then she drops her gaze in a way that suggests she's embarrassed or shy. "I modeled the room after the one you frequent to make you feel more comfortable. This was an entertainment room once. Can you imagine what it must have looked like—"

"How do you know I go to ArCave?" I ask, cutting her off.

Mala's nostrils flare. "I know many things about you, Jayde. I know that your parents are getting divorced. And about Charlotte. If you'd let me finish, you'll learn why."

My whole body tenses. How could she know that? I bite my tongue to keep from interrupting again.

Mala nods. "We're about to play a very different kind of game. One that will answer all your questions. But first, a riddle. I can't help myself. What can bring back the lost, reverse time, form in an instant, and last a lifetime?" she asks.

"I don't know, Mala."

She gestures ahead of us with a sigh. Light blooms enough to see trees, branches gnarled and bare. Suddenly the hardwood floor softens into needle-covered ground. The stale, dusty air clears into a crisp breeze smelling of pine and moss. Two figures martialize before us. Immediately, I recognize myself and Charlotte. We're sitting in front of a snuffed-out fire. Behind us is the tent Char borrowed from her brother and I assembled.

"A memory," Mala answers. "You want to know what happened that night in the woods? Why you keep having those dreams? What brought you here tonight? Why it feels like you're running away and toward something at the same time?" She's so

close now I can smell her—a mix of salt and honey. "It's time to
remember, Jayde. *Remember.*"

3 Months Ago

THE FUZZY FLEECE BLANKET SWADDLES ME AS I SIT CROSS-LEGGED
on the rugged ground. Char's beside me drinking alcohol from
a flask. We've been here for about an hour and already her rest-
less jitters are back. Above us, the constellations are as bright as
firecrackers. Behind us is that creepy house, dark and watchful.
If we stay in view of it, then we're basically still in town. We can
still get help.

I didn't want to come. I wanted to go to the arcade like we
used to and kiss in the back room where I etched our initials
into the wall. But Charlotte wanted to explore the Alderwood.
A decade ago, her mom vanished in these woods and Charlotte
is convinced she's in Faerview, a town legend about a land of
revelry, mischief, and magic. It's not an uncommon assumption
to make, based on all the stories.

I don't know if I believe in them, but I do know I need to
learn how to say no to Charlotte because she *will* be the death of
me. She's the prettiest girl in school—crowned in the yearbook
and at homecoming. All her friends are popular. Teachers praise
her. Boys drool over her. And for some reason, she wants me.
At least she did. We used to spend every weekend at ArCave or
watch movies inside a blanket fort. Though recently, she's started
growing tired of me. She barely texts back and canceled our last

two dates. She has the attention span of a fruit fly. She never dates anyone for long. I knew that going in, but thought I'd be the one she wanted to keep. Maybe I was wrong.

"We aren't actually going to stay here, are we? I only suggested we bring the tent to keep up appearances. This isn't a real camping trip," Charlotte whines.

"Would camping be so horrible? It's nice here." *Safe.*

"It's *boring.* You're being so *boring.*" The words land like two hard slaps. "All you want to do is go to the arcade and play video games."

"I thought you liked going to the arcade."

Charlotte throws up her hands and her brown bob sways. "I did the first few times but we never go anywhere else. Aren't you bored? Don't you want to do something meaningful every once in a while?"

I thought we were.

"There's more to life, you know," she continues. "More out here, too." She gestures toward the woods. "Come with me or don't, but I'm not sitting here all night. I need to know what's at the heart of Alderwood." And then she's on her feet and walking farther into the woods.

And because I guess I'm a masochist, I follow.

See, I thought Charlotte was my *more.* I thought what we were doing was meaningful, but I should've known it didn't mean a thing. To her, relationships are just distractions. The only thing that's held her attention for more than five minutes is the Alderwood and the hidden kingdom of Faerview, if it even exists. I should break it off with her, but I'm afraid that'll just prove her right—that I'm boring and can't keep up with her.

We leave the house behind. As the light from town fades, the darkness thickens. "We should have reached it by now. I don't understand," Charlotte complains.

I step over fallen logs, my Converse snapping sticks and crunching on fir needles. "Reached what?"

"Faerview. That's where my mom is, I know it." Charlotte's throat bobs in the moonlight as she swallows hard. "Anyway, there's a portal in these woods they use to cross into our realm. We're looking for a ring of mushrooms."

I stop in my tracks. "Fae aren't real, Char. They're—"

A twig snaps from somewhere deep in the tree line. Pure, unfiltered panic racing through my veins. Inching out of the dense forest and into the small clearing are two creatures, one with moss-green skin and ebony horns that curve around his face. The other has silver scales that flash in the moonlight. They're at least six feet tall, lean, and covered in bright draping fabric that glitters with what can only be described as wealth.

Not boys, then. Fae. The creatures our bedtime stories warned us about, the very thing my so-called girlfriend Charlotte is after, and they are standing right in front of us.

"We need to find another way to the mortal realm. This one ruins my shoes," the one with horns is saying. When he spots us, his easy expression turns sly and hungry. "Now where did you two come from?"

The hair on the back of my neck prickles. Charlotte's mumbling something to herself. I only make out the word "real."

"We were just leaving." I grab Charlotte's arm but she yanks free of my grip.

"You're fae," she murmurs.

"Very good," the scaly one says.

"What's your name?" the boy with horns asks.

Charlotte doesn't reply. Instead, she says, "Take me back to Faerview."

They exchange a look. "We cannot simply take you with us. We require something in exchange. Since you won't tell me your name, offer me something else." He crosses his arms and drums his nails against them in a steady, unsettling rhythm.

"Charlotte, don't," I warn.

"Wh-what do you want?" she asks, ignoring me.

"Hmm." He pulls out a strange fruit from his pocket. It has a silver ribbed skin and a red stem. He holds it out. "Share some with me?"

"I . . ." Charlotte rubs her hands together nervously.

"Or you could tell me your name?" he tries again. His eyes twinkle in the moonlight and not in a good way.

"Don't listen to him." A higher-pitched voice says.

Stepping out from the shadows of two trees is a stunning fae with long black hair and deep brown skin. She's striking and I can hardly look away. "Leave them alone, River."

River, the horned boy, clicks his tongue in annoyance. "Ugh, Mala. Always the bore. And it's *Prince* River to you."

"I mean it," the girl replies, reaching her hands in her pockets for something out of sight.

"Or what? You can't do anything to me. You shouldn't even be in the mortal realm. Don't you have court duties?"

"She's probably visiting that house again," the scale-covered boy says. "So pathetic."

"Shut up, Finn," the girl, Mala, hisses.

"Hey!" Charlotte calls out. She snatches the fruit from Prince River and takes a giant bite.

Mala groans and knocks it out of Charlotte's hands, but it's too late. The ruby-red juice from the fruit dribbles from Charlotte's lips. A dazed look splashes across her face.

"What's your name?" Prince River asks again.

"Charlotte."

No. No. No.

"Come here, Charlotte," the prince says, and to my horror, she does. "Are you hungry?"

"I'm hungry," she mumbles beside him.

Mala's fists ball at her sides. "Stop it, River."

I don't know who Mala is or why she's helping us, but I am grateful for the distraction. I reach for Charlotte again, but River twists her out of my grasp, and Finn sweeps my feet out from under me. The air knocks from my lungs when I hit the ground.

Mala puts herself between us, using her body like a shield.

"Do you want to come with us?" Prince River asks of Charlotte.

"Yes. Please." Charlotte grabs a handful of leaves off the

nearest tree and shoves them inside her mouth. "I'm so hungry."

My stomach roils. I'm too shocked to speak.

Mala steps forward but Finn is there, slipping a thin blade, the handle decorated with vines, from his boxy sleeves. Mala pulls her own out of her pocket, rubies and gemstones twinkling. Both are far too beautiful to be weapons.

"*Tsk. Tsk*," Prince River clucks. "No interfering, remember? Your sympathy for these *mortals* stops now, Mala. My father will hear about this. You like going to that ugly house so much, I'll tell him to banish you there, confined there until you can learn to have some fun." Finn and Prince River share a horrible laugh.

Mala looks stricken. "The king wouldn't—"

"He would. He tires of you. You aren't really one of us, anyway. Your mother might be favored by the Summer Court, but your father was less than nothing and she should've left you with him."

"You want so badly to make me your enemy, fine. But it will be your greatest mistake," Mala warns.

Prince River's grin belies the tension in his shoulders. She's rattled him, and I can't help but feel pleased. I know how some threats can cut so deep they hit bone.

Meanwhile, Charlotte gorges herself on twigs and grass and moss. I think I'll be sick. "Charlotte, we should go," I whisper to her while the fae bicker.

"But I'm so hungry," she mumbles dazedly, grabbing a bunch of twigs. I knock them out of her hand. She turns to me, and for a second, clarity shines through. "Run, Jayde," she says. "Run!"

I don't want to leave her, but as Mala slashes her blade in an impressive arc, cutting through the fabric and into the scales of Finn, my survival instincts kick in. A fight is imminent, and if I don't leave now, I risk getting caught in the crosshairs. If I run, I can get help. We couldn't have strayed that far from town.

"I'll come back for you, I promise," I tell Charlotte. I spin on my heel and start through the trees. Darkness swallows me as I run. I don't make it far before my feet catch on a protruding root. Then the world is spinning and gravity grabs ahold of me and pulls.

I'm falling down, down, down a ravine. Stars and shooting pain blind me as my head hits the ground.

When I come to, Mala is there, a deep gash on her shoulder. Her mouth forming words I can't yet hear. It takes a minute for my brain to work properly again.

"What's your name?" she's asking.

"Jayde."

Then the darkness comes and I let it take me.

Present

MALA SNAPS HER FINGERS AND WE'RE BACK IN THE GAME ROOM. I feel against my head where the skin is slightly raised, and my hair is thin. "What . . ."

"The mind can play dirty tricks on us. It's the best trickster of them all," Mala tells me. She looks almost sheepish when she adds, "Though, in your case, I suppose I gave it some help."

"You made me forget?"

"I glamoured you. I'm not proud of it but I thought it'd be better if you didn't remember and you could go back to your life."

"That was not your decision to make!" Mala raises a single eyebrow in response. I remember that beautiful blade of hers and reel in my anger. "You also told me to come find you. That's why I've felt a pull to this house." Mala doesn't deny it. Doesn't say a word. "Charlotte—

"Is in Faerview."

It stings to hear, but that's what she wanted. Our entire relationship was based on her wanting a distraction and my desperation to have someone to call my own because I'm lonely and hopelessly gay. I deserve better than that, and Charlotte deserves better than Faerview. I have to make this right.

"Why did you bring me here?" I ask of Mala.

"I wanted to see if you were well," she replies cooly.

"Nah, I don't buy it."

Mala purses her perfect lips. "Fae can't lie."

I chuckle humorlessly. Now it's my turn to wait for an answer. I may not know as much about them as Charlotte, but I know fae can skirt the truth.

"And," Mala continues begrudgingly. "I wanted to see you." There's something behind her eyes. Something so familiar, so *desperate*, I have to tear my gaze away. "There are terrible, monstrous things in the world, Jayde. For a time, I was one of them. Then I met you." She fixes her mouth into something like a smile. Her hands are cold on my arm; her touch like pinpricks of ice that simultaneously sting and caress.

The last of the memories come flooding back with her touch.

Cold fingers on my cheeks, swiping at my tears. Cold hands pulling back my hair and checking the knot on my head. Cold against my swollen ankle. And warmth. Warm food. Warm clothes. A warm bed.

Mala brought me back to this house, wrapped my twisted ankle, and fed me roasted meat, tart berries, and fresh water. We spent three days here just talking, not a game or distraction in sight. I was worried about Charlotte, but Mala promised we would help her, as soon as I healed. While I recovered, she told me stories about her kind—their reputation for loose morals, a love of games, and tormenting humans. I told her things, too. Like when I was little, I was always asked to show off what I learned in school, on the playground, or from the television. "Show us that new dance the kids are doing!" "Twirl around so we can see the dress Auntie bought you." "Smile!" I told her how I thought things would be different with Charlotte, but they were exactly the same. She only wanted me as entertainment.

I can't believe it took me so long to find Mala again.

"How about a deal?" Mala asks, her voice barely above a whisper.

"No deals."

"Humor me. If you can guess what I want, I'll let you go. I'll leave you alone. I promise." When I don't respond right away, she adds, "Please."

It's the please that finally breaks me. The human desperation softens me. I look at Mala. Really look. Medusa be damned. Her catlike eyes flash, but that's not what steals the air from my lungs. It's the way she's looking at me. Throughout my entire relationship with Charlotte, I wished for her to look at me the way Mala is right now. Like I'm the most interesting person in the world just by existing.

I know then what I need to do. "Fine. One question first, though. Why did you help me?"

Mala fidgets with her dress. "When I saw you and your friend in the clearing, I recognized someone in you. And you didn't want anything from me. Everyone always wants something."

I step closer and raise my chin. "I have a riddle for you. What's young but old, looks sweet but is bitter, and has finally met her match?"

Mala parts her lips. "What?"

I flash her my most devilish smile. "You," I answer. "I know what you want. I want it, too. You may pretend to be Maleficent, but even she had a heart for Briar Rose."

Mala's eyes sparkle with intrigue. "And what, dear Jayde, do I want?"

I shrug, but I'm smiling because I've won. "Someone to like you exactly the way you are and ask for nothing in return."

"Hm."

"I'm right, aren't I?"

She doesn't respond. Instead, she tucks a stray curl behind my ear. She looks content. No. Resigned?

"I suppose I should release you then."

Mala snaps her fingers and the room changes. The arcade is replaced with elegant wooden chairs half covered by white sheets, long-dead plants, and an old grand piano. It's a game room, just one much, much older and ravaged by time like the rest of this house.

"Is this real?" I ask.

She nods once. "I first met my father in this room. He was an old, old man by the time I was able to find him, but he was playing the piano more beautifully than any faery."

"This was his house?" I ask, and she nods. "So the arcade games . . . ?"

"Were Illusions. That's what I'm good at. My kind like to be entertained."

She doesn't have to say that she was part of their fun. I know she was by the tight set of her jaw and that night in the Alderwood.

"I understand," I reply quietly. "They may call us boring, but we don't owe them our entertainment." I didn't believe that until Mala showed me another path—one where I don't have to worry about being cool or funny or smart. I'm enough just as I am. I spent too much time trying to win Charlotte's praise when all along, mine was all I needed. As I watch Mala, I wonder if there are other things I need, too.

Mala nods in agreement and then averts her gaze. "I cannot leave. Not for some time. Punishment for going against Prince River one too many times."

I think of how I'll be spending my summer hiding from people; classmates who think I had something to do with Charlotte's disappearance; my divorcing parents and their not-so-subtle questions about who I want to live with. All I'll be doing is burying myself in arcade games.

Or.

I could be with Mala—a trickster faery with a kind heart. We could plot revenge against Prince River and the king who trapped her here and rescue Charlotte in the process like Mala promised we would.

"How will you spend your time?" I ask quietly.

She looks at me then. "I'm sure I'll think of something." It's said like a challenge. A dare.

I've been waiting my whole life for someone to really see me and appreciate me. In Mala, I've found it. "Would you like some company?"

Her responding grin warms me.

"I thought you'd never ask."

WHAT LIES IN SILENCE

Justine Pucella Winans

D EATH IS SILENCE. NOT FOR THE ONES WHO DIED, BUT THE ONES left behind. It's not the kind of silence where you can't hear anything at all. Despite everything, the world keeps turning, the birds keep chirping, the buzz of electronics and roar of engines and beeps of construction don't cease. It's the muted kind of silence. Like being underwater, where the waves morph the sounds to something unsettling and unrecognizable.

Like the soundproof walls of a dim room that was once filled with light and music.

That's why I like it in here now.

It's a vacuum kind of silence. Where I don't have to pretend that things are okay, that I am okay, because even though it's been months, every time I think of it, my lungs collapse and my eyes water and there's nothing.

When I was with Nonno, there was music everywhere. Not just in this room, where he'd lift his accordion or his guitar and his rough, wrinkled fingers would find the right strings and keys to create a sound that was as close to magic as this world gets. But in the birds, the electronics, the engine, in claps and snaps and stomps and whistles. There was always music to be heard.

Since he died, there's only been this damn silence.

If I close my eyes, I can almost imagine it's like it used to be. Rushing home after school, nearly slipping up the front porch steps and down the hall as the sound of his music led me to this room. I'd push open the heavy door to catch the padded walls, the grand piano, the drum kit and the guitars on stands, and sheet music everywhere, mixed with old CDs and even cassettes that Nonno never wanted to get rid of. Relics of the past, a captured moment of emotion and talent that lost its bitterness over time and only sounded sweet because that past was something I didn't know, and the present still held everyone I cared about.

In the middle of it all, he would sit in the chair, looking strong and healthy, his accordion on his lap as he lost himself in the sound of his music and his voice. The skin around his eyes would crinkle further as his head leaned back slightly on a long note.

He would stop only when seeing me. For a quick smile. A called out, "L'uccellino, canta con me," and it wouldn't be a question because it didn't need to be because I always would.

In my mind, his face is clear, the way it looked before he

got sick. His voice is strong, and I can hear his smile in the nickname he kept, something that always fit, even after I changed my pronouns and shortened my name to Luce. The scene is vibrant in my head. Loud. Alive.

But when I open wet eyes, I'm alone.

There's still the same piano, a small layer of dust gathering over the keys. The same guitars on their stands, the same sheets of notes and lined-up tapes. The same accordion, out of its case and resting on his chair, strap drooping toward the carpeted floor. I keep it clean, but haven't been able to put it away. When it's out on the chair like that, I can almost imagine that he's not really gone.

That he'll come back. Pick it up. That the scene I took for granted will play again.

I blink my stinging eyes and cross the room toward it. I lift the accordion, pulling the harness he added over my head, undoing the bellows strap and setting my hands in place. My phone is uncomfortable in my pocket, I toss it onto the chair.

Then it's just me and this strange, little box my Nonno loved. I glide my fingers over the keys, over the array of small black buttons on the right side.

I pull my hands out to stretch it before closing again. It releases a breathy note that reverberates through the room.

A chill passes over me and my hair stands on end.

There's the strangest feeling. Like someone is watching.

Which is impossible. I'm in a closed-in room with no dark corners or places to hide. Only the instruments the rest of my family left untouched and me. Logic doesn't stop my gooseflesh and, despite everything, I open my lips.

"Hello?"

I haven't heard my voice in a while. I've been speaking, here and there, when I absolutely have to. A few words that normally blend in with the other sounds of the world around me.

Not like this, when my one little question feels so loud.

For a moment, there's no response.

Then, the voice of a woman. Singing an *ah* in the exact note I played. A beautiful, ethereal voice that sends a chill up my spine. Panic surges in me. Something inside urges my legs to move with a *run, run, run*, but they don't listen.

Instead, I adjust my fingers and play a new chord.

She responds, perfectly matching with her angelic voice.

My arms tremble against the weight of the instrument in my arms.

"Who are you?" I ask.

"A friend," she answers.

I jump at the voice. This can't be happening. There's no one else here. There can't be anyone else here. I keep scanning the room, but nothing's out of place, and there's definitely no one else inside. No one else in my family even comes inside. It was always only me and Nonno. Now, it belongs solely to me and a ghost.

My heart pounds in my throat. Ghosts don't exist. Not like that. Sweat coats my palms. I have to be imagining things. I have to be.

I grip onto the instrument tighter and try to move, but something weighs me down, almost like hands are pushing onto my shoulders.

"You haven't been singing lately," the voice says, right in my ear. "I miss your voice. His too."

I jump in my own skin, but can't move much with the pressure. My breaths are short and quick. Shoulders still locked in place, I manage to turn my neck. No one's there. But then who is talking? Where is the voice coming from? Tears sting my eyes. I should focus on how to get free, but my mind grasps onto the voice's last words.

"You knew my Nonno?" I ask.

My voice sounds too high, too young, and I hate it. I've hated it for months, but I want to cringe at how weak I sound now.

The voice laughs, and it sounds like wind chimes. "I know everything about this house. Everyone who has lived here, everyone human . . . and everyone not."

With that, the pressure is gone, and I try to dart forward. The floor shifts and stretches under my feet, and I nearly drop the accordion, the weight yanking the strap down on my neck. I catch myself, finally steadying.

The lights go dark.

I can't see anything. It's quiet. Enough that I can only hear my heart pounding in my throat and my breath catching.

My arms shoot out to try to feel for anything: the chair, a stand, something to give me some spatial awareness. But I'm reaching into empty darkness.

Until the lights slam back on and someone stands there. A little scream escapes my lips. My mind struggles to catch up and make sense of it all. It's a woman, probably college aged or a little older, but there's something off about her. Her legs are almost glued together under her dress, seeming impossibly small. Her long, willowy arms break out into fingers that are much too thin and long, extended like a bird's feathers. A black veil covers the top half of her face, shielding her eyes entirely. She parts her red lips to give a smile, and all her teeth are pointed.

"What's the rush?" She says softly. "I only want to talk. Maybe sing a little."

I'm frozen in place. My mind begs me to run, but there's something about her voice that traps me here. Compels me to step forward. Closer.

Her right hand lifts, those stretched-out fingers all colored ash white at the tips that bleed into claws. She tickles the side of my face, deliciously gentle. "What do you say, Luce? L'uccellino. Canta con me?"

My pounding heart skips, breaks, and shoots to my throat.

"I can't," I say. "I don't sing anymore."

She lets out a low laugh. It's like wind chimes on a summer day. A skillful scale of fingers gliding across the piano keys. And something underneath. Something that makes an icy cold shoot up my spine.

"It's a shame. I really do love music. It's the one thing that keeps me sane." Her hand drops from my chin, but she doesn't step away. It's hard to tell her expression with the veil covering half her face. Yet my chest freezes when it feels like her eyes meet mine. "Would you like to hear a story?"

It's phrased as a question, in the same way my Nonno would

ask his questions. There's really only ever one answer that follows. The accordion lets out a short puff as my hands tremble. She's directly blocking the only exit, and with the way she towers over me, I wouldn't have a chance in hell in getting around her.

"Does it have a happy ending?" I ask.

The woman snorts. "Depends on who you ask."

"I'm asking you."

Her red lips curl up into an impossibly big smile, razor sharp teeth glinting in the light. "Then, yes."

"Okay," I say. "I'd love to hear it."

Going along with the wishes of the potential demon that has me cornered in a soundproof room seems like a good idea. I don't want to make her angry, especially not before I have a plan or any means of escape. My eyes dart down to my phone on the chair, where the right corner shows the X of no service.

I have to get to the door. I have to somehow get around her and run.

Run, *run*, run every nerve in my body seems to buzz.

"This story starts a long time ago," the woman says. She paces in front of me, no longer facing me, yet for some reason, it still feels like I'm being watched. "Before Italy was even a country, but somewhere in the mountains of what is now Molise."

My skin crawls. The province where my family's from.

"There was a young woman who fell in love with a musician. She was beautiful, so much so that no matter what other talents she had, she was only known for her beauty. But she was talented. Not in music, like her lover. Not in farming, like her parents.

This young woman was talented in magic."

Any questions that arise stay lodged in my throat. There's something in the way she sounds that makes me think she doesn't want to be interrupted. That this is a story she's longed to tell for a while.

I take a small step to the right.

"Her musician lover wanted this kind of talent for himself, so he begged her to use her magic for him. To allow him the ability to make his own magic through his instruments. It was a dangerous idea, to give magic to someone who didn't work for it, who wanted it because of his own arrogance and greed. But she loved him. And who hasn't done something dangerous for someone they loved?"

There's something about the woman's voice that seems nostalgic. But at the same time, is laced in a grief that I recognize in my own.

I take one more step. Slow enough that my foot falls silent.

"She did what she had to do, sacrificing a piece of herself to complete the spell. To give her lover everything he wanted. His music became magic. It held power. Enough to keep evil at bay, to make people fall in love. She gave him *everything*." The words comes out like a curse. Halfway through my third step, she twists back toward me. I freeze. "And what did he do? Worried that she would take his magic away, he killed her." While her eyes are still covered, it almost looks like a tear tracks down her pale cheek. "Now, because he killed a strega, his rotten family would be protected from our curses, our magic, for seven generations.

Is it fair? No. But what in this life is?"

Our magic? Does that mean the story is real and this woman is a witch?

My Nonno used to tell me about stregas: how his mother passed down stories of women who sold their souls to demons for power. I do remember something about being protected for seven generations, but I don't remember the context. In all the stories, I had still foolishly imagined some kind of *Strega Nonna* old woman with a broom and some telekinesis. Not *this*.

She starts to walk toward me, and I can hardly focus on processing the story or the parts of it that feel eerily familiar. I have to get out, even if it's risky. I dart around her, ducking under her long arm, and rush toward the padded doors. Desperately, I twist the handle. It doesn't budge. *No, no, no.* These doors can't lock. She chuckles from behind me, and the door handles themselves crumble to dust. I watch as the space between the padded doors melts together, shutting us in entirely.

"I'm sure you're wondering why I'm telling you all this," she says from behind.

Twisting the accordion to my back, I slam the side of my body into the door. My eyes water and my chest aches, but it doesn't move. I can feel her approaching, closer and closer behind me, but it won't budge.

I'm trapped.

I'm trapped and no one can hear me.

"Your Nonno was the sixth generation," she says. "Guess what that makes you?"

With her clawed fingers, she reaches out to take my chin in her long nails, lightly guiding me back to face her. She smiles, wiping away my tears with her sharp thumb. Her veil drops, revealing eyes that are crusted around the edges with dried blood, the whites a sickly yellow and the irises bright red.

"La mia vendetta," she purrs, before sinking her claws into my jaw and neck and throwing me across the room.

MY THROAT IS ON FIRE, MY BODY ACHES, BUT THE CRASH ACCOMPANIED by guitar strings, crushed wood, and fluttering pages feels distant as the room around me changes. Not to a different location, but to a more comfortable and familiar version of the same one. My Nonno sits in his chair, the accordion in his lap, playing a version of "O Sole Mio." His voice cuts off at the end of the final note and he looks at me.

He's alive. He's in front of me.

"Perché non canti?" he asks. "Did you forget how?"

It takes me a minute to find my voice. I can't believe I'm hearing his. Just like I remember. Just like it should be.

"No," I say. "How can I forget?"

He gives his signature *ehhhh* kind of grunt as he moves his hand like he's tossing me away. "Might as well. How long has it been?"

Without him? A few months now, is it? Without him like *this*? Even longer.

Too long. I wipe at my eyes and laugh.

"Mi dispiace, Nonno, I . . . I haven't felt like I had a reason."

He gives me a look. "Then you are lying to yourself. Why do you need a reason? You like it, so do it. Reasons will come."

"I'm not even that good," I say. Not like the other kids who actually got into show choir because they can sing pop and not just specific songs that suit their range. Not like the teens my age already writing their own songs and singing in bands. I'm good, but not enough to go anywhere with it.

His eyes, like watercolors that spilled both blue and green, look right at me. "Who gives a shit?"

"Nonno!" I half expected him to defend me and hype up my talent. He always was a little too honest.

"Life is short, L'uccellino. La vita è breve, sì, ma anche bella. So sing. It's when you stop doing what you love that you stop living."

"You didn't stop," I say. "Or you didn't mean to."

He laughs. "Well, I never said life was fair." He reaches out his warm, calloused hand to take mine. "I don't think you are done with it yet, though."

I shake my head. "I don't want to be."

"Ciao, Luce L'ucellino. Ti amo."

It's almost like the real goodbye I never got. Since by the time I actually said goodbye, he wasn't himself. In some ways, he was already gone. My tears burn my eyes, but I focus on this. The image of him, with his accordion. Making music.

Something like magic.

"Ciao, Nonno. Ti amo. Sempre."

And with a remembered will to live, I once again face my death.

MY EYES SNAP OPEN, ONE OF NONNO'S GUITARS BROKEN UNDER ME. It is a new kind of pain. I guess a part of me thought I'd be able to keep all his instruments forever. The accordion harness snapped, but the instrument itself is thankfully in one piece. Each dent it holds deepens my wounds. My chin and throat both throb where her claws broke the skin. My shirt is stained in streaks of blood. Pieces of the broken guitar push into my aching muscles.

La strega stands over me, my fresh blood still dripping from her right hand.

She bends down in front of me, bleeding eyes wild. "I don't think this will do much to help you now." She lifts the gold cornicello hanging from a thin chain around my neck and yanks it off. "The malocchio is the least of your problems now, dear."

She holds the charm between two claws and runs them over my eyebrow, cutting into the skin. I try to shove her arm away, but she's an impossible kind of strong.

"Why are you doing this?" I snap through the pain.

"Because I've waited so many years, because I can." She licks her pointed teeth. "If it makes you feel better, because you were born into a family that was doomed to be cursed."

I move my hands under me to try and sit up, back away. It's hard with the broken neck of the guitar. I don't know what I need.

Time can't hurt.

"So because I had a selfish asshole in the family hundreds of years ago, you have to kill me?" I spit out blood that slipped down my face and between my lips. "Seems kind of shitty."

"It is what it is. Seven generations of protection has to end sometime. It's an eye for an eye, no? Your family took one of mine, and I take you. Any soul of your bloodline would do, but . . . guess you're just unlucky."

I've felt that way a lot, but it's never really almost led to my death before. I can't die like this, though. Not when I haven't even graduated high school, or sung in front of people outside my family, or fallen in love, or . . .

Not to mention the fact that I'm just really fucking scared.

La strega grabs the lower half of my face, skin stinging as she forces my mouth open and holds me still. My left eye burns from tears and blood, and I twist and shake but I can't get out of her grasp. Her red lips part, past her sharp teeth, her tongue slowly unfurls and extends. The edge of it is sharp, but hollow like a straw.

It's hard to believe the sight in front of me, but it doesn't go away.

My hands flail around, patting the ground and the rubble of my Nonno's guitar for something. Anything. I accidentally smack my hand into the old cassette player, loaded with a tape that Nonno made himself.

She leans in, red eyes almost glowing as she moves her mouth closer and closer to mine, like she's going for a kiss. Her tongue pinches the inside of my cheek, drawing blood and sucking it in.

She wants to rip me apart, drain me from the inside out.

My throat trembles in fear as her tongue drops down. I can't breathe. I gag. Tears still sting my eyes as panic rises in me.

The music starts to play. My Nonno's fingers touching chords on the accordion keys. His voice carrying across the air and filling the room.

"Che bella cosa na jurnata 'e sole

N'aria serena doppo na tempesta"

Struggling to stay calm and choking on my own bile, my frantic fingers touch a guitar string, snapped off from the instrument. With her tongue literally sliding itself down my throat, I have no time to think. I toss the guitar string around her neck and scramble to grab it on the other side.

I pull tight.

She screeches, yanking away from me, tongue rolling back out of my mouth and between her pointed teeth. She gasps for air as the wire cuts into the chalky skin of her neck. Her claws scrape at me, but I can hardly feel the pain. I push her down onto the floor and straddle her.

I only feel the warmth of my Nonno's voice. For one last time, I sing with him.

"Ma n'atu sole!" we belt. *"Cchiu' bello, oi ne."* I pull the guitar strings tighter, a thick, brownish blood spilling from her neck. She screeches, but it's drowned out by our voices. *"O sole mio sta 'nfronte a te!"*

"You can't kill me!" she screams. "I'm too powerful. I'll come back for you. Over and over until I tear you to shreds!"

I can't hear her. All I hear is music. My throat hurts, I didn't warm up, but it doesn't matter. It has all of me in it. Loud enough to reach my Nonno wherever he ended up.

"*O sole, o sole mio.*"

A sickening squelch sounds in the moment I take a breath, followed by the crunch and pop of her spine snapping as the guitar string cuts through her neck. Face still twisted into a scream, her head rolls.

"*Sta 'nfronte a te . . . sta 'nfronte a te!*"

Vision blurring with tears and blood, I take my bow, imagining my Nonno's smile as I crumble onto the floor.

I ALWAYS HAVE MUSIC PLAYING NOW. ON MY HEADPHONES, HUMMING to myself, making a rhythm out of the noises around me. The moment it goes silent, she'll be back. That strega, with her red eyes, beautiful voice, and deadly tongue. I can feel her, in the pauses between songs, a suffocating pain ready to tear me from the inside out.

In each moment of silence, the memory of that pressure fills my throat. I gag, I vomit, a trickle of pee escapes before I can stop myself. If it goes too long, I hear her call back to me. Searching for the magic that was stolen. The magic still in the music I make.

Once she calls out, it's already too late.

One of us has to die, and if it's her, she'll wait in the silence until we start that song once more.

"Are you ready?" Mom asks.

I almost don't hear her over the music. It was the car horn that got me. She already has all my suitcases and boxes in the car, packed up and ready to drive across state lines to where I'll start my freshman year.

As a finance major. I decided that singing wasn't something I wanted to make a career of. It is something just for me.

I look back at the house. The towering turrets, the aged stained glass, and all the ghosts it has inside. The warm memories of the music room that became my salvation. And the not-so-warm ones, like the brown bloodstains I had to cover up after I awoke and la strega's body was gone. The guitar strings that I used to kill her, buried in the backyard on the shore where the rocky dirt swallowed them up as another secret.

"Until next time," I say. "Arrivederci."

I join my mom in the car and turn up the volume on my one earbud.

It's music that saves me, and more than that, when I'm listening, it's like he's still with me. I hear Nonno in every song. His love, his light, his unfortunate magic.

Death is silence, but music lets us live on.

ME I'M NOT

g. haron davis

SOMETIMES, IN THE STILL OF THE NIGHT, THE HOUSE WOULD laugh at me. A cruel, knowing laugh that was enough to freeze my spine even within the throes of that muggy, scorching summer. I told myself it was nothing but my imagination, that old houses had old bones and old bones creaked and cracked and groaned. But it was hard to convince myself of these being old-house noises when the sounds skittered through the halls and clawed their way into intelligible syllables, words, sentences.

Like, *You should have saved them.*

You shouldn't have lived.

You should never have come here.

As if I'd had a choice. As if I asked to be thrown to the wolves masquerading as the grandparents I'd only met twice—with one of those times just weeks prior, letting damp earth crumble through our hands in a symbolic gesture my parents didn't even believe in, let alone want. They'd wanted cremation. They'd wanted a small, casual, joyful celebration of life and a simple scattering of ashes in their favorite forest. The wolves refused to comply.

The grandparents gave me four days to gather anything salvageable that I wanted to keep because the rest would be taken to a landfill. When I tried to keep Dad's favorite jacket, well-loved and tattered and just a tiny bit musty in the best way, Grandmother informed me I would never be allowed to bring it into her home. It had been left mostly intact, so I didn't see the problem. I sneaked it out of the trash just minutes later.

My conditioner overpowered Dad's scent now, as I'd transitioned the jacket into my pillowcase. Every few days I spritzed some of his cologne—also smuggled from the trash—on it, but it wasn't the same. It was his scent, but it wasn't *his* scent. It wasn't his sweat anymore, or his tears he'd let loose for something as trivial as a video online with a too-cute kitten, or food stains that never fully came out because of how messy he ate, or the undercurrent of Momma mingled in because they hugged and touched and snuggled enough that it embarrassed young me to no end.

I'd have given anything to have them back, to be embarrassed all over again.

Instead, I suffered alone, quietly, with grandparents that acted more like hostile roommates than family. They acknowledged me by obligation—they fed me at appropriate times, they enrolled me in online school, they bought a few outfits for me, they even found it in their miserable empty hearts to grace me with fifty dollars each week. But they weren't kind. They weren't loving. They hadn't once even asked how I felt after losing my whole world.

For years I'd wondered why I only knew Gigi and Papa Mock, Momma's parents who lived in Jamaica, until the day they no longer lived, even though Dad's parents lived less than an hour from us. I came to understand just after Momma and Dad died. I'd fought with and lost against the grandparents when it came to handling the situation. I'd lost about being allowed to stay with a friend and finish junior and senior years at the same school. I'd lost every battle with them and the war was far from over. Part of me still held out hope that they would become the stereotypical grandparents from the small screen. Foolish, naïve.

We'd driven to this house once years ago, a very quick stop on a road trip to better places. I hadn't liked it then, either. Dad told us to wait in the car, parked on the opposite side of the street at the curb rather than in the driveway. He told us it would take less than five minutes. He took some deep breaths, dark eyes closed like he was psyching himself up for a public speech. He protected himself with the sign of the cross, rolled his eyes, and launched out, immediately jogging across the street.

The front door yawned open and the inside of the house showed us nothing but darkness and part of a wrist near the knob. I squinted as if that might help see through the black hole, but all it did was make things blurry. The darkness enveloped Dad, and I felt my stomach knot. I started a timer on my phone just in case we needed to execute a rescue plan.

A minute and sixteen seconds later, he hustled back out the door. He carried a navy blue folder with his name, Darrien, written on a little white label. He kept it tucked beneath his leg as he drove, like he wanted to make sure Momma and I didn't touch it. Momma asked no questions, so I did the same. But I could see the start of Dad's tears in the rearview mirror.

That folder sat at the top of a stack of other things in Dad's office safe. Grandfather burned it before I got the chance to look inside. I asked the house once if it knew what was in there. The house said nothing.

Life with the grandparents consisted of routine. Waking up with the sun, powering through online school, performing child labor to keep the house in good shape, eating dinner in silence, lying awake in the evenings counting nothing on the ceiling, wondering if or when or how this house would collapse in around me. Sometimes it became so hard to breathe I felt dizzy. Sometimes I prayed I wouldn't wake up. Those nights, the house tormented me especially relentlessly.

Tonight was one of those nights. Tonight the cicadas stayed quiet. The wind jostled oak branches without so much as a whisper. Not even the house made a sound. Something about that unnerved me. I sat up and reached for my touch lamp. The room stretched farther than the pale lilac light could go, but at least the space immediately encircling me felt a little safer. Slipping on my fancy headphones brought even more comfort. I still felt panic biting at the back of my throat, but my music did its best to beat that sensation back down.

It felt wrong. I couldn't even articulate what "it" was. A nebulous feeling of dread commonly overcame me here. But this . . . this was a new feeling. Like being light-headed and heavy-hearted and surrounded and utterly alone. I turned the music up, slinked farther into my uncomfortable bed. I hadn't been able to take my four-poster bed from home because Grandfather said it was too heavy and too much trouble for the movers to carry out. They sold it along with the house and some other "too-heavy" furniture and stuck me with a too-firm twin with one needlelike spring just left of center that stabbed me at every turn.

My sweaty hands clung to my sheet tighter. I never slept without something over me, even with the grandparents' refusal to use air-conditioning and the sizzling heat that comes with living on the third floor of a very old house. They at least conceded to buying me a box fan.

I glanced at the fan and realized that even it made no noise. The blades remained still. I reached for the remote. Pushed and held down and banged on the power button. Nothing happened. This old house had power outages sometimes. But I could see my laptop's charging light blink from atop my desk. Batteries seemed the next likely issue. I reached into the nightstand drawer, felt around for backup AAs. Leaned over to do a visual check. Dumped the whole drawer out onto my bed and rifled through the mess. I sighed.

It happened sometimes. The house moved things. Put them back in odd places. Simply never returned them again. It knew I would be boiling up here. It did this on purpose. But I had

resolved to not let the house break me. I wouldn't overreact.
I wouldn't show fear. I would do nothing more than cross the
expanse of the room over to my desk and get batteries from there.

I swung my legs off the side of the bed to prepare for the trek.
As soon as my toes touched the scratchy carpet, everything in me
locked up. The unnerving, oversized ventriloquist dummy that
the grandparents wouldn't let me remove glowed and grinned
from the darkest corner. Nearly my height, propped up with a
mannequin stand, forest fire-red curls and blotchy brown freckles.
Its mouth hung agape with that stupid grin frozen forever
and its hands rested on its skinny hips, as if a dummy had any
business being in a power pose. The letterman jacket engulfing
it belonged to Dad, but I hadn't asked if Warren sported a pair
of his old jeans, too. I couldn't understand why the grandparents wanted this weird white dummy. And I especially couldn't
understand why whoever made this abomination chose to give
it glow-in-the-dark eyes and teeth. If this thing was why Dad
left and never looked back, he had my complete support on that
decision.

Since my second night here, the dummy stood under two
blankets with an empty trash can on its head to make quintuply
sure that I'd never see its face. I kept that dummy covered
precisely *because* its creepy face made it even harder to sleep. So I
shouldn't have been staring at the glow at all. And yet . . .

Sweat cascaded down my back, down my front, down every
possible spot. The dummy, Warren, had been covered when I got
into bed. And the fan had been on high. Warren and I stared each

other down, and I half expected him to say something. To admit that he'd unplugged my fan or stolen my batteries or committed any other demonic gremlin shenanigans.

Nothing appealed to me less than even just the idea of having to fetch batteries from Warren or anywhere near him. I considered heading downstairs to sleep on the couch instead; the living room, at least, was air-conditioned. But if Grandmother found me down there in the morning, I could look forward to even more menial chores as punishment for coming out of my room. It was difficult to say if I felt more scared of Warren or of Grandmother.

Look.

"Not now," I told the house. I needed to concentrate on working up the nerve to approach the dummy.

Look. Look. Look look look look look look look look look.

"Look *where?!*" I covered my eyes as I whisper-yelled.

Rather than a verbal answer, the house responded through Warren. A tight creak, the sound of clothing rustling. I opened my eyes again and all my sweat turned to ice. I couldn't help but shiver. His right arm, no longer positioned by his hip, was flung out away from his body. His fingers were curled into pointing. I followed the line of his index finger and found myself looking out of my now-open bedroom door.

A shadow rushed past my door, left to right. Long enough to draw my attention out of my horror but too quick to tell what I'd seen. The grandparents hated noise, and existing outside of my room created noise, so I was practically forbidden from roaming the house after they'd gone to bed for the evening. But the shape came back again, entering the staircase from the right side of my view. Walking down the stairs. I launched up and off of my bed before I could think better of it.

I lived on this floor by myself. The grandparents didn't come up here unless it was to inform me of how exactly I'd screwed up once again—a Dr Pepper can resting on cherrywood without a coaster or laundry forgotten in the dryer. But I hadn't gone downstairs at all in the last eighteen hours, and if one of them was up here to scold me, they'd forgotten to actually do it.

I made it to the winding staircase just in time to see the top of a head disappear. Closely cropped curls, so gray they were practically white. Grandmother. I called out, picked up my pace a little to catch up to her. No matter my speed, she remained just out of reach. An illness had taken most of her hearing as a child, so I reminded myself to speak louder; she often went without her hearing aid within the house because, as she put it, nothing in the house was worth listening too closely to.

I jumped off the final two steps just as Grandmother slipped into the kitchen. The skirt of her cream nightgown billowed out and reminded me of movies with fragile white women wafting through castles forlornly while carrying candelabras. Grandmother was the exact opposite of them.

I shouted for her, but the door to the backyard crashed closed without her giving so much as a glance my way. She didn't like me, to be sure, but she hadn't ever flat-out ignored me before. I groaned and stopped in my tracks. In my time in the house,

I hadn't once disobeyed the grandparents to come downstairs after bed. A coldness spread in me upon realizing my mistake.

The kitchen at night felt foreign, a liminal space that begged to be immortalized in Internet urban legends. Like so much of the rest of the house, it consumed all attempts to illuminate any surroundings. A couple of night-lights tried their best but ultimately only shone in a two-inch radius. Light bled out in a straight line off to my left, the dumbwaiter light seeping through a gap in the door.

The light on the stove hood remained on, too. A habit I recognized in Dad. Maybe the only habit I could glean that he'd carried over from his time with his parents. Like a ghost light at a theater, Momma explained to me once. A little light so the ancestors wouldn't be kept completely in the dark. But I couldn't imagine any ancestors wanted to be in this house at all.

Even with the few attempts at light, everything existed only as harsh lines jutting through nothingness, slicing through dark to create vague approximations of a kitchen. That might have been the stove, sure, but it could also have easily been a rusty cage waiting to entrap me. The fridge may as well have been a guillotine prepared to slice through my neck.

I wanted—no *needed*—to go back upstairs. To sit back in my room and pretend I hadn't seen a single thing at all. I'd put Warren out and do my best to sleep soundly and never think of this moment again. I'd bury the thoughts just like I'd buried my parents.

My breath quickened. I should follow Grandmother outside,

but the backyard would be even darker than the kitchen. No one seemed to believe in streetlights out where the grandparents lived. I thought I knew dark. I didn't know dark at all before this house. My phone sat upstairs on the alchemy symbol charging mat that Joy bought me before I was forced to leave, so I didn't have a flashlight. Rummaging through the kitchen drawers was out, since it would make too much noise and potentially wake Grandfather.

I morphed the whole scenario into a screenplay in my head to put myself at ease. Something I could film when my friends and I were reunited at college. Maybe this house would inspire my thesis film. Maybe this moment would be the inciting incident. I thought of Joy in the role of protagonist and the pang in my heart replaced a little of the anxiety. My girlfriend had been more upset about my move than I had. Turning her into a movie star would be the least I could do.

Wherever Grandmother had gotten off to, she was likely long gone by this point. I tried to accept that she had no desire to speak to me. One of the entrances to the attic was near my room; she'd probably been up there among boxes of old dresses and tattered love letters or whatever it was old women put in attics.

Turn around.

The sharpness of the house speaking again, *growling*, startled me. I felt off-kilter, almost nauseous. In the darkness, in the distant shadows of the den, I could see him. Warren. Highlighter-green teeth, mouth stretched too wide, like he knew a secret that he'd never share with me.

I gasped as I backed up with a start. My hand smacked against a cup of assorted wooden spoons. Every single spoon within took its time clattering out onto the countertop. I gasped as I whipped around to try and stop it.

Eye whites glowed not even two feet from me, narrow and accusing and hardened by things I likely couldn't even imagine. I slid my headphone cups off of my ears slowly.

"What do you think you're doing?" Grandmother moved out of the shadows, slow and deliberate as a big cat cornering prey. She tightened her bloodred robe's belt and it felt like a threat. The house hummed with amusement.

My mouth malfunctioned. I could only sputter. Each noise I croaked brought Grandmother closer. A final spoon bounced to the floor, far too long after the others had already fallen. We both glanced to it, then at each other. Another battle was soon to be lost.

"Answer me when I address you, Carlotta."

She spoke only moderately above a whisper, but it registered like a scream. Humming evolved into quiet rolling laughter from the house. The already dark kitchen became increasingly dimmer, tighter. The thick line of Warren's smile shrank and shrank and shrank until nothing was showing at all. I wobbled where I stood.

"I . . . saw you." I choked the words out in a way that only marginally kept the contents of my stomach in place. "I watched you leave."

Grandmother hardened her face. I saw small bits of Dad in her broad nose, her high forehead, her frown lines. But mostly,

I saw a stranger. Someone convinced that they were in the presence of a dangerous individual. Someone trying very hard to mask her fear.

"How many times must we go through this?" Grandmother threw her arms up in exasperation. "You need to stay in your room. You can't roam about as if you're on a scavenger hunt. What would happen if you . . ."

Grandmother's voice faded the closer I came to fainting. But before the floor and my body collided, I stared behind her, into the living room. I expected to see Warren again, to have him and his ridiculous slack-jawed smile reveling in my admonishment. But he wasn't there.

Instead, the other Grandmother, the one I'd been chasing, stood. Her smile was too big for her face. Her eyes reflected maniacal glee. She stepped toward the kitchen, though it was more like treading water—fluid and weightless and defiant of gravity. The nightgown swirled around her while she glided, all the while her smile somehow grew larger and larger. With each inch forward, Other Grandmother's skin grew ashen, tight, too small for her body. Seams of her arms split, her forehead cracked open, her cheeks practically caved in.

The laughter from the house turned near hysterical as my legs buckled. Other Grandmother hovered over me, and her gown's hem dusted against my face as everything turned black.

235

I AWAKENED TOO EARLY. BIRDSONG FLOATED THROUGH THE BAY window, though light still failed to come through. Downstairs, bacon sizzled and the air around me tempted me to slip downstairs and steal a piece or two. I almost think I'm happy. That I hadn't lost my two favorite people. That Momma was the one cooking a big fancy breakfast as Dad worked on his world-famous hot cocoa even in the middle of summer. That I'm not imprisoned in this gloomy, uninviting house by gloomy, uninviting relatives. I sighed as a throbbing started up at the base of my head.

Just to my left, on top of the walnut nightstand, a glass of pale juice sat accompanied by two small white tablets. A quick sniff into the glass revealed cloying sweet citrus and banana. I took a small sip, glanced to Warren the dummy, and frowned. The trash can–blanket combination was back in place over him. His arms were back on his hips. Everything looked back to normal. But I felt unsettled.

They're poisoning you.

"Stop." I tried to sound firm, to be assertive and imposing. But quivering whispers never intimidated anyone. Never mind how ridiculous it was to try and stand my ground against a house.

The juice tasted fine. It wasn't poison. It *wasn't* poison. And the pills were likely acetaminophen or ibuprofen or some other innocuous painkiller. A tiny show of slight concern for me hitting my head on the kitchen hardwood. Though, I couldn't imagine why either grandparent would choose to care about me now after so much time doing the opposite. I struggled to swallow. Maybe it *was* poison.

Sometimes, if I thought too hard about something, it manifested. Like if I thought too much about my throat malfunctioning, about forgetting how to swallow, I suddenly struggled to push anything down past my uvula. I felt it coming on, felt my throat muscles tensing too much and the pills sitting just at the back of my tongue filling my mouth with an acrid bitterness that I couldn't spit out. I was stuck. I was dying.

Pathetic.

Tears slipped out of my eyes. My stomach heaved, acid flooding its way up toward my mouth and burning every inch on its way. I opened my mouth to let everything dribble out, and more than just the disgusting pill-juice sludge came out. Bile and undigested dinner flowed. I brought my hands to my mouth as if I could push it back in, but all I succeeded in doing was forcing it to burn through my nose.

It lasted too long. Vomit soaked my hands, my thighs, the bedding, the mattress, the floor. I couldn't get my throat working well enough to even cry about it. Disgust didn't begin to cover how I felt.

When it finally stopped, I slid out of my T-shirt carefully, slowly, to avoid getting puke on my bonnet. I stripped off my underwear, my bedding, tried to sop up the mess with my balled-up bedsheet as my head pain bubbled up from near my neck to fill up near my temples. The house was right; what kind of childish loser couldn't even swallow simple Tylenol? What was wrong with me? How could I have let—

Floorboards creaking behind me interrupted my guilt spiral.

I froze. Nothing clean was nearby to grab and cover myself up, but I tried using some of the fitted sheet. I'd just have to accept one of the grandparents seeing an uncomfortable amount of my birthday suit.

"Hello?" I called out. I craned my head to peek over my shoulder. Only Warren looked back at me. At least, it felt like he looked at me. Thankfully, he remained covered up. Shuddering, I went back to cleaning.

Seconds later, another creak. This time, closer. Practically right at my back. The feeling of someone standing behind me overwhelmed. A quick whip around and . . .

Nothing. Nothing was there. Only the dummy, covered and quiet. I analyzed his position—had he moved at all? Was he closer? Had the trash can shifted? But there was nothing. The fan whirred, birds chirped, and I was losing my mind. A few deep breaths marginally calmed me, but the feeling of being off-kilter overwhelmed.

Scritches at the window redirected my focus. The trees outside didn't grow close enough to the house to scrape the glass, and I didn't see any birds or other creatures that might attempt to enter through the window. Nothing seemed near enough to be responsible for the sound.

A bench beneath one of the magnolia trees normally stood empty. The grandparents rarely sat outside, and I'd only used the bench a couple of times on my better days. But there on that concrete slab, someone sat hunched over something that I couldn't quite see. Their tightly coiled hair flopped into their face, obscuring their hands. A phone, I assumed. They wore all black—long-sleeved shirt, straight-legged pants, nondescript shoes—despite the heat. It had to be sweltering down there if the temperature in my room was any indication.

I hadn't seen a single neighbor come close to this house, let alone loiter on the property. So this person on the bench must have been beyond desperate for a seat. I glanced along the street for signs of an emergency. A stalled car or a drowning puppy or something. But the street was empty as always. Whoever sat down there had walked, then. I wondered if I ought to alert the grandparents that someone was outside. Or if I should warn this person to stay as far away from this place as possible.

They snapped into sitting up straight so abruptly that I nearly fell backward from being startled. I tried hiding myself behind the heavy, black curtain. They lowered their hands into their lap, and their head began craning around painfully slowly. Toward me. I couldn't breathe. I suddenly didn't want to see their face but my feet had been superglued to the floor.

Little by little, their face came into view. Soft features, full cheeks, bright sad eyes. I knew that face intimately.

It was mine.

And it was giving me the same empty, lunatic smile that Other Grandmother had. Other Me rose from the bench as if someone had grabbed their head and pulled them straight up. As they stared up, I realized I could see what was in their hands without issue now. Other Me held Pua, Momma's favorite figurine. A goofy white hippopotamus in a ballet pose, en pointe,

reaching an arm to the sky. The first gift Daddy ever gave her—
she was a ballet teacher, and she loved hippos, so it fit perfectly.

When I was three, I'd decided so much white wasn't pretty
enough for her, so I set out to fix it. Momma didn't quite
appreciate all the red nail polish and permanent marker scribbles
all over her bed and only partially on the figure, but I'd chalked
it up to her not understanding my artistic vision. She kept that
mess anyway, proudly nestled within a shelf of books about art
history and museums and the fragile mental states of creatives.
One year Dad and I even made a little museum plaque for it.

I'd buried that figurine with Momma.

Pua danced again, Other Me guiding her with erratic
rhythmless twitches, as I would make her do years ago. But Other
Me lacked grace and caring and appreciation for Pua. And then,
Pua raised up in the air and smashed down against the sidewalk
in a second.

Other Me smiled more while looking at the shards of Pua
littering the concrete. Then, they raised a hand and flicked it
to the side briefly. A strange, jerky wave. Then slow, floating,
weightless steps like Other Grandmother had taken. Along
the stepping stones. Up the winding drive. To the front door. I
smashed myself against the window to see down, to keep track
of this copy of me.

Downstairs, the front door creaked open, then slammed
closed.

That was enough to snap me out of fearful freezing. I sprinted
toward my bedroom door, nearly taking a tumble on a slick,

uncleaned spot on the floor. Footsteps stomped up the stairs with an echoing, menacing slowness that tensed every muscle in me. The door felt a thousand miles away and rising as I struggled to reach it in time to shut and lock it. I could see the top of Other Me's deep black hair and the way they practically glided closer.

My knees stung as I dove for the door and hit the uncarpeted hardwood. I didn't have time to think about pain—I scrambled forward and kicked the door to close it just as Other Me began coming into view. A scream bubbled out, and I half-crawled half dragged myself away from the door. It hadn't latched closed. I needed to get up and run.

"Leave me alone!" I screamed. "Stop fucking with me, you stupid *fucking* house!" I scrambled under my bed to roll to the other side and put distance between myself and Other Me. "Fuck you! Fuck this house! Fuck everything!"

"Carlotta!"

Grandmother sounded so far away that I thought she was calling from downstairs. But she stood at my door, one hand in a death grip on the knob, the other covering half of her face, and one thin brow quirked. I knew I must have looked unhinged to her—flailing around my bedroom, naked, bits of sick all over. Trying to explain would have been pointless. So I simply stared.

I waited for the house to laugh. To tell me I was crazy or stupid or unreasonable or something that would break my spirit. But neither the house nor the grandmother said a word.

Blood began to seep through Grandmother's hand on her face. She briefly moved it, and I felt my insides clench.

Grandmother's nose was bleeding. I had kicked a door right into my grandmother's face. I hadn't seen myself at all. Nothing in the room had vomit covering it. This was all another trick. The house was playing games, and I was losing.

This was a punishment. It had to be. The house was choosing to punish me for letting my parents die.

For hearing the shattering of glass and doing nothing.

For ignoring the heavy-footed, crunchy stomps and the anguished screams and the blood and the blood and the blood and the blood.

For choosing to save myself above helping my parents survive.

When it happened, I didn't cry. I didn't scream, or panic, or lash out. I locked the door to my room, sat on my bed, and waited. They'd break the door down, I'd told myself. They'd run in and kill me, too, and then I wouldn't have to carry on life as an orphan. But I didn't even know who they were. At least that was my statement to law enforcement. Warren and I both knew, though. I had the letterman jacket to prove it.

Since moving here, I've cried almost every morning. I've screamed into a pillow pressed hard enough to my face that I wished I could suffocate. I've thrown clothes, books, shoes, dolls, myself. I've flooded my brain with the help of the house constantly echoing my thoughts that

I should have saved them

I should have saved them

I should have saved them

I *could* have saved them

if I'd only just done *some*thing. The house and I both hated me. And so I was seeing ghosts.

Breathing started to feel like a chore that I had no desire to carry out. Tears slid into my ears as I looked to the ceiling, an uncomfortable feeling, but I didn't bother doing anything about it. I deserved this. I deserved to lose everyone I love and get rehomed with strangers and be forced to tiptoe around and never leave this awful place. I deserved it. I was here with these ghosts and this madness because of my own actions.

"Grandm—"

I screamed before I could get the rest of the word out. The second I looked back toward where Grandmother had been, I saw myself instead. Other Me, bloody faced and bewildered. Screaming. As if *they* were the one to see a ghost. I wanted to scream, too. To let them know I was the one with the right to be terrified. But my open mouth only choked out laughter. Loud and ugly and cruel.

Like the house.

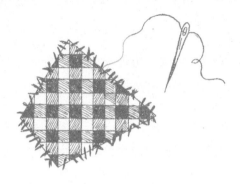

LIKE MOTHER

Gina Chen

A COLLEGE ACCEPTANCE LETTER OUGHT TO BE A CAUSE FOR celebration. Evelin had been clutching the thick envelope for so long, her fingernails were cutting through the paper.

"I'd qualify for financial aid," Evelin said, almost shouting. The stove vent was whirring on high. Sweet, oily steam misted her face as she put herself in her mother's way. The kitchen was small for hosting an argument; the sooner Mami agreed, the better for both of them. "Money won't be an issue. I could do work-study, too."

"Still expensive." Her mother nudged her aside to pick up the ladle and used it to skim off the fat from a pot of chicken jujube broth. "There are a lot of hidden costs. And I can cook for you at home. Cafeteria food will be no good. What happened to the other college, the one forty minutes away?"

State college. At least four of her friends were going. "That one accepted me, too," Evelin said slowly. "But the pre-med program is even better at Southbury."

"*Tsk.* They are all the same. It's not like you got into Harvard."

"Being independent is an important part of growing up," Evelin said, trying a different tactic.

"Why? Stay close to family." Her mother must have caught the distraught emotion that passed over Evelin's face, because she hastily added, "There's plenty of time for independence later, and you don't need to go across the country for that. Anyway, what was the other question you had?"

Evelin's nostrils flared. For Evelin's entire life, Mami had told her, "Work hard and get into a good school. That's your only responsibility." Southbury was a *great* school; why was Mami suddenly adding conditions?

And Evelin knew it wouldn't stop at college, either. Afterward it would be "Find a job nearby," then "You need someone to look after your kids," then "Who will look after me?" She was swimming upstream, her mother a current that recognized no force but her own gravity. Maybe Evelin would like living with her more if she went away for a while, but she'd never know now, would she?

She had a week left to respond to Southbury's acceptance letter. She'd figure something out, but it'd have to be soon.

Evelin let the envelope drop to her side. "Um, I just need that old quilt—the one you sewed. Do you know where it is?" She spoke fast, mixing more English with her Cantonese than usual.

"There's a group project for AP Lit and we're doing a skit, and—"
Mami's expression clouded with confusion—"never mind, I just
need it for school."

"It's in the storage room. Pink shelf, in the back."

EVELIN WASN'T A PERFECT DAUGHTER BY NATURE. AUNTIES
misunderstood her when they stroked her hair and praised her
for being guai. "Evelin's grades are so high," they would cluck
to their own children, as Evelin would meet her cousins' eyes
apologetically. "She takes Mandarin classes—piano, too! She
didn't quit her lessons after they got hard. She never goes to
parties or go do this or that. Learn from her."

The only alcohol she'd had was wine at a wedding
and she didn't even like it. The rest of it—the grades, the
discipline, the dutifulness—was simple. Mami had given her
everything—birthing her, feeding her, clothing her—so it was
natural that Evelin owed everything in return. Perhaps this
was transactional, but Evelin could not say it was unfair, and
Mami herself had described this as love. After all, what could
be more precious than giving her daughter the tools to thrive?
Not everyone was as lucky as Evelin, certainly not herself when
she was Evelin's age, and Evelin could not argue with that,
either.

So Evelin was as painless of a daughter as possible; she would
not leave Mami's house with any debts.

Her mistake had been assuming she would be able to leave.

A tantrum swelled within her as Evelin marched over to the storage room. On the bright side, she might calm down in the three hours it would take to find the quilt in there. It was a disaster zone, a sorted landfill at best. She shouldered open the door and felt along the wall until she found the light switch, then flicked it on.

Evelin yelped.

In the back of the room, crouched by the pink vinyl shelves, Mami was putting away a stack of labeled shoeboxes.

"Shit, you scared me." Evelin breathed. She stepped into the room carefully, shimmying between a tower of fruit crates and a broken vanity missing its mirror. "Weren't you . . . just in the kitchen?"

Mami coughed and stood up. She was wearing a patterned jacket Evelin had never seen before—or had she? That bright floral print . . .

The quilt. It was the same fabric as the quilt.

Then her mother turned around, and Evelin stumbled backward.

"You're not Mami," she blurted.

The imposter looked like her mother if you smoothed out her sunspots and wrinkles. Its hair was an even, elegant gray, not the unnatural black that tattled of dye. It wore lipstick and did not hunch.

It was what Mami had looked like in the oldest pictures of the family photo album.

"Evelin." The imposter did not get her smile right, either; the lines around her eyes were too fine. "Are you OK?"

"Y-You're—" She backed into the stack of crates, sending it crashing, and she yelped again. Something made of glass broke and nipped at her heel.

"Evelin! Are you OK?" Mami shouted from the kitchen.

The imposter put a finger to its lips. Evelin, wide-eyed, heart thumping, opened her mouth but did not scream.

What would Mami think if Evelin had gone insane? Evelin never thought of herself as superstitious, but standing before this replica of her mother, her understanding of the world shifted: Demons were real, and she was looking at one.

In her family, only Nai Nai ever told folktales, but they were mostly about weather spirits and wise animals that changed the fortunes on her farm, stories that didn't transplant well to the concrete suburbs. The suburbs must have its own monsters, ones that Nai Nai never encountered. Mami would be of no help here when she was the least superstitious of all. The demon would probably disappear if she came to check, and Mami would only find her fraying daughter, then blame the wrong thing for the mess on the floor.

"I'm fine!" Evelin shouted back to her mother, hoping her voice carried. She thought about where the toolbox was stashed, but she didn't want to reach for a weapon yet. The demon was here for a reason, and Evelin knew how to negotiate like a good daughter. To it, she asked, "What do you want?"

The demon's smile waned. "What every mother wants, Evelin.

For you to succeed."

"You're *not* Mami."

"I didn't say I was."

Evelin bristled; it really did sound just like Mami, the touch of petulance and all, a tone Evelin inherited.

"I am not your Mami," it continued calmly, "but I could be."

"I don't need another mother."

"Listen please, Evelin. I did not say I would be another."

She pulled its threats into the light. "You want to, what, replace Mami?"

"As though you are fond of your current one." The demon took a step toward her.

"She's a control freak, but—"

"You love her?"

"I do everything she asks," Evelin hissed, before she knew what she was saying. "She never asked me to love her."

For a split second, the demon's mouth spread into a grin that she'd never seen on her mother, or any human at all. Wide enough to drink her thoughts, to laugh while doing it. The toolbox, Evelin remembered, was on the top shelf behind her, out of reach.

"Evelin!" Mami—the real one—interrupted. The walls were thin and, for once, that made Evelin feel safer. *"Still looking? Try later. Dinner's ready! The food will get cold."*

"I have to go," she told the demon. If it wanted to play as her mother, then it should understand.

It nodded and stepped away. A strange feeling twisted in

Evelin's stomach. That was easier than she expected.

She took an old towel and used it to sweep away the broken glass on the floor, and kicked aside the fallen crates. When she reached the doorway, the floorboards creaked behind her.

"Wait," said the demon. "Take it."

The demon held out a quilt. Evelin had completely forgotten about it.

The demon was also no longer wearing a jacket. It looked skeletal without it, as if the life had been squeezed out of her mother's stocky body. The single yellow ceiling light made its skin look jaundiced, nearly green.

Evelin stood frozen. The demon pressed the quilt into her grip. "You need this for class?"

"Um—yeah." It had been a jacket moments ago, with sleeves and a collar, she'd swear it. But when she shook it out, there was only the quilt she knew, the one Mami had sewn when she was pregnant with her: a faded patchwork of eclectic patterns—retro, but not in the trendy way. She used to be embarrassed by it lying around, which was why she put it away in the first place.

"Take it," said the demon. "But, bring it back when you are finished. I am powerless without it."

"Powerless?" Evelin stared into its face. It looked less like her mother with each passing moment, yet there was something real fueling its illusion that kept her mind confused. "Why would you tell me that? What if I don't bring it back?"

It shook its head and folded its empty hands. "You are a good girl, Evelin. You would never do that."

Swallowing, Evelin did not reply. Unsure whether to leave the lights on or off, her hand fumbled with the switch as she backed out of the room. It was strange either way—pretending to be hospitable to this thing or leaving something who looked like her mother in the dark.

She chose the latter and pulled the door closed behind her. Her mother's outline stood in the darkness, unmoving.

FROM THE RARE OCCASIONS OF REPRESENTATION ON-SCREEN AND from Internet forums, Evelin understood that Chinese mothers showed reserved displays of affection through bowls of cut fruit, but it was a love language that Evelin could not decipher, and besides, she could cut fruit herself.

In the rarer occasions Mami or the other adults in her family opened up about the past, Evelin understood that emotions were a fragile, dangerous commodity when Chinese mothers grew up. When pressed about their lives before they emigrated, the adults spoke vaguely of famine and unrest, sidestepping specifics of how they survived because they still feared their homeland's shadow. Sometimes they would wave away the question entirely; the past was pointless or boring or troublesome, depending on which excuse they felt like reaching for. In any case, they would ultimately say, young people these days with their glittery iPhones and seven-dollar milk teas could never understand. It was a lost cause of a conversation.

And Mami was the best at turning conversations awry. She could pick up a thread in any conversation and make it about some deficiency in Evelin, then go on about it for what felt like hours in even-toned Cantonese.

"The neighbor's dog barked all night yesterday—*aish*, I could hardly sleep," Mami chattered over dinner, a stir-fry of leftover vegetables and a plate of steamed black-bean spareribs. "Remember when you wanted a dog, Evelin? You wouldn't have taken care of it. They cost so much money to raise, too, practically another child. Did you know we thought about having another one, your dad and I? He wanted a son, I wanted another daughter. It was a good idea—having a sibling would make you more responsible."

A dog would have done the same thing, Evelin thought of saying, but she didn't want to turn Mami's rambling into a real argument. Mami did not ask about her classes or the skit, in which Evelin had used the quilt to transform into Frankenstein's monster. The group project had been very silly, but that had been the point; classes hardly mattered now that seniors got their acceptances, and her Lit teacher knew it, too. Mami was never curious about her classes beyond her grades, although she generally didn't understand a thing Evelin studied.

"Have you been in the storage room lately?" Evelin asked. The quilt was still rolled up in her backpack, unreturned. She did not walk past the storage's hallway anymore, and she locked her bedroom door at night even though it was getting stuffy near summer.

"Yes, you left such a mess searching in there! I had to clean it up."

"You didn't see, um . . ."

"See?" Her voice hardened, suspicious. "See what?"

"Never mind. I thought I left something there and I . . . never mind."

"You are lucky you have me picking up after you, spoiled only child," Mami teased as she deposited more spareribs onto Evelin's plate. "You don't know how to take care of anything but yourself yet. That is why you want to go far away to college. Sometimes, I think . . . no, since your dad died, it is good we did not have another. One is too much when you are raising alone. When you are a mother, too, maybe you will understand."

A heart attack had claimed Dadi when she was six. She had few memories of him, but she remembered that week—the plastic smell of the hospital and Mami's wailing. Mami didn't cry again after they left the hospital; there was a funeral to prepare. Dadi's brothers were in China and Colorado, except the youngest one who lived two hours away and was useless. Nai Nai was too old and grieving even more, so it all rested on Mami in the end to take care of the paperwork and bills. There was no space for tears to smudge ink.

An auntie, one of Mami's same-village friends who emigrated to the same neighborhood, looked after Evelin during that time. She took Evelin to her favorite noodle shop three meals in a row, and on one of those trips, told her in English, "Your mom is so strong. She has gone through so many things in her life, and now again, God has given her this new hardship. But she will fight through it, for you. You are all she has now, so you must take care of her."

Evelin had taken this to heart, as well as what was unspoken: Learn to endure, and you will grow up well, too.

Mami went back to work as a hostess at a banquet house after that. After school, Evelin would be shuffled around more aunties and briefly, a home-run day care, until Mami deemed it too expensive. Evelin had liked it there because the other kids taught her card games. Some months later was when Evelin had begged for the dog, and Mami had scolded her for being ridiculous and for asking too much. She never asked again. Evelin didn't understand until she got older that she wanted one because she'd been lonely.

Hadn't Evelin endured enough by now? Yes, she would be leaving her mother alone if she attended Southbury, but she would return during breaks, and maybe over summer if she didn't get an internship. She wished she could *explain* to Mami. Her Cantonese lacked the nuance to express much without sounding like a workbook. Money and grades—these they both understood. But feelings and dreams and worries—these had no numerics, no objective truth. Evelin could say she would pay any cost to leave this house for four years, and Mami would call that a waste.

Evelin finished the last rice grain in her bowl as Mami started clearing the table. Evelin reached under her seat and brought out the thick envelope that held her Southbury acceptance letter and the forms saying she'd accept. All she needed were Mami's signatures and a deposit.

"Mami," Evelin said, taking a deep breath. "This would mean so much to me, and I swear I won't make it a burden on you. I really want to go. Don't you want me to be happy?"

Mami looked bewildered. She didn't pause while wiping the table. "You *are* happy."

The scraped-together hope in Evelin's gut sank. Nodding, she put the envelope back on her lap.

MAMI WENT TO SLEEP, AND EVELIN TOOK THE QUILT AND RETURNED to the storage room.

She flicked on the light switch. The demon was still standing in the same spot, though the broken glass and toppled crates had been cleared away.

"You came back," it said. It still sounded like her mother, its mockingbird talent, but the time away from the quilt had transformed it into a greenish creature with waxy skin and black hair that seemed melted to its face. Horrified as she was, she pitied it. "Did your project go well?"

"I—um." Evelin never thought about how to explain it in Cantonese. "Yeah, it was silly. But it was fun. It was based on a book called *Frankenstein*. I don't think you know it." She wasn't sure if she meant those words for the demon or her mother.

"No, I don't, but that is OK."

"So, what are you?" she asked, not crossing the threshold.

"I am a creature trying to live, just like you. I make my home in the hollows of homes, and there is so much space here in your mother's life."

"What do you know about Mami?"

"I have followed her for a long time, even traveling across the ocean with her. She was like you."

She laughed. "Stubborn?"

"Stuck. Stuck in a country where she could not breathe, so she married your father for citizenship and emigrated. She was the first of her family to leave, you know."

Evelin knew, but she could never weasel out the details of why and how. "Did anyone hate her for it?" She never met her grandparents on her mother's side.

The demon shrugged. "Perhaps. But guilt is not necessary for the things one does in order to survive."

Mami would agree with that. "And why do you need this?" Evelin held out the folded quilt. She expected the demon to lunge for it, but it did not move at all. Maybe it couldn't. "It gives you the ability to look like her?"

"Only because I infused it with my own magic." It gazed at the storage room's clutter and dust. "I draw a little bit of power from the life abandoned here and I turn it into something that allows me to go out into the world. I, too, am tired of living in this house."

"If I give this back, you will go away?"

"I don't need that quilt if you can give me something better, Evelin."

Evelin shuddered, shutting her eyes. When she opened them again, the demon was smiling.

"You already know," it said.

She had done some research. Difficult to find sources online and she'd run so many articles through translation, but she couldn't stop thinking about their first interaction. The offer it had implied.

"You are really a piece of Mami, from long ago?" she asked. "A part she cut away?"

"You seem to know of my origins better than I do. But is it surprising? Every part of her is stubborn and survives." The demon reached for something around its neck and extended an arm to her. "Come here, Evelin."

Evelin approached slowly. The demon pulled a chain out of its undershirt. At the end was a round, corked vial tied with a black ribbon. Thick, clear liquid oozed inside. "Make your mother drink this. Put it in her broth when you reheat it for her."

Evelin wasn't so naive; she knew, when she voiced it, that a wish was a dangerous thing. She plucked the vial from its knobby fingers. "It won't hurt her, right?"

"Just the opposite. It will soothe her. She won't feel a thing."

The demon's words jumbled in her head. Evelin could sense what was being said and unsaid, but she brushed the thoughts away, feigning ignorance to keep her conscience clean. "I don't want to hurt her."

"I know." The demon pressed a palm against Evelin's cheek. The touch felt paper-thin, and she thought there must be nothing but smoke underneath its skin. "You grew up well."

Evelin reminded herself that she didn't hate Mami.

EVELIN HAD LEFT THE QUILT WITH THE DEMON, BUT THE NEXT morning, she found it abandoned on the storage room floor in a crumple, like the shed skin of a lizard. The middle panel of fabric was marred with strokes of paint, like someone had pressed a face full of makeup against it. When she brushed a finger against the marks, they flared hot, hissing smoke.

She folded up the quilt as tightly as possible and squeezed it into a shopping bag. Cloth bulged unevenly from the plastic as she tied the bag's handles together, but the less space it took up, the better she felt.

She took the bag outside to the back of the house and tossed it into the trash bin.

The bin's lid clattered down. Evelin's heart panged for a beat. She really loved the quilt as a toddler. As her hand hovered over the lid, a warning prickled at her skin, electric, and she recoiled. Her mother might have felt something similar on that plane out of China, a reminder that regret could destroy a person quicker than any poison or country.

The garbage truck came around every Tuesday. The quilt would be gone by tomorrow evening. Evelin closed her hand

and went back inside the house.

"Did you take out the kitchen trash, too?" Mami called from the dining room.

Evelin shucked off her outdoor slippers and slid into fluffy indoor ones. "I did it this morning."

"OK. Come here. You should check these forms, make sure I signed them right."

Evelin went over and sifted through the application for any unfilled parts. Truthfully, it would've been very easy to forge Mami's signature on any form she needed, but Evelin still lived in Mami's house. Her slate would stay clean until she left.

The signature lines were all filled. Evelin beamed. "Thank you thank you thank you *thank you.*"

Mami's laugh was fond and strange to Evelin's ears. "Of course, Evelin, it's no problem. Education is the most important. I save money for this reason. Don't be afraid to ask for things if it means a better education. Just study hard."

"Mmm, I will." Evelin leaned over and hugged her. She didn't remember the last time they hugged. Mami relaxed against her, and Evelin was more certain that she'd done right. They were alike in many ways, and they'd both been suffocating in this house.

As she pulled away, her hand brushed against a straight ridge of raised skin along her mother's back. Evelin had worked the needle all last night. Her sewing wasn't as clean as Mami's, but it was good enough to hold in a demon's soul; with time and love, it would soften like the quilt, and no one would notice a thing.

She glanced up at Mami's gray hairline. There was a trickle of dried blood where the stitches ended. Evelin held her breath until the wave of nausea came and passed. She licked her thumb, wiped the blood away, then made herself forget that the red had ever been there.

Grounds

IN DEEP

C. L. McCollum

"T HAT IS *NOT* A POOL." I SCOWLED AT THE GNARLED BUSHES I'D all but fought my way through as I left out the back door of the bed and breakfast. I'd passed what I thought to be trellises against the back of the house, or more like the *remains* of trellises that had long ago collapsed beneath the weight of the same bushes that now grew over the back of the house and colonized most of the yard leading out to my destination.

I already regretted the tank top I'd thrown over my bathing suit before heading down the creaky stairs from my assigned third-floor room. It was one of my favorite bi pride shirts, but it left my arms unprotected against the bushes' grasping thorns. I made it through, but I paid for my passage with blood.

And to think, I'd paid it for *this*. "Take a swim out back, she says. The water will be refreshing, she says."

The pond must have been what the B&B's landlady meant for us to swim in—or well, she'd technically only told *Ben* he was free to enjoy a refreshing swim. Instead of my brother, though, I was the one who'd dared to venture back here after our arrival.

Ben and Gabby were too busy "checking out the bedrooms" and ensuring *they* would share the double room as opposed to what was originally planned.

But I wasn't bitter or anything. Really.

I tried to shake off the thought of the couple inside and regarded the pond with its rickety dock emerging from the shadows of the old house looming behind me. It did look deep enough to dive off, technically, but that was all the pond and dock had going for them. The water itself lay still and murky, reflecting nothing back but a brackish, green glimmer in the afternoon shadows. Other than the dock, there was no clear path to the water, as other plants ringed the edge, hiding where the ground fell away as if to deliberately trap anyone walking along the bank. Between the sharp-looking blades of the leaves and other wicked-looking thorns to match those tearing up my arms, I imagined few creatures dared get anywhere near the place.

Still, the end by the dock wasn't *that* unappealing with its few patches of sunlight gleaming back at me off and on. Especially compared to the far end out past the remnants of a picket fence that looked like a failed attempt at human control of the mess of vegetation. There, the mossy hued pond all but faded into blackness under sprawling oak trees. Their roots dipped out to disappear in the water, and branches hung down as if reaching to shove someone or something underneath the surface.

I shuddered. On second thought, it was really too chilly to swim anyway. March had once again missed the memo that spring break should be hot enough to party instead of cloudy with a lingering dampness that had my short hair shifting from wavy to static cling.

Not that I was in any mood to party. Or for much of anything except avoiding the sight of Ben making out with my crush and former friend. Maybe that wasn't fair. Maybe Gabby and I would be friends again. Eventually. Whenever the sting faded from her going out with my brother less than a month after kissing and then rejecting me.

The latter action I could forgive—if she was straight, then she was straight, and I couldn't blame her for it, even if it *was* kind of crappy for her to make out with me to test whether she was into girls once and for all. I already would have forgiven her, if not for . . . well. There had to be some kind of code against her dating Ben, right?

She could at least *not* be all over him in front of me. Granted, Ben didn't know about our little make-out session—no one did, and I promised I'd keep it that way—but she didn't have to rub my face in it.

I looked back at the ragged old B&B and scowled again, not wanting to go back inside. Not when I was 90 percent sure they were long past making out by now and hadn't even noticed I'd come out here.

Sibling vacation, my ass.

"You coming in or what?"

I jumped and spun around, hissing as the bushes took another bite of my forearm. A girl looked back at me from the far end of the dock, her arms holding her out of the water high enough to reveal a glimpse of a dark green bathing suit that blended in with the green tint of the water.

I blinked, scowl falling from my lips and bad mood temporarily forgotten. I hadn't heard anything but the leaves rustling a little anytime the breeze picked up. I hadn't seen anyone in the pond, either, let alone a girl like this one—pale skin dotted with freckles and wet hair hinting at a glorious red at the crown when the sun hit it just right. I felt my mouth drop open, and her lips curved slightly at my shocked expression. Had she been under the surface this whole time? Or hiding under the dock? How had I not noticed *her*?

"Well?" she asked, voice amused and holding a hint of an accent I couldn't recognize. "That towel's no use if you don't get wet."

"Umm," I started, then coughed and silently cursed my disaster bi self. "I—yeah, I just thought it might be a little cold, you know?"

She shook her head and slipped back into the pond completely. Her arms floated back and forth below the surface lazily, holding her head above water, with what looked like no effort at all. "It's nice once you're in. Honest."

Despite my earlier decision to stay far away from the murky depths, I found myself walking onto the dock and toward the edge.

"I mean, if you think so, I might as well try it, right?"

Before I could talk myself out of it, I stripped off the tank top and my shoes and sat down on the edge of the dock to dip my toes in the water.

It was, in fact, every bit as cold as I expected it to be, and I struggled not to shriek and pull my feet right back out again.

"Come now, you have to get all the way in. At least get your hair wet or what's the point?" The girl pulled a few strokes farther away from me to leave room to get in, lips pressed together in amusement as if she knew damned well I did *not* want to do this.

"How are you not cold?" I clenched my hands against the edge of the dock, then unclenched them again as I immediately gave myself a splinter—of course. What else had I expected from the way this sad excuse for a vacation had gone so far? I tugged the splinter free and let the bit of wood fall into the water along with a couple drops of blood. I hissed and sucked on the spot, forgetting my audience for a moment. I looked up to find her watching me with an oddly intent expression on her face. I dropped my hand from my mouth and bit my lip self-consciously.

"Splinter," I explained unnecessarily, and she laughed a little and nodded.

"Happens to the best of us." She swam back toward me, finally accepting I wasn't getting in at this point. Her dark eyes flicked up and down me, and I forced myself not to hide my thick tummy where it showed in the strip between my bottoms and my tankini top. She gave me a closed-mouth smile that might almost have been shy if not for the wicked glint in her eyes. "I'm Mila."

"Umm, Reece. I'm Reece. Do you live around here?" I asked, gesturing vaguely to the stretch of forest and fields around the B&B. We hadn't seen many houses when the tow truck driver dropped us off.

Mila shrugged. "Mm. Mrs. Genov doesn't mind me swimming here. Our families go way back." She reached up to pull herself up to sit on the dock behind me, somehow avoiding any splinters. I kept perfectly still so I didn't lose any more blood, but she seemed comfortable. "What about you? What brings you out to our neck of the woods?"

"Spring break road trip. Or what was supposed to be a road trip before our car broke down." I couldn't keep the bitterness out of my voice. I really had looked forward to this trip, before my best friend dropped out at the last minute and my brother invited Gabby without telling me (or our parents who'd have thrown a fit over Ben travelling with his girlfriend with only me to "keep them from getting into trouble" which . . . My parents *had no idea* what their son's reputation was at school). I'd thought about telling Mom, but it was bad enough both Ben and Gabby were seniors to my junior. They were also so much more popular than I was that snitching on either one of them would be social suicide. Neither family loyalty nor a former friendship would protect me if I betrayed them like that. In retrospect, that was probably the only reason Gabby felt it safe enough to experiment with me.

She knew I wouldn't dare share the secret.

Also in retrospect, our friendship hadn't really been much of one, had it?

"Our?" Mila's question broke me out of my thoughts, and I scrambled to pull myself together enough to answer.

"Yeah, there's three of us. We were supposed to make it to the beach, but only got six hours into the drive when this happened. Ben and my parents told us to get the SUV towed and find a hotel." I nodded over my shoulder to the B&B. "This place was the only option for miles."

Mila hummed and nodded. She started to say something else but the opening of the back door cut her off. We both turned to see Gabby standing on the back steps, carefully avoiding the grasping branches of the bushes. Her dark eyes narrowed as she looked from me to the strange girl.

She didn't exactly have the right to judge me sitting with another pretty girl, now did she? I raised my eyebrows and stared back. Gabby huffed, crossing her arms defensively over her chest. I tried not to notice Mila watching with an amused tilt to her lips.

"Dinner's ready, Reece. Ben said to come get you. Unless you have something better to do," Gabby said, pointedly. I was tempted to snap back that I did, in fact, have something better to do, but at that moment, my stomach growled like some creature lurking in the reeds at the edge of the pond.

Mila burst into laughter, and Gabby's eyes hardened at the sound. Fat shaming always did piss her off. It was one of the reasons I couldn't stay as mad at her as I wanted to. She snapped, "Rude much?"

Mila stopped laughing abruptly and blinked. "No?" She blinked again and looked at me, eyes widening in comprehension.

"Oh—no. No, not that, Reece." Mila reached out and ran a hand down my arm. "Not that, I promise. The sound surprised me is all. You're hungry. One should always eat when one is hungry."

As if on cue, I heard my brother's voice before he appeared behind Gabby. "Reece, what's the hold up? I'm starving, man. Get in—" He paused as he noticed the newcomer, and I saw the familiar too-charming smile slide onto his face. "Who's that then?" In front of him, Gabby's lips tightened into a thin line, and I couldn't help but wonder again why she'd said yes to Ben, of all people, considering how many girlfriends he'd cheated on previously. "Hey there, I'm Ben. You eating with us? Looks like the landlady made enough for an army."

Mila tensed beside me and cocked to the side as if to hear him that much better. I sighed; so much for a pretty girl flirting with me instead of my brother. I should give up and get used to it. Mila's eyes darted over to me and then back to Ben, and for a moment I thought she looked almost regretful.

"So, dinner?" Ben asked again, clearly missing all of the awkwardness he'd caused between us three girls, or more likely, just not caring.

"No . . . No, I'll get my dinner later." Mila shook herself, as if forcing her gaze away from my brother, and looked back to me. "I should finish my swim before it gets too dark," she added and gave me a smile that almost pushed away my disappointment. "But I'm sure I'll catch you later if you're around a few days, yes?"

I nodded, smiling back despite myself. "I'll hold you to that. Night, Mila."

"Good night, Reece." She flashed a smile toward Gabby and Ben. "Night, you two."

She dove back beneath the surface and out toward the middle of the pond without bothering to wait for them to answer. In the waning light, Mila looked strangely insubstantial. She didn't look back at me, but then she didn't look back at Ben either.

Enjoying the brief moment of triumph over my brother, insignificant thought it was, I toed on my shoes and followed them inside, trying not to focus on how my name in Mila's mouth sounded like a caress.

I knew better than to get my hopes up that way.

DINNER SUCKED FOR A MULTITUDE OF REASONS.

If this meal was anything to go by, Mrs. Genov's customers rarely ate here unless they had no other choice. Even if the food hadn't tasted wrong, as if the rolls and pot roast started to spoil as soon as she cooked them, I would have been put off eating after the first comment about my weight and appetite from Ben. He and I were built similarly enough that him cracking fat jokes was more than a little hypocritical. Not that he'd believe it. He was a football player, after all—he was athletic and so couldn't possibly be as fat as I was.

Not that fat was a bad thing, or so Mom kept trying to tell me and I kept trying to remember. She told me I was pretty *and* fat, as opposed to pretty *but* fat the way most people would say it.

Still, my extra weight was definitely talked about negatively a lot more often than Ben's.

Guys got to be "built like a lineman." Guys could be "big— but it's mostly muscle!"

Girls were just fat. And girls who called out that double standard were fat *and* defensive.

Through all his comments, Gabby looked . . . uncomfortable, but she followed Ben's lead and avoided my gaze.

Funny how a stranger making what she thought was a fat joke was somehow far less acceptable than when Ben did, huh?

Equally as obnoxious as Ben being more himself than usual was Mrs. Genov all but fawning over him, refilling his tea constantly and bringing him seconds without him asking. And all the while as she flitted about the dingy dining room with its torn and faded wallpaper, she answered his not remotely subtle questions about Mila, singing her praises like she was a daughter instead of a family friend.

Gabby kept quiet. Mrs. Genov gave her and me strangely jealous glances more than once, and I wondered if she had the gall to keep all but arranging a hook up between my brother and her neighbor while his girlfriend sat *right there*.

As dinner ended, I wished, not for the first time, that Gabby picked me over my brother, but—and this was for the first time, I admitted—I wished it as much for her sake as mine. It didn't change anything, and it wasn't like she didn't follow Ben up the creaking steps to their room when he beckoned, but I wished it all the same.

I wished it even more as the clock ticked toward midnight, but I couldn't sleep. I'd stayed downstairs, helping Mrs. Genov clear the table as much to delay heading up as to be polite. The landlady had gone all but mute, clamming up and dropping the solicitous act as soon as Ben was out of the room. The cold-shoulder silence hung uncomfortably enough on the air that as soon as the last of the dishes were in the sink, I finally forced myself to head to the stairs. I climbed them slowly, one by one, reluctance slowing my feet on the ragged carpet covering the steps like mud might have done. It gave me plenty of time to look around the shabby surroundings.

On the grimy walls of the staircase hung pictures, most looking at least fifty years old or older. I paused by one, caught by the flash of red. In the picture, two girls probably around my age stood wrapped around each other on the dock with their back to the camera. One, with dark hair, turned her face toward her friend, and the profile reminded me strongly of the old woman downstairs. The other, though . . . I peered at it. I couldn't see the girl's face, but the hair and the shape of her shoulders made me think of Mila. I thought they must have been related. If I was right, Mrs. Genov really had been a friend of her family for a long, long time.

Something about the image haunted me. Something about Mila haunted me, too, though I couldn't put my finger on what exactly.

It still haunted me, adding to my unease and sheer aggravated sleeplessness due to certain *sounds* coming up through the thin floors to remind me that Ben and Gabby's room lay beneath mine. I tried putting on my headphones to block some of it out, but the sharp knocks of a wooden headboard into the equally wooden wall right underneath me kept breaking through my audiobook. With decent Wi-Fi, YouTube or Netflix might have drowned them out, but like everything else on this fail of a trip, Mrs. Genov's Internet disappointed me. I should have opened more tabs or downloaded a few episodes of the new *Wayward Daughters* season before we left home, but hindsight did me no good now.

After scowling up through the dark at the ceiling of my room a while longer, I sighed and rolled out of bed, fumbling for shorts and shoes by the light of my phone's flashlight. Maybe I'd get some signal outside on the dock, and if not, at least both of our assigned bedrooms faced the front of the house. Hopefully, I wouldn't hear them way outside.

Creeping down two flights of stairs in the dark in a strange house wasn't something I ever wanted to do again. Every creak of the stairs and thud as I misjudged and hit the wall sounded like gunshots going off. I kept waiting for a bedroom door to open to Ben "joking" again about me sounding like a whole herd of elephants on the worn rug-covered hardwood floors. He didn't, thankfully, and I tiptoed my way across the peeling linoleum of the kitchen floor and out the back door.

The rusted hinges on the screen door sounded so much louder in the night, like some strange creature shrieking its rage as I disturbed its sleep. I cringed and did my best to close it without letting it slam.

I was more exhausted by the escape from the house than I had been by the noise of Ben and Gabby, but it was too late to retrace my steps. I'd been lucky enough to avoid notice on the way out—there was no way I'd manage it twice. I resisted the urge to lean back against the door and cry. Knowing my luck, that would make the door creak underneath me again.

Only because you're fat! Ben's mocking voice in my head made me smother a growl, and I pushed off from the door to make my way toward the dock.

Strangely, even with only the nearly full moon to light my way, I didn't catch my skin on the bushes this time.

Not even once.

I shivered; the lack of that expected contact added a sense of the unreal to an already stressful night. I shook my head, resolving to ignore it.

Surely nothing could be worse than hearing Gabby's voice from the floor below.

I reached the dock and sat down, surprised again when I avoided any splinters in my thighs. I rested my head in my hands, ignoring my phone as I took a few deep breaths, trying to regain some bare bit of calm after the hell of the day.

I almost didn't hear them coming. The door that had been so painfully loud when I left barely let out a whisper as it shut behind the odd little parade. Instead it was the unexpected rustling of the bushes that seemed to signal a warning.

Mrs. Genov led the way, dragging Ben and Gabby behind her like sleepwalkers. They stumbled along in her wake, tangling their arms and legs in the thorny branches. Despite the pain I knew from experience they *had* to be feeling, neither made a sound. Mrs. Genov marched them down through the grasping vegetation to the pool's deep end under the trees, passing me and the dock as if we weren't even there. Under the trees, she stepped onto a thick root stretching down into the pond, balancing carefully and leading Ben and Gabby out with her on the precarious perch.

The surface of the pond rippled.

I felt myself freeze in place as Mila broke the surface of the pond and swam sinuously forward, seeming insubstantial despite her visible effect on the physical world.

Despite her lingering effect on *me*.

She very clearly was *not* wearing the swimsuit she had on when I'd first met her. Her nudity, gorgeous though she was, somehow only added to my growing terror, and a sense of foreboding crept down my spine

Mrs. Genov smiled toothily down at Mila and pulled Ben forward to stand at the edge of the big root where it hung suspended over the water.

Then she pushed him in.

My brother hit the water with a splash, and it was as if the sound suddenly freed me to scream. "Ben! No!"

My shout and the water splashing up to drench her bare feet shocked Gabby out of her fog, and she lunged forward, trying to reach where my brother flailed weakly, somehow unable to do more than keep his head above the water. That wasn't right—I knew he could swim well. Why wasn't he pulling himself out?

I thought again of the landlady refilling his food and drink over and over. Had she dosed him? I went cold as I remembered Gabby sleepwalking right alongside Ben and the near paralysis I'd thought due to my terror but now wondered if it might be something much more sinister.

Had the woman dosed *us*?

Mrs. Genov moved, and with a strength I hadn't expected of the old woman, she grabbed Gabby and pinned her arms behind her. She held the sluggishly struggling Gabby in place, grinning viciously all the while.

Then Mila spoke, and I found myself frozen again, limbs heavy and focus somehow transfixed by the seductive tone to her voice even though she didn't speak to me. Could never be meant for me. Even in the midst of a screwed-up situation like this one, the thought hurt. "Look at him, Gabby. Look close."

Ben noticed her in the water now and reached for her, looking for help she wouldn't provide. She dodged his hands easily and laughed before addressing Gabby again. "You don't *really* want to help him, do you? You know what he's done, Gabby. You *know* how he's betrayed you." Gabby stilled in Mrs. Genov's hands, transfixed as Mila swam side to side and crooned her vicious words. "I was like you, Gabby. I loved a boy once, a boy just like *him*."

Quick as a snake, she darted forward and shoved Ben's head under. Mila let go and let him come back up, coughing and sputtering. His eyes were huge and panicked in his face, and I felt a sob escape my throat, though I still find the strength to move against the spell of Mila's voice.

Mrs. Genov looked straight at me over Gabby's shoulder, and in the pale moonlight, I almost thought she winked at me.

Mila ignored her accomplice's action and my presence behind her, instead continuing that strange, poisonous seduction of Gabby. "But that love chose another. And another. All the while saying pretty things in my ears, promising this one was the last or this one or that one. But boys like him, they never stop. Do they, Gabby?" Slowly, so painfully slowly, Gabby shook her head, her eyes wide and mesmerized. Mila smiled. "Do you know what I did? I drowned for him. Drowned right here in this pretty little pond at the very spot where you stand.

"But I wasn't the only one. My boy drowned here, too, not three years later. Then, my dear friend's faithless husband." She lifted her hand to gesture lazily at Mrs. Genov, who stared back at her with a look of mad devotion. "She's brought me so many over the years, Gabby. So many men who broke their promises. But my dear friend is getting old."

At those words, Mrs. Genov quivered, and she lifted her eyes to give me that same hateful, jealous look from dinner. Why so much anger toward me? Gabby was the one Mila had chosen. Must have chosen. Wasn't she?

Mrs. Genov's rage made me wonder.

Still, Mila seemed to ignore this look from her "dear" friend, too, focusing on her quarry. "Soon I'll be alone, with no one to help me punish boys like him."

She swam forward to dunk Ben again, her eyes never leaving Gabby as she did so. I could tell his strength was failing him, and still frozen, I wondered when he'd finally give up and sink.

Mila lifted her hand to Gabby, offering it like a suitor might. "You understand me, don't you, Gabby? You're just like me. You could stay—could help me, couldn't you?"

Something in me snapped.

"She kissed me first!" Without knowing I intended to speak, nor that the truth in the words would hurt so much, the words burst free of me like a shout, breaking through the odd paralysis and letting me step forward.

Mila spun around, breaking her stare with Gabby. Behind her, Mrs. Genov's eyes grew somehow even more angry, and her grip slackened on her prey. As it did, Gabby blinked slowly and looked around her with a dawning horror and then determination. Their responses and my own words gave me an idea, a desperate plan that might save the girl I'd wanted to love so desperately once. Might even save my brother, though that didn't matter near as much.

I made myself focus on Mila and her beautiful face with its terrible expression. I swallowed hard and walked to the very end of the dock. "Gabby isn't like you. She's like *him*. She kissed *me* first. Then left me alone for *him*. She wouldn't understand you. Not like I would. Not like I do."

It was the truth, the one I'd promised to keep locked inside myself. A truth that might damn me in Gabby's eyes even as it saved her.

I heard Mrs. Genov scream and then a loud splash, but I didn't dare look to see what was happening. Mila didn't, either; instead, she swam toward me as if as mesmerized as Gabby had been only moments before. I vaguely heard Gabby sobbing Ben's name and more splashing, but I kept my gaze fixed on the girl in the water. "She betrayed me, Mila." My voice shook. "She kissed me and then chose my brother. She doesn't deserve you."

All at once, Mila's eyes went soft and filled with a pride that sent a sick sort of satisfaction rolling in my core. "Oh, Reece. I knew you would understand. I could taste it with your blood in my waters." She swam forward a little closer, and I tried not to crave her nearness. "I just couldn't know you'd have the courage to admit it."

Just then, Ben and Gabby, both soaked to the skin, crashed through the foliage, stumbling as they raced past me and the dock to the house. Before I could turn to follow, they ran inside.

The door slammed behind them, and a lock slid home with an audible snap.

I stared at the house and the closed door, numbness creeping over me. They'd left me. I'd been the one to distract Mila and Mrs. Genov long enough for them to get away, had ripped myself open emotionally to save them, had drawn their predator's attention to myself instead of them, and *they left me.*

Mila spoke again, her voice surprisingly gentle. "Oh, Reece."

Slowly, I turned back around to face the pond and Mila. Behind her, not even bubbles broke the surface. I wondered if Mrs. Genov escaped while I looked away or if she joined Mila's other victims at the bottom of the pond. I had a feeling it was the latter, and that her *dear friend* had let her drown without a second thought.

"Reece," Mila said again, her eyes strangely fond as she looked up at me. "Are you coming in?" she asked, echoing our first meeting.

I thought about my brother laughing at the dinner table and Gabby pretending I was invisible. I thought about the sounds from their room that had driven me outside tonight in the first place. I thought about the locked door behind me.

I thought about the dark depths of the pond and the slim chance that anyone would ever find the bodies of so many drowned, faithless lovers.

I licked my lips, mouth gone dry. "Will you let me get back out?"

Mila smiled slowly, for the first time showing every one of her teeth, all sharp enough to gleam in the moonlight. She shrugged, but didn't answer.

I dove in anyway.

BLOOM

Tori Bovalino

Y ou're in the backyard when I wake up. In these hours, the hours when my eyes are open and I can think and things are happening, things are changing, you're always in the backyard. It's only in the hours between, the times when my body is resting but my mind is vivid as always—that's when I find you behind the door in the living room or in my closet or huddled under the kitchen table, tucked away, waiting.

But not now, because now I'm awake, and now you're not waiting, and now you have teeth and jaws and lips and tongue.

I track you through the windows as I go through my routine. When I roll out of bed and rest my forehead against the cool glass, you are lying prone in the edge of the bramble, milky eyes open, staring straight up at nothing. If you were alive, you'd feel the scratch of the past-ripe blackberry bushes against your skin, the sting of the poison ivy. The trail between the trees is there, just past the jelly sandal that clings to one of your feet (the other foot is rotten or bitten off, ending at a polished ball of ankle bone), and through the trees, the lake is gold and glimmering with sunlight. When I make it to the bathroom, do my business quickly so as to not miss you, you've shifted and rolled onto your side, arms reaching forward, reaching for nothing. I duck away, spit out the toothpaste, and when I look back I can see the flesh clinging to your ribs and the spoiled-meat-purple of your muscles below your mottled skin.

Back to my room. Into jeans and a sweater—*your* sweater, actually, given to me by your mom in the days after you died. Hester Lake Track and Field. Your mom still loves me, or says she does—says she's forgiven me, though there's no way she knows the extent of it and I don't think she would if she did. I wear your clothes, the remnants of your closet merging into mine as if that's repentance. As if that keeps your memory alive. Keeps *you* alive.

You told me, once, about what happens to lambs when they're being given to a new mother. Sometimes, when a sheep's baby dies, the farmer will skin the dead lamb and put the flesh over a new lamb, freshly born. Convinces the mother to take it in. Convinces her it's her own spawn, her own baby, something to be kept alive and protected.

That's how I feel, in your clothes. It would be no good if I tried to skin you now—there's so little of you left, so little of you whole—but the effect is the same. Everyone will love me more, will keep me, if they think I'm the piece of you that's left behind.

Outside, you've rolled to sit, your knees tucked to your chest. I prefer you this way, with the worst of the sinew covered. They never found your body, out in the lake. Eventually, they just stopped looking.

It doesn't matter. I know you're here, with me.

The only thing I hate is the way you watch me. Your eyes, or what's left of them, tracking me through the windows the way I track you.

Downstairs, focusing on the front of the house. I can't bear to turn and see you at the window, your broken nose pressed against the glass, milky eyes watching.

This is the one thing I didn't expect, in the time after it happened. All our lives, the entire messy time of it, I kept track of everything you did. I followed in your wake. You were my sun, my moon, my stars, my morning and night. You were the law. And I would've given anything for you to turn around, to look and see *me*.

That's the main difference. Now, you just won't stop looking.

YOU DIED FOUR MONTHS AGO, ON THE FIRST DAY OF SPRING THAT felt like it could almost be summer, when we finally thought we'd escaped the cold for good. We used to count down, in February and then March, creeping closer to April. You would check the temperature in homeroom, hemming and hawing over the shifting degrees until finally, *finally*, you said, "This'll do."

It was our thing, our very own rite of spring, every year since we were eleven. April it was, always, on the edge of being too cold. Your brother Paul could never believe we did it without alcohol, but that was the point: For it to count, we both had to be sober. If not, the luck just wouldn't work.

That's what it was about, after all. Luck. We thought that that first swim, that first icy breakthrough of the year was enough for everything to go okay for us year-round. And now, with both of us looking toward our futures, this year was the most important of them all.

It was a half hour past sunset when you got to my house, wearing soft shorts and jelly sandals and an oversized gray crewneck over your bathing suit. I went upstairs to change—the luck didn't work if we didn't match; the luck didn't work if the universe didn't see us as one and the same; and though I never told it to you, I was always certain that was the mechanism—and then we were trudging across the backyard, searching for fireflies that weren't there. It was too early.

We pulled the boat out of the shed near the water, and you sprayed it down with the hose to get rid of any spiders while I grabbed the oars. After that, it was the easiest thing for you to sit in the back of the little boat while I pushed off, yelping at the icy water up to my calves. I launched myself in with you, both of us giggling as the boat rocked perilously.

Then we were off. In the days since, I wondered if anyone was watching from their deep back porch or their dock as you and I rowed out into the dark stillness of the lake. If one person leaned to the other and said, *Bit cold, don't you think, to go out?* And the other replied, *Foolish, this time of year.*

I wondered, too, if anyone was watching when I came back, as the little boat trundled home and ashore. Before the call, before the red and blue lights and the crying and the divers, there was just me and the boat, and no you to speak of.

WHAT DO YOU BELIEVE?

You know, with your rot, and I know, with my persistence, to keep going. But perhaps we should explain—elucidate, in that SAT-prep way you were using words and explaining the meanings as if I didn't know all of January through March.

So, let's break it down. Let's say that you and I were on the boat. We'd rowed far enough out that the trees that lined the lake were dark shadows, punctuated by the glittering lights of houses and headlights. It was colder on the lake, cold enough that my legs and arms were stippled with gooseflesh. You pulled your oar out of the water and sat back, balancing the wood across your hips, your elbows propped against the flat edge of the stern. I brought my oar up, then, because you'd decided on your own that we'd rowed far enough, and I wasn't going to push us farther and farther in circles.

"Paul says I should cut my losses," you said, halfway through a conversation in your own head, unwilling to share the beginning. You had your head tipped back, bold nose pointing skyward.

"In what way?"

"Take a year off. Get a job. Put some space between me and The Incident."

That's what we called it now: The Incident. It would be a bad time to say *I told you so*, to remind you that I thought it was a horrible idea for you to scribble answers on your thighs and peek during exams from the very first time, to say I warned you. It seemed fun, at first, like a game or a bet: how far could you go before you got caught? What even were the stakes to this little trick? Time after time, you giggling in the corridors as you whispered your tactics—it all lost its edge, until someone finally found you out.

It wasn't just one incident—you'd been cheating on tests since sophomore year. It was a matter of time before you got caught, and we both knew it.

It's just, I don't think either of us expected it to cost you quite so much.

"Do you think that will work?" I asked.

The glare you turned on me was positively venomous, but you were the one who brought it up. "Of course it will work," you said. "If I take a year, let things settle, retake some exams— everything will be okay again."

"What will you do, in that year?"

You shrugged. "I don't know. Maybe Paul has the right idea.

If I take a year, then you and I can get jobs, and maybe an apartment, and next year . . ."

You must have seen it on my face as you trailed off. I chewed on my lip, and it was only by force that the words came out next—"What about next year?"

"Next year," you said, so slowly, like you were writing the words into existence for the very first time. "We can go."

I closed my eyes. I hadn't expected the caution, that anyone else would be right about you even as I assured them they had it wrong. "When you say you and I," I started, searching for words. My voice was thick in my throat. I swallowed, but the lump remained. "What do you think I'm going to do this year?"

For the first time, I watched the hesitation on your face. That little seed took root and spread as you realized what I was saying—my heart pounded as I understood what you wanted.

"You and me. Us. It's always been us."

My nails dug into the wood of the oar, a splinter clawing its way under my thumbnail. "You want me to stay here."

"Deferring won't be that bad," you said.

But I was already shaking my head, the impossibility of it all sinking in. "Katie, I can't wait for you."

"But—"

"I'm sorry," I said, my throat thick, but that was the truth. It had always been the plan to be inseparable, to go to the same colleges (or, at least, ones close together) and spend those years as roommates, or visiting each other at weekends. We were supposed to go to the same parties, join the same clubs, take the same classes.

The point is, it was supposed to be you and me. It wasn't supposed to be me out there, living my life as if nothing had happened, and you here in Hester Lake for another year of rotting. I saw it in your eyes, how much the idea killed you.

"Please don't go," you said, barely a whisper. You lurched forward, rocking the boat as you grabbed my hand, your nails digging into my skin. "You can't leave me."

"I can't stay," I said. There were offers from colleges, scholarships—Mom sat me down the day after the punishment was handed down, the day after your schools were notified and the offers were rescinded. *She made her choices*, Mom said, her fingers tracing circles on my forearm as if that would ease the blow. *I know you love being in Katie's shadow, but you have to live your own life now.*

And I, fool that I was—I never thought you'd ask this of me.

"You *promised*," you said, the bite coming into your voice.

I know. I did. I can't.

"I know," I said, "but I'm not the one who did this to you."

Before I could stop you, you lunged forward, your hands going to my neck. There was something in your eyes, something I didn't understand, something I'd never seen before. I couldn't breathe—you were holding too tight, pushing too hard.

Your knee on my stomach. Your hands on my throat. Your voice, screaming, calling me so many names—and maybe then, maybe now, I deserved them. My own tears, salty on my tongue, as I could not breathe and could barely think.

Then I kicked at you with both feet, and your eyes flew wide as the boat lurched wildly, and I bit your arm. You recoiled and the whole thing tipped, spilling you and me and both oars into the dark, murky cold of the lake.

I came up sputtering, calling your name, but there was no answer. I found the boat, the oars. I set things to right.

But we never found you.

Rewind. Start over.

You and me, in the boat, in the middle of the lake. My mother's voice in my head as I looked at you, your head tipped back, staring at the stars, talking about a future that you yourself had ruined. You, saying *you and me*, as if I fit into your small personal tragedy, as if I had no dreams of my own.

"I hate you for it," I said, unprompted.

Your head snapped up and you looked me in the eye. "What?"

"I hate you," I said, "for what you did. It was supposed to be us. You and me. And you *ruined* it."

"What are you talking about?" you said, your voice taking on that mean edge. Mom had heard that edge before, a couple of times, when we were younger. She got quiet every time, and then after, in the car, she reminded me that I didn't have to be friends with people who were not nice to me.

But we weren't just *friend*s. You were my person, and I was yours. If I tried to feel us apart, to find which parts belonged to whom, I had the feeling we'd be all mixed up: two incomplete mosaic people without the rest of the pair.

Except—you and me. You and I. *We can stay in Hester Lake*, you were saying, in this place that I hated even as the claws sunk in deep. I wouldn't stay.

"I'm leaving, Katie. I can't stay here with you."

That meanness hardened. Your fingers tightened on the oar, the corner of your mouth quirking down. It was getting darker, and shadowy; we were always fools to go out at night. No one would be able to see if something went wrong.

"You can't leave me here," you said, like it was a foregone conclusion, but I was already shaking my head. That's when the note of hysteria crept into your voice: "I can't stay here without you. You have to—"

"I don't have to do anything." I looked at the water, at the little ripples, and wished we'd never come onto the lake. The oar felt too heavy against my hips.

"I'll tell them you helped."

"What?" The word tore out of me as my head snapped up to look at you.

"I'll say you did it, too. How could they prove it? How could they know?"

Cold, uneasy dread spread through my veins. Everyone knew we were inseparable. It wouldn't be that hard, annoyingly—in fact, it would be even more difficult to prove that your transgressions weren't mine. "You can't," I said.

Your nose was already blotchy, your breathing hiccup-y and

uneven. Maybe if I was less devastated, it would've mattered to see you so torn up at the thought of me leaving. So torn up you'd ruin me instead.

"I won't let you," I said, my own voice ragged. I didn't recognize the feeling in my stomach. It was lead hot, anger and frustration and resentment, all poured over an uneasy measure of love.

"You can't stop me. You can't prove anything." There was that edge of fear creeping in, then. You'd never been afraid of me before, but you were then as you tucked your knees to your chest.

"You just had to be the best at everything," I said, the tears thick in my throat. I hated thinking about it, about you here alone as I went away, about all the dreams we'd had that would never come to fruition. "You never were the best, or the smartest. You just pretended."

You recoiled as if I'd struck you. "You don't get it," you said. "I needed the scholarships. I needed to qualify for——"

"You're such a fucking fool, Katie."

Your eyes darkened. "And you're coming right down with me."

I don't know why I did it, even now. Why I picked up the oar, the heavy weight of it in my hand, picking up speed as I swung. There was nothing inside of me but a dark pit of rage, and then the oar connected with your head. I watched the flesh of your scalp as it crunched in, your face of shock. The blood dripped over your eyebrow, down your face, into your mouth, and all we could do was stare at each other.

All it took, after that, was one swift kick. One reflexive jerk, and you were over and sinking and gone.

Stop.

There's another option, that none of this is the truth at all. That it wasn't me and the oars on that night in April. But it's easier to pretend that I was there, that I had some hand in it. If I pretend that it was me, that it was *my* fault, it makes more sense.

It's better, this way, to imagine your hands on my throat or the oar in my hands. To picture *me* being the reason your head dented in and the breath left your lungs as the lake water invaded. At least, then, I can understand.

But that's not the reality at all, is it? Let me walk with you. Let me follow you on that day, the weekend night in April, days before we were supposed to do our own ritual. Let me come with you, you crying broken thing, Katie my Katie, my friend my only—

You went without me. Left your car just a bit down the road from my house, in the middle of the night. You told Paul we were having a sleepover, and no one thought to check with me. I don't know how long you sat in your car, waiting for all of us to go to sleep. I wonder if you were drinking, or if you took something, but there was no body that anyone else could see and thus no tox report, and it's not like I can go to the coroner and tell him that I know where you are because you stare at me through the windows with your sad, milky eyes.

The motion detector camera on the neighbor's house caught you as you staggered down the strip of grass between their land and ours; our trail cam picked you up down by the dock, dragging the boat down to the edge of the lake.

Imagine if I woke up then. If I dragged myself out of bed by some unseen force and went to the window, if I looked down at you on your own private adventure. Maybe I would've dragged myself down the lawn, caught your arm before you could go.

I didn't wake up. And if I did, if I did look out to the moonlit lake to see you silhouetted, I only remember it as a nightmare.

You pushed off and rowed yourself into the middle of the lake, to the place we used to go every year for the rite of spring. Maybe you looked out at the land, where the trees were only shadows, and the houses and headlights glittered, and maybe you thought that you just couldn't handle this world anymore.

I wasn't there in the boat and the chill. I wasn't there for the push-off, the moment of decision; no one saw you jump into the lake and never come up again. What followed was all I had left of you: the red and blue lights and the crying and the divers; your mom and your sweatshirt and all the things you left behind.

Katie, I would've followed you anywhere. I even would've stayed here, in Hester Lake, for a year or a million, if you'd only asked.

And then you slipped away. We found the boat, and the oars, and your car, but we never found you.

You watch from the edge of the trees as Mom backs the car up close to the garage. Your eyes don't leave us as I drag out box after box. It's too much, I know; too many suitcases, too many boxes of trinkets, too many *things*. But you always knew I was a maximalist. I can't leave anything behind without the guilt coming like a punch in the stomach.

It takes nearly an hour to pack the car. Mom and Dad play a delicate game of Tetris as I watch, leaning against the wall in the heat, wearing your crewneck. Twenty minutes before we're supposed to go, another car pulls into the driveway. It's your mom and Paul, bearing yet another box of your clothes. Mom eyes me, but she does not protest when I push and shove at the boxes, making this last box fit.

Your mom holds my hand in hers, and says nothing. She doesn't look out to the place where you lurk in the shadows. She doesn't look at the lake at all. I wonder if it's too painful for her, if she would leave here if she had any real choice.

Paul kisses me on the forehead like he used to do to you. "She would've wanted you to go," he says, which is a bald-faced lie and we both know it. I let him say it. I swallow down the lie.

When they're gone, Mom and Dad shuffle their feet and look at the clock and say, "Well, we're burning daylight." I nod and say nothing else, then get into the back seat, among my boxes of your things, as Dad fiddles with the radio and Mom pulls up directions on the GPS. I press my face to the glass of the window, and I look out at you. You're watching—you're always watching—as I move farther and farther away from the points where we diverged.

When I go, you don't follow.

THE SHOE

Alex Brown

N ANAY'S FAVORITE STORY STARTED LIKE THIS:

A man was once warned to stay on a certain path as he walked through the woods.

He did not listen.

WE DIDN'T MAKE IT PAST THE THIRD STEP ON THE PORCH—WHICH was a bummer, 'cause I'd spent the last few hours decorating the inside of the house for an epic promposal. No one really did them anymore, but I knew Jess would love it. It was cheesy, romantic, and the kind of thing that I'd always dreamed of doing for my first girlfriend.

All we had to do was make it inside the house.

"Davina," Jess said, "I can't come in." The wood on the second step creaked under her feet.

"Just ignore the squeak," I said, turning back around to face her. "You won't fall through. I promise."

Jess looked over my shoulder at our bright red front door. I hated that thing. Whoever lived here before painted it that way, and no matter how many times we tried to cover it with a different color, it remained the same shade as a stubborn scream.

"It's not that," Jess said, slowly. Patiently. "I don't think I can do this anymore."

"Do what?"

"Be with you."

"Oh," was all I said back. I couldn't bear to look at her, so I stared at the porch instead.

The wood was old and splintered. Splattered with drops of discarded paint that never stuck to that damn bright red door. Splotches of blue, black, white, gray—even purple, though that one hadn't been my idea—surrounded our feet. Those little tiny dots highlighted all of the wood's imperfections. The splinters we inherited. The way the planks that got too much sun had faded into a pale beige, while the ones left in shadow were still closer to some shade of dull, unfortunate brown.

"Jess?" I said, letting her name fall out of my mouth as a question, because it couldn't just be "Jess." If I said her name just as it existed—like it was a thing that no longer had the power to hurt me—then it really was over.

I wasn't ready for that. Not when there was a promposal waiting just behind that bright red door.

Jess took a deep breath, exhaling with a sigh so sharp it made me wince. "Look, it's been fun, but—"

One of Nanay's favorite sayings went something like this: Everything someone says before the "but" doesn't matter.

"But?" I asked.

"But," she continued, "This isn't gonna work out."

"Why?"

"It just won't. I'm sorry."

I didn't mean to laugh but I couldn't help myself. Sorry was what Nanay said the last time she saw me, before she left the house for good. Sorry was always what someone said when they wanted you to believe that they meant it.

But they never did.

And oh. There it was again. That word.

"But—" I said, trying to salvage a sinking ship.

All I ever wanted was someone who would come inside. See my room upstairs. Hang out in the kitchen. But between the old porch, red door, and black shuttered windows, everyone was always a little too creeped out to follow through. Not that I blamed them. I didn't even like this house. It was the kind of place where someone had definitely been murdered in an upstairs bedroom like fifty years ago and they just put up some tacky floral wallpaper to cover up the blood splatters. The abandoned oars in our garage—remnants of whoever lived here before—probably had something to do with it.

"We can still work this out, right?" I asked, knowing the answer before her lips rounded out into a profoundly solid no.

"There you go again," Jess said, shaking her head. "You never listen to anything I say, Dav. We always do what you want to do. Or what you think I want to do. But have you ever asked me a question and waited to see what my answer would be?" She leaned in close, poking her index finger into my forehead. "No. You're too busy making up your own answers in your head. I don't exist there, Davina. No one does."

"Well," I said, gesturing to the street, "I guess that's it, then. See you in calc."

Her eyebrows shot up into her jagged bangs. She staggered back, as if she wasn't expecting such a quick dismissal. But what was I going to do? Stand there and beg, cry every time I took a step? Squeak out a plea for her to stay that matched the peal sounding from the porch's slowly rotting wood? Hell no. I was a Rejection Champion. She wouldn't see me break.

No one would.

"Uh, yeah," Jess said, a brief bit of hurt flashing in her light blue eyes. "Guess so. Bye, Dav."

"Bye."

I stood on the top step of the front porch, watching her go. Nanay's rocking chair creaked as the wind blew around me.

We still had it, even though Nanay's never coming back. She wasn't dead, or anything like that, but one of her kids got very sick back in the Philippines and she left to take care of them. She didn't want to leave me, even though she knew she had to. My parents reassured her it was fine. I was old enough to take care of myself.

When my godmother left, she took her stories with her.

But the rocking chair stayed. A reminder of all the things she used to tell me to help me cope with how quiet the darkness could be. But now, there was nothing to help. No stories. No distractions. Just me, as I've always been.

Sad. Alone. Heartbroken.

Jess swore from down the driveway. Her footsteps echoed as she jogged back to the porch. "Uh, hey," she said, shoving her hands in her pockets.

"Hey," I said, hope filling my chest with nervous flutters as I waited for her to tell me it was a mistake. To take it all back and wrap her arms around me and tell me she couldn't live without me.

Instead, she looked down at the porch and said, "I can't find my keys."

"Oh," I replied, because what else could I say? "I took them."

"What?"

I held them up. They glinted in the dim porch light. It was easy to pretend to stumble as we walked up our winding driveway, slipping my hand in her jacket pocket before we made it up to the house.

"It was a joke," I said, even though it wasn't. It was unfair of me to do it, but I didn't regret it. Part of me hoped that if I kept her there, she'd realize she'd made a mistake. She'd choose to stay. But another part wanted to punish her for the months she stole from me, and the promposal that, now, was never gonna happen.

"What is wrong with you?" she asked sharply, snatching her keys out of my hands. "You can't take things like this, Dav.

That's not okay."

"I wanted to ask you something. Had to make sure you came back."

"What was so important that you stole my keys?" she asked, her voice rising dangerously close to a shout.

"Do you wanna go to prom with me?"

Jess laughed. It was a cold, harsh sound. It cut through the air, making me wince.

She stared at me, light blue eyes burning with fury. "Are you serious?"

"Yes. I don't want to go alone."

She scoffed. "Well, you're not going with me. And Dav, do me a favor? When you see me at school, don't talk to me." And just like that, she walked away.

Tears filled my eyes as Jess's car roared to life.

I didn't know how long I stayed there, mourning something that hadn't really ever existed. But I did. I bawled until my eyes were sore. Until I couldn't find more tears to cry.

And that's when a voice called out from the darkness.

"What's wrong?"

THE MAN WAS DUE TO BE MARRIED, BUT HE'D BEEN LEFT AT THE ALTAR earlier that day. He refused to acknowledge that he'd done any-thing wrong, as most men do. And so he wandered into the woods and continued down the path that he insisted on forging for himself.

It was only when the moon broke through the clouds that he realized he had no idea where he was going.

There was a clearing up ahead, and along with that, the faint glow of a fire. The wind blew through the trees once more as a warning drifted through the air. It urged the man to turn around. To return to safety.

He did not listen.

SOMEONE SLINKED OUT FROM BEHIND THE BIG OAK TREE IN THE front yard. The first thing I noticed were her legs—maybe because that was how she stepped into the moonlight. Legs so long it was almost unbearable, a waist so tiny that it looked like it was in danger of being split in half if the wind blew the wrong way. And her eyes—an inky void that would swallow everything up and never let it go.

Maybe she'd let me lose myself in them. If only for tonight.

"Hi," I said, because I wasn't sure what else to say.

"Hi," she replied. She ran long, slender fingers through her hair.

I swallowed, wishing that her fingers would run through mine instead. I pushed the thought away as I asked, "Are you new here?"

"Hmm?"

I cleared my throat. Put my hand on the back of my neck as I rocked on my heels. "It's just—I don't think we've met before."

"I don't think we have." There was definitely a hint of sadness in her voice at that. "I'm so sorry if I startled you. I was on a walk and heard some crying, and—"

"Oh." Warmth rushed to my cheeks. Could she see me blushing in the darkness? "Yeah. That. Sorry."

"Why are you apologizing?"

"It's, uh, a family thing. We don't really do PDEs."

"PDE?"

"Public Displays of Emotion."

"Ah. I see." She took a few steps closer to me. Her tan skin glowed under the moonlight. "Well, I won't tell if you won't. This can be our secret." She held her hand out, waiting for me to take it.

A spark jolted through my body as my fingers slid down hers, gliding down to her palm. "I'm Davina, by the way," I said.

She smiled. "Davina."

A car pulled into the driveway. I let go of the other girl's hand, running to meet the driver. My heart skipped a beat as I got closer. It was a sedan, just like Jess's car. Maybe she realized I still had one of her keys. It was a small one to an old bike lock that she stopped using years ago. She must've figured out it was missing and decided that she was wrong. That she'd let me keep the key and also go to prom with me!

"Jess—" I started to say but stopped as soon as I got a good look at the driver.

It wasn't Jess. I was wrong. She wasn't coming back. She left, just like everyone else.

"Hi, Mom," I said, as she opened the driver's-side door.

"How'd your promposal go?" she asked, the smile on her face fading as she saw my expression. "That well, huh?"

"Yeah."

"I thought I saw you talking to someone when I pulled up. That wasn't Jess?"

"Oh, no. That's my new friend," I said, turning back to the girl who'd been standing by the porch. But she wasn't there. "She . . . just left, I guess."

Mom frowned, looking around at the yard. "It's getting late. We should go inside."

I nodded and followed her up the porch steps, past Nanay's rocking chair. Something rustled in the top of the big oak tree, sending a crow flying out of it. I looked out into the darkness one last time before I closed the door. But no one was there.

THE MAN SHIVERED AS HE WALKED THROUGH THE TREES, FOR HE WAS only wearing a thin barong and pants that were not designed to fight the wind.

Although he did not start the fire up ahead, going to it seemed like a good idea, as he knew it would bring him warmth. He was hopeful that he'd find a kind person sitting by the flames. One who was, perhaps, willing to share their food with him.

Branches hung so low and dense that they started to obscure his vision.

"Hello?" he called out, pushing some of branches out of the way. "Could you help me?"

But there was no response. He took a few steps forward, more cautious this time than he had been all day. "Excuse me," he said again, still moving closer. "I seem to have lost my way."

The wind blew through the trees once more. This time, the man heard a woman's voice whisper along with it.

Stop.

"STOP LYING TO YOURSELF," I MUTTERED, TURNING MY PHONE FACE down on the porch. It'd been three days since Jess broke up with me and she hadn't tried to call. Or text. She even avoided me every time she saw me in the hallways during class changes.

Whatever. At least I still had her history textbook. And her old, useless key. She wasn't getting those back anytime soon. And I didn't need her, anyway. I had the porch, and the front yard, and the cool, crisp night air.

I leaned against Nanay's rocking chair, letting out a deep sigh. Blinked a few tears out of my eyes. Jess Collins wasn't worth crying over. We hadn't been going out for that long.

So why did it still hurt?

"We've gotta stop meeting like this," a voice called out from behind the big oak tree. And there she was, the mystery girl from a few nights ago. She slowly drifted toward me; a specter bathed in soft moonlight.

"Like what?" I asked, wiping away at my eyes. I scooted down to the bottom step on the porch. "Me, a complete mess, and you, all put together?"

She nodded. "I thought PDEs weren't your thing?"

"They're not supposed to be. But they are." I shrugged. "It's not really public if it's just me angsting on the porch. Even if there *is* an audience."

She smiled. It was bright enough to turn the night into day. "Well, I think it's great that you're crying."

"You do?"

"Yes. That's what makes you human."

"Well, at least I've got something going for me." I sighed, putting my head in my hands.

"It's wonderful that you can feel sadness. And joy. I—" she stopped, snapping her mouth shut. Cleared her throat before she continued. "I don't think you should let this get you down."

She stepped closer to me. Stopped right in front of me, kneeling down next to the first step. Her hand dipped under my chin, lifting my head up to meet her gaze. Her eyes were even more beautiful up close—pools of darkness that begged me to dive in. "You have so much love to give, Davina." Her voice was nothing more than a whisper. "Someday someone will see that."

I tore my gaze away from her, scrambling up the steps. She was wrong. No one would see that I was worth loving because I didn't have any love to give in return. All I did was take. I couldn't help it. Sometimes, people left things lying around and I had no choice but to steal them. Jess's keys. Melanie's pen. Steve's sunglasses.

It was the real reason Nanay ran back to the Philippines as fast as she could. We all talked ourselves into believing that her son was sick. But really, she was just sick of me.

Maybe Jess was right. I spent so much time building people

up in my head—pretending they were who I wanted them to be—that I couldn't see them for who they actually were.

I wanted to be different. I *had* to be different. But I wasn't sure how.

"Davina," the mystery girl said, lingering in front of the first step. "Don't give up now. You're close to finding love. I'm sure of it."

"I'm not."

She laughed. Moonlight danced in her dark eyes. "Then you should trust me."

I gave her a small smile. "How can I do that when I don't even know your name?"

"You'll find a way."

"That sounds like something a serial killer would say."

She laughed. It wasn't like the other times. Before, the sound had been light and free. Happy. But now, it was like her laughter had teeth. Like it was lurking in the darkness, ready to strike. The sound a wolf makes before it takes down a deer.

The front door creaked open once again. I turned around to find Mom's head poking head out from behind that bright red monstrosity. "Dav? You should come inside."

"I will," I said, turning back to face the other girl. "Once I'm—" my thought hung in the air. She disappeared. Again. "—done." I said, quietly.

"What was that?" Mom asked.

"I'm done," I replied. I scrambled up off the porch, facing her with a smile that pulled too tightly at the corners of my mouth.

"Thanks for getting me."

"Of course," Mom said, shifting so I could walk past her. "You shouldn't sit out in the dark alone, anak."

I nodded, walking upstairs to my bedroom.

I didn't tell her that I wasn't sitting alone outside in the dark. She wouldn't believe me, anyway.

She'd just say that Nanay's old stories were getting to me.

DESPITE THE WARNING TO STOP, THE MAN MOVED CLOSER TO THE FIRE. No one was there.

I COULDN'T SEE HER, BUT I KNEW SHE WAS THERE.

This was the fifteenth night we'd spoken. Me, talking out into the darkness. Her, replying. Sometimes she'd come close to the porch. Other nights she stayed by the oak tree. And then there were times I didn't see her at all. Only heard her voice.

It was strange. But I didn't mind it.

"Do you believe in love?" I asked the darkness, waiting for a response.

She paused for a few seconds longer than usual before she replied. "Yes."

"Have you ever been in love?"

"A long time ago," she said, something wistful drifting into her tone. "And then never again."

I wasn't sure why the thought of her never loving again

carved a hole deep in my chest. But it did.

"Do you think you could?" I asked, twisting my hands together.

"Could what?"

"Love again?" I swallowed. I wasn't supposed to dread the answer to that question. But I did.

"Perhaps," she replied. The word weighed heavy in the air.

"Even if the person had never been in love before? If all they did was take, and had no idea how to give?"

"If they wanted to learn, I wouldn't mind teaching them." She paused. "Do you have someone in mind?"

A nervous laugh fell out of my mouth. "No. No, I don't think so."

But I did.

"That's too bad, then," she replied.

Silence stretched between us. Every now and then, I'd see a pair of eyes flash from somewhere in the yard. At first, I thought a cat was wandering around; it had that same holographic glow. But there weren't any sounds that indicated an animal was running around in the dark. There weren't really any sounds at all, except for me picking and picking and picking at the front porch, and Mystery Girl answering my questions.

"I think you're wrong, you know," Mystery Girl said.

"About what?"

"Taking my free advice. If you ask me, you shouldn't punish yourself for not knowing how to give. It's a thing we all learn in time."

"But what if there's no hope for me?"

"That's for you to decide." The shrug was evident in her voice. "Why do you think you're hopeless?"

"Everyone always leaves," I replied, the words flowing out of me before I could stop myself. "I always think people are perfect. Not just perfect for me, but perfect. Melanie was. Steve. Jess. Especially Jess." Bitterness filled my mouth at her name. "She was right, you know. She said I loved the idea of her, and not *her*. But I . . . I think I'm broken. I don't know how to love someone. Like, really love them. The real them. Not some perfect version I've cooked up in my mind."

There was a long, uncomfortable silence. I used Jess's key to carve more random patterns into the porch, trying to ignore the gnawing feeling that I scared her away.

Finally, after an eternity stretched on, she said, "I can help you with that. If my help is something you'd like to take."

"What do you mean—" I started to ask, but Mom opened the front door, hurrying me inside.

And that was the end of our fifteenth night.

"HELLO?" THE MAN CALLED AGAIN, EDGING CLOSER TO THE FIRE. "Who's there?"

"WHO ELSE IS OUT THERE?" I ASKED, DIGGING MELANIE'S FAVORITE pen into the paint splatters on the porch. I drew lines between them, connecting them together in what could maybe pass as a rough sketch of the Big Dipper. "Dating pools are kind of limited, you know."

"There are lots of people in the world," Mystery Girl replied. That night, she made it all the way to the top step. She stretched to reach the porch, her head propped up on her elbow. Her free hand rested lazily by my leg. If I wanted to, I could shift a little and we'd touch. And maybe I wanted to. A little. Her body was turned toward me; her torso was draped in darkness, lost to the part of the porch that the light didn't touch.

She delicately traced the lines I'd roughly cut into the wood. "You can always try again."

"And get hurt."

"Maybe. But people could surprise you. If you give them a chance."

Her eyes met mine and that's when I knew I had to try. I turned, ever so slightly, so that her hand could brush my knee. And when I did, I swear I caught a glimpse of the area where her torso *should* have been. Only . . . it wasn't there.

"Davina," she said softly, gently touching the bottom of my chin. She guided my head back to her face, watching me carefully with her beautiful, dark eyes. "There's something I should tell you."

"Yes?"

Something broke a nearby branch, sending a harsh *crack* through the silence. Her head snapped to the sound.

"What was that?" I asked as I pulled out my phone. I turned the flashlight on and shone it in the sound's direction. Something retreated into the bushes.

If I didn't know any better, I'd say it was a pair of legs.

But I *did* know better. Legs were always connected to *something.*

"I should go," she said, retreating into the darkness. "It's getting late. I'm sorry."

She vanished faster than should've been possible.

I sat on the porch, alone, listening to silence.

A GIGGLE DRIFTED DOWN FROM ABOVE HIM.

"Don't be afraid," someone called out to him. *"I only want a friend."*

"WE'RE FRIENDS RIGHT?" I ASKED A FEW DAYS LATER, WAITING FOR her to make her move.

She looked down at the tic-tac-toe board I'd drawn on the porch. "Of course we are." She placed the *X* in the top left corner of the board. Not where I thought she'd go, but it still worked in my favor. She handed the pen to me. I took it, trying to hide my smile.

"Then I hope you won't mind *this*," I said, placing the final *O* in the bottom right corner. "That's seven out of ten. I win."

She held her hands up. "I surrender. On one condition."

"What's that?"

"This was supposed to be your prom night, right?"

I looked down, covering the tic-tac-toe board with my hand.

"Yeah."

She lifted my head so that I'd meet her inky black gaze. "Will you dance with me?"

"Here?" a nervous laugh bubbled inside my chest. "On the porch?"

"Yes."

"We don't have any music."

"We don't need it."

"Are you sure?" I asked.

She held out her hand, helping me up off the top step. "I'm sure."

THE MAN LOOKED AROUND THE CAMPSITE, FINALLY FINDING A PAIR OF legs poking out from behind a tree. He thought it was odd that someone would be laying down so far away from the fire, so he crept over to see if she needed help. Once he moved around the giant tree, he stumbled back, screaming.

Where there should have been a person, there were only legs.

He pushed himself to move forward. But before he could take another step, something sharp latched onto his shoulders.

HER FINGERS CURLED AROUND MY SHOULDERS AS WE GLIDED around the porch. Eventually, she guided me down the steps and into the yard. We waltzed under the big oak tree to a tune she hummed.

"This is perfect," I said, closing my eyes as a cool spring breeze danced around us. "You're perfect."

She pulled me closer to her. "I have something to tell you," she whispered. "A secret to share. But I can only give this to you if you'd like to take it."

"Of course I would," I whispered back.

I opened my eyes as she let go of my hand. She vanished into the darkness.

THE MAN LET OUT ANOTHER LONG, TERRIFIED SCREAM. BUT THERE *was no one around to hear it.*

"I've been alone for so long," the voice said. Now, it was much too close. "It'll be nice to have some company. If only for a while."

Blood poured out of the man's wounds as he was dragged into the sky. His vision darkened as he got farther away from the fire where the legs were supposed to be.

"Don't be afraid," the voice said. "I'm nothing to be scared of."

"DON'T BE AFRAID, DAVINA" SHE CALLED OUT, FROM SOMEWHERE above me. "I'm nothing to be scared of."

Something lowered down from the branches above. My breath caught in my chest.

There was no way this was real.

It was the intestines first. That's what made me back up. I looked up, trying to see who was climbing down from the tree and was greeted by intestines. And then the rest of her came into view. Or, well, whatever was *left* of the rest of her.

She only existed from the intestines up. Large wings sprang out of her back, folded up as she climbed down using only her hands. Her fingers had curled into claws, nails protruding out of them like talons. Her dark eyes were wild. Hungry. Black hair flowed over her shoulders and down her back. She smiled at me, fangs glinting in the moonlight.

Apparently the mystery girl I'd been talking to wasn't much of a mystery at all.

"Manananggal," I whispered, scrambling back to the porch. I tripped over a pair of legs—her legs—and screamed.

THE MAN SCREAMED AS THE MANANANGGAL LIFTED HIM HIGHER INTO *the air. Her intestines tangled with his legs. They wrapped around him so tightly that he began to lose sensation in his limbs.*

The monster dug her claws so far into this shoulder that he was sure they ripped all the way through. Shadows crept into his vision as the man struggled to stay conscious. It was a battle he wouldn't win.

"Why?" he managed to say, breaking another rule that was given to him. The word scraped out of his mouth, dripping with desperation, as he tried to free himself from her grasp.

The manananggal laughed. "You were warned to stay on the path. You should have listened."

The creature opened her jaws as wide as a snake and tore the man's head cleanly off of his body.

He didn't have time to scream again.

"You were supposed to be perfect," I shouted, kicking the manananggal's discarded legs out of my way. Adrenaline coursed through my veins, pushing every muscle in my body to its limit as I made a mad dash for the porch. "You lied to me!" I screamed in the darkness.

"I didn't," she said, flying above the legs she'd abandoned and stopping at the first step.

My hands curled into fists. "You said you were my *friend*," I snarled. "You told me to get back out there. That I could find someone who loved me. But you just wanted me to suffer. That's what you do, isn't it? Feed on people who're left at the altar?" I barked out a laugh. "A promposal's not quite the same, but it's close enough, isn't it?"

The manananggal bristled. "Heartbreak has always been a part of our stories—but not the way you think. They want you to believe I'm a monster who feeds off of pain, but those are lies that jealous men told. That's not what I want, Davina."

Breath hitched in my chest as I asked, "What *do* you want?"

"You," the manananggal said, gliding closer to the porch. She lingered right in front of the first step before she flew away, returning with her hands closed around something small. She held it out to me.

"A shoe?" I asked.

Moonlight caught on the intestines that hung down loosely

from her abdomen. Blood dripped down them, watering the ground. Her large, bat-like wings flapped slowly as she hovered in front of the house. She ran a clawed hand through her hair, looking away from me before she met my gaze again.

I'd been raised to think that her eyes—as dark as the bottom of the ocean or the far reaches of space—were terrifying. And maybe they were. But there was something so beautiful about that darkness. It was hard to look away.

I didn't *want* to look away.

"I haven't spent every night speaking with you because I wish you harm," she said, voice soft as rain that fell after the fourth time we talked. "All I've ever wanted was someone who wouldn't be frightened by who I am. Someone who could look past the monster they saw and love me in spite of that." She reached out for me, but her hand fell as I took another step back on the porch.

Jess said that I spent too much time in my head. That I didn't really get to know her—the *real* her—and I fell in love with the idea of her instead. But what I had with the manananggal was different. We'd spent the last month and a half becoming friends. Building something that could last.

The manananggal was wrong, though. Love shouldn't happen in spite of who—or what—someone was, but because of it.

Somewhere between that rain-filled fourth night and our dance in the darkness, we'd gotten to know each other in a way that was more meaningful than stolen kisses and broken promposals.

She wasn't some perfect, idealized version of herself. Or a monster.

She simply was who she was. And I loved her.

I looked up at her, barely able to hold back a smile. "I've got one question for you."

"Yes?"

"What's with the shoe?" I asked.

"It's a gift," she replied, holding it out to me. "Take it."

"I—" I said, reaching out for her gift.

The door creaked open. I turned around as Mom crept out onto squeaky wood, standing next to Nanay's rocking chair. "Dav?" Mom asked, looking over my shoulder. "Who's that?"

THE ONLY THING THEY EVER FOUND WAS HIS SHOE.

"Mom," I said, heart pounding. She was *WAY TOO CALM* for someone who just saw a monster with loose intestines and giant wings in our front yard. "I can explain—"

"I'm Tala," the manananggal said, interrupting me. The porch's steps creaked behind me. "It's nice to meet you, Mrs. Amano. Dav's told me so much about you." She nudged me forward, moving to my side as we both stood in front of my mom.

I turned to look at the manananggal—at Tala. I nearly fell over. Her legs were back and her intestines weren't dangling out of her exposed torso. Instead, she was in a long black terno. The sleeves puffed up at her shoulders. Silver embroidered flowers filled her skirt.

"It's nice to meet you too, Tala," Mom said, holding out her hand. "Would you like to come in?" she asked, as Tala took it.

Tala turned to me. "As long as that's what Dav wants."

My mouth hung open for a few seconds before I snapped it shut. No one I'd ever brought home before actually made it *into* my house. We'd only ever gotten as far as the front porch.

"It is," I said, sliding my hand into hers. "I'd love that."

We both walked past Nanay's rocking chair and stepped inside the house. Mom shut the door behind us.

TALA'S VERSION OF NANAY'S FAVORITE STORY WENT LIKE THIS:

One day, a man walked into the woods.

He'd just been left at the altar and was angry.

He found her.

When she tried to be his friend, he tried to hurt her.

So, she ate him.

OUR FAVORITE STORY STARTED LIKE THIS:

We weren't perfect.

But we were happy.

A HELPING HAND

Linsey Miller

WAS THE FAMILY BIBLE THAT STARTED IT. THE WHOLE THING was an easy twenty pounds, weighed down by the ink of a hundred birthdays and death dates. The front cover flipped open, plastic protector crinkling, and the pages turned in a haze of dust. They stopped on the latest entry scrawled across the endpapers:

Samuel Anthony Turner 23 May 1972–7 November 2020.

"Well, fuck you, too," I muttered. Dad had only been dead for three months and cremated for one. He hadn't wanted to be buried, fearing he'd be aware of his rotting for eternity because of some story he'd read once. He cared more for hauntings and nonsense than history. Mom had only been able to talk him into buying the house because the last owners had said it was haunted.

Haunting me was exactly the sort of thing he'd do, and the

pinch of loss in my chest made me gasp. I'd never really bought into it.

The pages rustled, Dad's page flipping back and forth. I was home alone—Mom couldn't stomach the place now—and all the windows were shut. The heat had clicked off an hour ago. Outside, the day was still and silent under a blanket of snow. I sat up on the couch.

"Is this a joke?" I asked, expecting nothing.

The page dog-eared on its own, and I pressed my back into the couch. The bareness of my neck, the thinness of the wall behind me, and the smothering solitude of the house came into sharp focus. Dad and I had always joked that the place was haunted, but that was only a bit of fun to annoy Mom. Ghosts weren't real.

The cloying scent of old paper grew, and the heat dragged its clammy fingers down my spine. Across the room, the thermostat read a balmy 72 degrees.

But the heat was still off.

I waited for fear to take hold of me, make my heart race as gooseflesh crept over my arms, but all I felt was hot and confined, like some great mouth was breathing down my neck.

"You couldn't have shown up while he was alive?" I asked, voice cracking with thirst.

Maybe a haunting would finally make me feel something, or maybe the haunting was me, all those missing emotions trapped in the house with nowhere to go. Unfair of my feelings to flee and leave me here with the nothing life has become. What stage of grief was poltergeist?

The Bible's spine creaked, pages flattening as if a hand were splayed atop them and pressing down, and the dry, rotting taste of old books flooded my mouth. An uncomfortable warmth curled around my shoulders, the weight too akin to an embrace.

"What do you want?" I whispered, sweat weeping down my face. "What are you?"

A shape that might have been a hand appeared in the dust and shut the Bible.

"Dad?"

For the first time in a good, long while, I *felt*—dread writhed in my belly. Time slithered slowly between us. The ice hung, only half sloughed from the trees outside, and water drops hesitated halfway down the frosted windows. The clock on the wall didn't move, the soft electric hum of its mechanism gone. The second hand shivered.

"What do you want?" I whispered.

And the hand, the void shaped by dust, turned palm up. I reached out, dust clinging to the sweat-soaked crinkles over my knuckles. My fingers passed through the air and found nothing. No familiar grip met mine.

The front door flew open. It slammed into the wall and bounced back. Mom kicked her heels together, shaking slush onto the rug, and sniffed. I yanked my hand back.

"So help me," Mom muttered. "Mel! You can't keep the heat on all day."

Ice crashed to the ground outside, and the thrum of electricity filled my ears. I wiped my hands on my pants.

"Didn't touch it," I said, glancing at the Bible. The spine was flat, the pages crinkled, and none of it moving. "Look—it's still on sixty-five."

Sure enough, the thermostat was set to sixty-five but displayed an indoor temperature of eighty-three. My mother cursed.

"I've had it up to here with you," Mom said, hanging her coat up in the closet and not gesturing at all. "You take the chicken out of the freezer? You sand the sidewalk? You get up off that couch at all?"

I shook my head. Mom was desperate to escape the house, but I was desperate to want anything.

I laid my hand on the family Bible, but the pages were still and dry. I'd imagined it, surely. Heatstroke from a broken heater.

Dad always said ghosts had real-life explanations. I should've known.

Mom sighed. "Go get the chicken."

"Got it," I said, and rolled off the couch.

There was only one way into the garage from the house. The kitchen had become a marathon of cruel reminders—the old family pictures on the fridge, Dad's favorite mug still speckled with coffee-stained fingerprints resting on the table, and the pile of condolence casserole dishes waiting to be washed. Cold air seeped through the bottom crack of the door separating the kitchen from the garage. Dad had always put off fixing it.

I didn't mind the chill so much now. Maybe he would come back to fix it.

The door creaked shut behind me, uneven hinges helping

me out. Mom's car, still warm, sat in the middle, and the empty space next to it was half-filled by the new freezer. We had needed a place to hide the flood of food from friends, family, and acquaintances who didn't know what else to do. The sight of it made something clench deep in my chest. It was like grief spun a wheel every week to decide what asinine thing would set me off.

I shimmied between Mom's car and the garage door, the metal rattling against my back. A ziplock bag of wrapped chicken, DEFROST TODAY written on the front, was at the very top of the freezer, and I leaned inside to grab it. The garage door rattled again, warm air breathing down the back of my neck. The hair along my arms rose.

Something slammed into the garage door. I turned, chicken raised, and hesitated.

A handprint, the littlest finger missing its tip just like my father, appeared on the plastic window of the garage door. Frost melted around it, and the window steamed. The freezer's temperature alarm tinged.

"Dad?" I asked again even though his ashes rested not fifty feet away.

And three knocks against the door answered.

WE WEREN'T RELIGIOUS EXCEPT IN THAT WAY MOST SOUTHERNERS were, the whole nation being built the way it was, but calling the minister felt wrong, so I skimmed online instead. There were all sorts of stories about people hearing from parents long after their deaths, most obviously fake. Dad had liked those the most and had plenty of books on how to talk to the dead, but if those had worked, he'd have told me. I found plenty of stories about knocking and how I should never answer, always answer, or only answer every third knock, and nothing about ghosts causing the temperature to increase. They almost always left rooms and people colder, and any handprints they left were frosted on the glass. Nothing ever melted or breathed.

Almost like ghosts weren't real at all and there were no answers to find, as if the warm breeze I'd felt were the breath of grief as it closed its great jaws around me.

"It was his hand, though," I mumbled, wedged between the freezer and the garage door for the second time this week. School didn't start till January, and my mom had begged off hosting Christmas this year. We were alone. Supposedly. "'Course, if my mind was playing tricks on me, then it would know what his hand looked like."

There'd been no more knocking, balmy air, or floating Bibles these last three days. There were cold spots and flickering lights, the standard evidence of ghosts or poorly built homes in winter, but none of it ever happened in the garage. It was the only place I could find a moment's peace. I'd settled for scrolling through methods of contacting the dead without boards or pencils or flashlights. All of those could react without input from anyone. I needed . . .

"A helping hand," I mumbled, reading a comment on a fake

haunting video. "The ritual is simple: At 3:33 a.m. in a dark room, open a doorway and reach into it with your dominant hand. Ask the dead person you're trying to contact for help by name. If no one takes your hand, remove it and shut the door. Do not turn on the lights. Leave the room without looking back at the door. You may try to contact them on another night. Ensure, though, that you use the same hand each time. Do not go through the door while the ritual is ongoing. To end it, let go of their hand, retreat without turning your back to the door, and turn on the lights. Then, shut the door. You must end the ritual once three minutes have passed."

It couldn't be serious. They'd used punctuation and everything.

But I'd seen Dad's hand. This was the only thing I'd found that didn't require a board, bathtub, or any blood.

"Maybe, if it was real, he spent all his energy getting my attention," I said, and checked the time. "I'll have to reach out first."

There was something powerful about that. All I'd been able to do about him dying was plan the funeral. Now, though, if this really was happening, then he needed to talk to me, and I could make that happen. Doing something was better than nothing.

That was what Mom said: keep moving and grief couldn't catch up, as if it were a beast stalking our steps.

"Think you can wait until 3:33?" I asked the empty garage. It was only about ten minutes away. I'd been fixing to head to bed for the last four hours.

My phone screen went to sleep. Darkness nestled into me,

cool and smothering. I liked the bite, the sharp teeth of winter that reminded me I was alive even when I couldn't feel anything else, and it was easier to picture my father before me without the betrayal of light. He'd be standing, knees locked like he'd never been taught better, beside the door to the kitchen, and his socked foot would be tapping against the cold concrete. He'd shake his head and laugh at my hiding spot. He'd turn on the light.

The garage light flickered on, and I startled. The shelves behind me shook, sending shadows skittering across the room. The light overhead sputtered but stayed on.

I exhaled slowly, my breath misting before me. The cold dug into me until it was hard to breathe.

"Dad?" I whispered. "Are you really here?"

The door to the kitchen rattled so hard the lock clicked into place, and I shot to my feet.

"Dad!"

The door handle was so cold I couldn't touch it. The lock, too, had frosted over. I checked my watch, stomach turning at the 3:28 it flashed. I slapped the light switch off, plunging the garage back into darkness, and hit the garage door button. Hopefully, mom wouldn't hear it. She would have heard the kitchen door if I used it.

I hit it again once there was a two-foot-ish crack. The chilled night air crept in, lapping at my feet. The light flickered again, bright and painful, and I covered the switch with tape to keep it down. Dad and I hadn't talked the day he died; maybe he was as desperate as I felt.

3:31.

I settled down before the garage door, between Mom's car and the freezer, in the void that once was Dad's, and tried to picture him on the other side. He wouldn't appreciate having to scoot under it, but surely he wouldn't mind. I just wanted a few more talks and the chance to hear his voice again before I forgot how he sounded. I needed to commit him to memory.

If I forgot him and mom did too one day, then he'd really be dead.

3:32.

This was what the earth felt like on still nights when snow covered everything in sight and there was nothing to break the silence but the creak of snowflakes piling up. Frozen. Smothered. Peaceful.

3:33.

I reached into the dark beyond the garage door with my right hand. The cold didn't even hurt anymore.

"Samuel Anthony Turner," I whispered.

Behind me, the tape over the light switch crinkled but didn't give. The kitchen door stopped shaking.

"Dad?"

The dark writhed. I knew, knew it deep in my bones, that nothing was there, but that didn't stop my mind from filling in the gaps. Flashes of silver speckled my vision, and darker-than-black ribbons twisted just out of reach. My mind couldn't stop thinking of hands, and it saw them in the dark. Fingers curled around the bottom of the door. Nails dragged across the pebbled driveway. Knuckles creaked.

Except there was nothing there at all—no hands or fingers or sounds. There was only the normal dark and the growing void around my hand. It grew warm and heavy, but there was nothing.

No, my brain wasn't imagining anything there like it was everywhere else, as if the only true dark in the world rested at the tips of my fingers.

The heat spread. It prickled over my arms, needling into my skin. Breathing became thick and hard like it was a humid summer day, and the ice melted off of the door. The drippings were a curtain of movement in the blackness, not quite visible but visibly there. Then, something split the water in two.

The swirling implications of shapes condensed into a single smear in the pure void around my hand. Slowly, as if each movement were an unfamiliar lesson in pain, a hand gripped mine. It was warm and clammy. The rough calluses from guitar playing scratched my palm. A too-short pinkie curled around my fingers.

I couldn't see it, but I *knew*.

"Dad?"

It felt alive. The warmth, the sweat, and the weight all made it feel as though he were simply on the other side of the garage door. He squeezed my hand in answer, and I sobbed. He was here. He was here. He wasn't gone for good.

3:34.

Dad's thumb rubbed the back of my hand in slow, unsteady circles, and I finally found my voice again.

3:35.

"Are you OK?" I asked, and immediately felt stupid, but he simply drew a *Y* on the back of my hand with a finger. "I mean, you're not . . . it didn't hurt, right?"

There was a breath, the vague nothing covering my wrist and hiding my hand from view undulated with it, and then he drew an *N*. I sighed.

"Mom's lost. She's never worked so much, but I don't think she's paying attention to anything. Just drifting," I said. "I know I'm not much better doing this and all, but she keeps saying we can work through you dying and not ever actually thinking about you. She can't even look at the bedroom. She can barely look at me."

I laughed, and the odd nothing beyond the door thrummed.

It wasn't like the dark behind closed eyes. That was complete but bright. There were flickers and fractals there that made me think of color even if I wasn't seeing any. This was nothing. Pure nothing. Like one of those rooms so quiet people in them could hear the blood rushing through their fragile veins. Except it didn't feel empty. It felt full and waiting.

And in it, was my father.

"Can you come back?" I asked, gripping his hand so tightly it must have hurt. "If I call you again, will you come back?"

Pins and needles prickled over my hand as if it were asleep, and I flexed my fingers. Dad's grip tightened. A burst of cold air shuddered down the back of my neck, and I startled. My watch lit up at the movement.

3:36.

"I have to go now," I whispered. "I love you."

Dad squeezed my hand and let go first. I couldn't see either hand, but I felt the loss. The space where he had been was warm, and I slowly pulled my hand from it. It was like climbing a ladder out of a wave pool—there wasn't resistance until most of my fingers were free of the dark, and then I felt too heavy. Falling forward into the crack between the door and the ground would be so much simpler.

Another gust of cold air rustled across my back, and I yanked free. Backing up to the light switch, I shuddered in the sudden chill. The air was colder here, and the tape had curled up at the edges like someone had been one-handedly picking at it. I flicked on the lights.

The world beyond the garage door, the icy driveway and flickering streetlight, appeared as if they had always been there. I sniffed. That had just happened, right?

I glanced at my hands. My right hand didn't look any different; all fingers there and scars still in the same place. The skin was pink and tingling, as if I had been holding another hand tightly. I pressed my pointer finger to the button on the wall, and the garage door lowered to the ground with a groan.

My left hand, though, the one that hadn't passed through the dark, felt cold and wrong, and my watch somehow read 3:33 again.

NOT DOING IT AGAIN DIDN'T EVEN CROSS MY MIND. THE MOMENT I'D shut the garage door, a new doorway had opened in me. It was yawning and empty, begging to be filled. I had done the impossible, and Dad had been here. I had to see him again, I had to hold his hand again, and I had to figure out how to get Mom to trust me long enough to do it, too. I wrote down the ritual on a sticky note and stuck it under my keyboard. Eventually, I'd need that to explain it to Mom. Maybe she'd humor me.

The next night, I returned to the garage at three and waited in the dark. It wasn't as cold as before, and no odd chill haunted the entryway. The flickering street lights and snow-buried cars were distorted by a thin layer of frost on the garage door windows, and water droplets cut clean through them as the ice melted. I laid the back of my hand against the door, expecting heat. It was cold.

It was probably just snow melting off the roof.

I did the ritual exactly the same. Despite the light flickering in through the windows, the gap between the door and the driveway was black. I reached out, the dark still a new sort of emptiness I couldn't comprehend. It wasn't empty. It was brimming with nothing, oozing up my arm. Dad grabbed my hand, drawing a smiley face on the back of my hand. I laced our fingers together.

"If I reach out with my other hand, can I—"

A chill needled the back of my neck, freezing me in place, and I shook my head. I shouldn't get greedy.

"Never mind."

I let my eyes shut so that I could imagine he really was here. He let me ask questions again and mostly wrote out assurances that he wasn't scared or in pain, just a little lonely. He didn't confess to any secrets I should know, like hidden money or secret murders, and he refused to explain what death was like.

"It feels like nothing at all," he wrote out.

"Does it hurt to bend your thumb like that to write?" I asked. "I can turn my hand over."

"Other hand." He hesitated, fingers tapping against me and wrote, "No, nothing hurts here."

That sounded nice.

I opened my eyes, the black of the doorway so complete that even my shut eyes hadn't prepared me for it, and froze. The tips of my father's fingers were barely visible against the back of my hand. The littlest finger wasn't, of course.

But I could touch him. Talk to him. See him.

"How are you here?" I asked.

My watch buzzed—time was up—and I hesitated. After a moment, his fingers tightened and then slipped from mine. I backed away from the crack in the garage door.

How much of him could I reveal from death?

THE FIRST KNUCKLE. DAD DIDN'T WRITE MUCH ABOUT HIS DEATH OR bother revisiting the past. He mostly listened and reassured me that he was safe, but safety had nothing on being alive.

THE SECOND. I DIDN'T PULL HIS HAND CLOSER, BUT I DIDN'T REACH out as far into the void either.

IT WAS TOO COLD TO VISIT DAD WITH THE GARAGE DOOR OPEN, BUT I did anyway. It was never cold once I called him. The air was always warm and damp, a steady breeze blowing in and out of the barely open garage door. I reached into the dark, fingers trembling, and I could see the whole of his first two fingers curled around my wrist. A speck of blood stained his skin.

"What made you crash?" I asked, teeth chattering. The cold at my back sharpened until it hurt.

Dad's fingers twitched, and he slowly wrote, "No."

Once he was done, his other hand dropped to the ground. I could only see the tips, but the nails were bitten and broken. I had never known him to bite his nails. I hadn't known enough about him. I never would.

I swallowed, the scent of burning rubber and gasoline as clear as when I had arrived at the wreck, and nodded. "Sorry. I just . . . I didn't realize you'd be bloody."

"Not again," he wrote.

We spoke of other things.

DAD GOT IMPATIENT AND SLAMMED THE GARAGE DOOR TO THE ground before I could talk to him. Mom heard, so I couldn't risk going out there. I sat down in my bedroom, the lights off and the closet door open, and called out to him at 3:33. The dark wasn't right, too full of imaginary flickers like behind shut eyes. He didn't take my hand.

It was a new flavor of despair, this rejection. It wasn't like when he had died. There'd been finality.

I had known that sooner or later I would hit rock bottom, but now there was no guarantee of a bottom. My stomach was a swooping, hollow thing stuck in my chest and refused to settle. My mouth was sour and hot. He loved me. He'd come back.

The room grew colder. The temperature change came from behind me, not blowing like a breeze but simply existing. Frost crept over the carpet and creaked like thick ice under booted feet. The chill bit down to my bones and held on tight. What warmth there was fled.

3:34.

I pulled my hand from the closet doorway. I had to go to the garage tomorrow. No matter how cold it was or how annoyed Mom was or how angry Dad might be, I had to reach him. If I could just do it one more time, maybe I could pull him through. I wanted him, alive, with me again. Just a few more days, even. A few more memories to drown out the sight of the wreck.

I turned on my lights, and there, in the frost melting on my closet wall, were two words scrawled in a weak hand.

"No door."

I had to sneak back into the garage.

THERE WAS NO CHILL AT ALL THE NEXT DAY. THE WHOLE HOUSE FELT warmer, as if the winter had worn itself out. Even Mom noticed, double-checking the thermostat when she got home and narrowing her eyes at me while she passed. Her insistence that we carry on as normal didn't bother me for once; soon, we might be able to carry on exactly as we had before.

I held out my hand into the dark of the open garage door and invited my father in again. "Samuel Anthony Turner."

A single shiver of cold brushed the back of my neck. Then, a hand, my father's entire hand, grabbed mine and held tight. The heat of his skin made me jump, and I nearly fell back. My other hand gripped the garage door so tightly my nails cracked. Pain shot down my arm.

The airborne, free-fall feeling in my stomach slammed into me. I sobbed until 3:35, and he just held my hand. There was no awkward patting on my shoulder like he used to do, but his hand was solid and visible. He didn't let go.

"I can see more of you each time, you know," I said, and wiped my nose on my shoulder. "I don't want to think of you and remember the wreck and the funeral and the nothing that came after. Mom looks around for you sometimes, and I turn to where she's looking, thinking she's seen you. She's just on autopilot. There's nothing there. You're nothing. I hate it."

The cold returned, biting into my shoulder. Dad tapped my hand again. Warmth flowed over me and chased the cold away.

"I know. You're not nothing," I said. "It just feels like that."

As if death were a creature slowly gnawing at our heels and eating us piece by piece, memory by memory. Pursued and devoured all at once. Losing Dad and ourselves.

"What happens when all of you comes through the doorway?" I asked.

The tape over the light switch snapped. A shock of cold spilled across the room, freezing the air in my chest. The light flickered but didn't stay on. Maybe the ritual wouldn't fail.

"You can come in as far as you need to, you know," I said, and rose, turning toward the light switch. Light from the kitchen filtered in under the door. "Don't let go. I can reach it if I—"

Dad stood before the kitchen door. His hand was on the light switch, the vague fog of his body passing through it like he wasn't there at all. He was only a suggestion of a person, a space in the dark slightly more defined than the rest of it, and I couldn't take my eyes from his face. My memory filled in the gaps his ghost didn't.

"Dad?" I asked, breath misting before me.

His mouth moved, but I couldn't hear anything. The old radio in the corner crackled, static drowning out the rushing in my head. Frost spread across the wall where his hand passed through. Tears streaked his cheeks.

"It was you," I said.

Dad shook his head, and I ran to him.

His hand yanked me back. I slammed ass-first into the ground, and my joints creaked within his grip. I groaned.

"How are you there?"

Dad raised his hands. Hand.

The right hand with the little finger missing the tip was gone. The jagged bone of his forearm stuck out from a torn sleeve, and his blood dripped, pooling on the concrete as pale snow.

But his hand, that missing hand, gripped my fingers tighter and tugged me back toward the garage door.

Warm air ruffled my hair. Moisture gathered at the nape of my neck, dripping down my spine like sweat. I shuddered and tried to slip my sweaty hand from his. A second hand grabbed my elbow.

But Dad hadn't moved from the doorway to the kitchen. To back inside the house.

His gaze slid from my face to the doorway behind me, and his face twisted in pain. In the edges of my sight, a hand wrapped over my shoulder. Fingers slid around my throat.

My dad shook his head, but I couldn't resist. I turned around.

Hands. Chains upon chains of severed hands held together by the silver flecks I saw when I stood up too fast. The dark behind my eyes. In my head. Invited in.

They skittered through the narrow crack in the garage door and grabbed my other arm. They were hands of all sorts, severed but not rotting. They moved as surely as if they were still attached and struggling against whatever orders they were getting. My dad's hand flexed around mine.

It had been broken, bitten, torn off past the wrist, the frayed edges of his skin covering the hand holding it like a veil. I tried to see what was beyond them lurking in the dark. An impossible shape, more void than darkness, squirmed. More hands crawled through the nothing toward me.

Then, it folded. Moved not down or up or sideways but within itself. Threw some new part of it into the gap of the garage door. It wasn't possible. There was too much. Too little. All of it endlessly folding and revealing more and more.

Fingers worrying the edges of a maw of hands. An eye weeping hands instead of tears. Three tangled halos of interlocked hands sewn together by the strings of the universe spinning above a starving, crawling pit at the center of creation.

I blinked, and it was only my father's hand holding mine in the dark.

"Dad?" I tried to turn around and couldn't, fingers I couldn't see digging into my scalp. "Daddy, please."

His severed hand flinched. I tried to pull away, barely slipping free. His hand shot forward and grabbed my wrist again. Slowly, he—it—pulled me into the doorway.

It clawed at my wrist, fingers digging into the tender meat of my arm. There was no pain, but I still felt it all. The pressure. The heat. The threat.

Nothing hurts here.

I screamed. A hand covered my mouth, fingers wriggling

between my teeth. My skin tore, bursting open beneath the many fingertips. Blood welled in the holes, and Dad's fingers wedged between my bones. He pried them apart with a creak. A feeling like stretching after waking up oozed up my arm. Dad's hand twisted mine off like a bottlecap.

It held my hand aloft, and my father's ghost vanished. Slowly, another hand with chewed nails reached from the dark beyond the garage door and grasped the dripping wrist of my severed hand. The chain of hands shivered, every finger flexing. Then, so did mine.

My fingers curled together. My thumb cracked each knuckle. And I felt each movement.

My vision blurred, not silver snow in the edges of my sight but nothing. A waiting dark. Slowly, my own hand helped pull me through the gap.

And then it shut the door.

About the Authors

TORI BOVALINO (she/her) is the author of three YA horror novels, including *My Throat an Open Grave*, and is the editor of the Indie best-selling anthology, *The Gathering Dark*. She is originally from Pittsburgh, PA, and now lives in the UK with her partner and their very loud cat. Tori loves scary stories, obscure academic book facts, and impractical, oversized sweaters. She can be found on Instagram as @toribovalino.

ALEX BROWN loves rooting for the final girl—especially if she's a monster. Alex is the author of *Damned If You Do* and *Rest in Peaches*, and is the co-editor of *Night of the Living Queers*.

TRACI CHEE is a best-selling and award-winning author of books for young people, including the instant *New York Times* bestseller *The Reader*, Printz Honor Book and National Book Award finalist *We Are Not Free*, and National Book Award longlisted *A Thousand Steps into Night*. Her latest title is *Kindling*, a YA fantasy reimagining of *Seven Samurai*. She is currently on faculty at the Low Residency MFA in creative writing at the University of Nevada, Reno, and lives in California with her fast dog.

GINA CHEN is the *New York Times* best-selling author of *Violet Made of Thorns*. She tells stories about heroines, antiheroines, and the kind of cleverness that brings trouble in its wake.

KAY COSTALES (she/her) is a Toronto-based Filipino author and poet represented by Lesley Sabga of the Seymour Agency. As the daughter of immigrants and a daydreamer by nature, she imagines and creates all kinds of stories for the diaspora, whether they're fantasy, romance, horror, or contemporary.

G. HARON DAVIS is a New York–born, Tennessee-raised author, cat parent, and fishkeeper. Currently residing in the outskirts of Kansas City, MO, they specialize in horror and fantasy with a little bit of humor thrown in for good measure. In their spare time, they can be found playing video games, daydreaming about epic fish tank builds, and preaching the gospel of BTS. They can be found online as ghdis.me and @mxgeeTV on X, Instagram, Threads, and TikTok.

NORA ELGHAZZAWI is a Muslim Lebanese–American writer currently living in Boston, MA. She holds a doctorate degree in pharmacy, and her passions include travel, classical music, and fairy tales. When she isn't consuming inordinate amounts of iced coffee or reading beautiful books, she can be found working on her novel, writing out her own magical adventure.

COURTNEY GOULD is the author of *The Dead and the Dark*, *Where Echoes Die*, and the forthcoming *What the Woods Took*. She writes books about queer girls, ghosts, and things that go bump in the night. She graduated from Pacific Lutheran University in 2016 with a degree in creative writing and publishing, and now lives in Salem, OR, where she continues to write love letters to small towns and haunted places.

LIZ HULL received her master's degree in Education from Virginia Tech. Instead of teaching in a classroom, she's spent the past decade or so working in tech helping young people understand how to protect their privacy, safety, and well-being online. She lives in Portland, OR, with her family and a cat that has never forgiven her for bringing two human children into his home.

C.L. McCOLLUM (she/they) is a card-carrying disaster bi of a SFF author who can never make up her mind between YA and adult. Her adult debut *13 County Road 666* is coming soon from Falstaff Books. She has contributed to multiple small press anthologies, as well as Jolene Haley's annual "Spooky Showcase" event, and she also co-edits a charity anthology series known as "Clichés for a Cause." Currently, she is keeping it weird in the Texas Hill Country with her family and their various furry roommates. You can find her at https://linktr.ee/clmccollum.

Once upon a time, **LINSEY MILLER** studied biology in Arkansas. These days, she holds an MFA in fiction and can be found writing about science and magic anywhere there is coffee. She is the author of the *Mask of Shadows* duology, *Belle Révolte*, *The Game*, *What We Devour*, *Prince of Song & Sea*, *Prince of Thorns & Nightmares*, and *Prince of Glass & Midnight*.

SHELLY PAGE was raised in Chicago, maintains a long-distance love affair with New York, and currently resides in Los Angeles. By day, she's a practicing attorney representing homeless LGBTQ+ youth of color. By night, she's planning ways to bewitch her readers while simultaneously awakening their inner gay. Her editorial debut, *Night of the Living Queers*, is a QPOC horror anthology that received starred reviews from Publisher's Weekly and Shelf Awareness. Her YA debut, *Brewed with Love*, is a queer paranormal romance to be published by Joy Revolution in Spring 2025. She can be found online at shellypage.com.

SANDRA PROUDMAN (she/her/ella) is the editor of the YA Latinx SFF anthology, *Relit: 16 Latinx Remixes of Classic Stories* and the author of the YA fantasy, *Salvación*. When not busily immersed in all things publishing, you can find her spending time with her amazing husband and adorable toddler, catching up on all her shows, and taking care of her vegetable garden. Connect with her on social media @sandraproudman.

NOVA REN SUMA is the author of *A Room Away from the Wolves* and the #1 *New York Times* bestseller *The Walls Around Us*, both finalists for an Edgar Award for Best Young Adult Novel, among other acclaimed novels and short stories. She co-edited the anthology *Foreshadow*, and her next novel is forthcoming from Algonquin YR. She currently lives in a hopefully not haunted house in Philadelphia.

ROSIEE THOR began their career as a storyteller by demanding to tell their mother bedtime stories instead of the other way around. They spent their childhood reading by flashlight in the closet until they came out as queer. They live in Oregon with a dog, two cats, and an abundance of plants. They are the author of *Tarnished Are The Stars*, *Fire Becomes Her*, *The Meaning of Pride*, and *Life is Strange: Steph's Story*.

JUSTINE PUCELLA WINANS (they/she) is a queer and nonbinary writer who lives in Los Angeles with their husband and incredible Halloween-colored cats. Their books include YA mysteries like the critically acclaimed Indies Introduce title, *Bianca Torre Is Afraid of Everything*, and *One Killer Problem*. Their middle grade speculative horror titles include the acclaimed Stonewall Honor Book, *The Otherwoods* and *Wishbone*. When not writing queer, creepy, and funny fiction for kids and teens, they can be found training Brazilian jiujitsu, reading (a lot of) manga and webcomics, and actively avoiding real-life scary situations. Legend says they also haunt Instagram as @JustinePWinans and their website, www.justine-pucellawinans.com.